THE
JOAN CRAWFORD
MURDERS

BOOK II OF THE TINSELTOWN TRILOGY

PETER JOSEPH SWANSON

Stonegarden.net Publishing
http://www.stonegarden.net

Reading from a different angle.

For Tracy Hamby,
and also for all Joan Crawford fans from casual to crazy

Chapter One

The day had been so exciting that she drank way too much. Just as she was about to pass out, there was a knock at the dressing room door. She opened her eyes, opened the door, and saw a Joan Crawford in an old fashioned padded-shouldered 40s suit. She was confused. "Huh?"

"I'm Joan Crawford."

She answered, slurring, "Noooo, *I'm* Joan Crawford!"

"I'm the only Joan Crawford, so I'll have to kill you."

"BALLS! Look whah-you're *wearing*! It's goddam 1953, for chrissakes!"

"Bloody knife! Bloody knife!"

Joan squinted, trying to see straight. "Who *are* you?"

Three studio security guards rushed into the hall and two of them dragged the kicking and swearing impersonator away. A third guard stayed and asked, "Are you alright Miss Crawford?"

Only able to think about having had far too much to drink, she tried to keep her eyes open, and found that her tongue had became stuck. "Mah-*laaah.*"

He chuckled. "All right Miss Crawford. I'll lock you in now for the night."

"MGM can go-ta Hell!" She hiccupped as she slammed the door. She grabbed her razor sharp silver *From the Desk of Joan Crawford* letter opener and held it out to the room like a weapon as if she was still in danger. "Wha-ya want!" She sliced at the air. Then she realized she didn't see anybody else in the room. "Oh." She went to put the letter opener back but missed the desk by a foot and it fell to the floor, sounding a pretty chime. She didn't hear it as she fell to her knees knocking an empty vodka bottle to the side. Then she started to raggedly snore.

* * * * *

The phone rang. She woke up. "Goddam! Why am I on the floor? That must have been some party. Oh, my head!" She picked up the phone but it had stopped ringing, so she washed her hands, popped some aspirin and fixed herself a drink. While she washed her hands again, the phone rang again. She grabbed it. "You're speaking to *a star*!"

"Cranberry! You get to be Joan Crawford again! You get ... "

"Bill!" It was Joan's oldest friend, the ex-star, Billy Haines, who helped her start out in the silent days. "Bill!" Joan shifted the heavy metal telephone to her other ear as she began to rub freesia glycerin on her elbows. "Is that you? Bless you! How dear of you to jingle-ling me, *here*! How's my favorite fairy dust? How's your hubby, Jimmy? How are my favorite Hollywood homosexuals?"

Bill Haines said, "Oh we're fine, we're ... "

Joan cut him off. "WAIT a minute! What did you say? I get to be Joan Crawford again? Bill! You know I'm Joan Crawford - even when I sleep! What the hell are you trying to trick me up with, now. You should see me! I'm gorgeous! I lost ten pounds just for this picture! For my fans!"

Bill gasped. "Ten? From where? Where would you have ten pounds to lose? Did you cut your legs off?"

"Everywhere - but here." She grabbed one of the stiff jutting cones of her padded bra.

"You *were* a bit of a dumpling when you first came to town. With big beautiful peepers! And you weren't Joan Crawford yet."

"I'm always Joan Crawford!" She popped a mint and loudly crunched it between her great porcelain teeth.

Bill chuckled. "What I meant was, I remember when you were just called Miss MGM. And now you're back at that studio after all these years! So you get to be Joan Crawford again - MGM's creation. MGM'S ..."

"Hold on, I want to change my ring. There. Are you still there? Oh look at this ring! It's just gorgeous! Bill? You there?"

"Yep."

"Now what did you say?"

Bill attempted to continue, "You were ..."

"MGM's creation? Damn you! You put it that way and you make me sound like Boris Karloff in somebody else's wig! Joan Crawford ran right out of these gates ten years ago like it was a prison break!

I got away from those goons! I got away!"

"Oh, they love you at MGM," Bill quickly injected. "I heard…"

Joan interrupted, "The henchmen were very sweet when I came back – for this – for this *comeback*. Idiot starlets were waving at me. The *welcome back* banner they put up was cheap, but it looked okay for the photos and I suppose that's all that counts. At least in Tinseltown."

"I called the house and they said you've totally moved into your dressing room. What's going on?"

"I'm living here, now, and I'm not budging!" Joan sighed. "I need to concentrate to make a good picture. There's too many distractions at home. The last time I was there I was caught up on the roof in a fistfight with a lawyer."

"Lawsuit?"

"No. It was midnight. He was a date."

"How'd you manage a fist fight up on the roof?"

Joan explained, "Well, we started yelling on the balcony. I went up to the roof and he was nipping at my heels, the lousy bastard."

Bill gasped. "How do you get from your balcony to your roof? That's impossible!"

"Not when you're damn mad! So, I climbed up the wall, of course. What was impressive was that a fat lawyer could do it, too."

Bill asked, "But - the roof! You could have fallen!"

"Oh *pfff*. If you start sliding there's always the gutters at the edge. Speaking of almost getting killed – can you believe my life? Did you and your sweet hubby see my last picture many times?"

"Jimmy and I saw *Sudden Fear* four times. We were just amazed."

"Amazed that I didn't get killed?"

"Just … just *amazed*."

Joan laughed. "Bless you. I gotta go. I'm checking nail polish colors. They say *Torch Song* is going to be Technicolor, now, and everything has to be re-tested. It's a new law for the 50s, I guess – color is. I haven't been in color in awhile. I'm so needles and pins! I haven't done a dancing picture in how long? Can I still do it? The styles have changed. I'm a nervous wreck."

Bill chuckled. "If you can climb from your balcony to your roof then you can do anything in a dance number!"

"You're right, I suppose I can do any kind of a back flip as long as I have a cocktail in my hand. Oh! Gotta go! Speaking of crap, a fang has just walked into my dressing room!" Joan slammed the phone down and ripped adhesive patches off the laugh lines of her face, Frownies and Wrinkies. She smiled and clenched her teeth.

Henry Berman wrinkled up his nose at the heavy mixed-up smells of grease paint, astringents and expensive stinging sweet perfumes. Then he noticed a sinisterly simple-looking small white envelope that had been inauspiciously slipped under her door. He asked, "What's this?"

"How long has that been there? It's mine, obviously. Give it to me."

"Slipped under the door?"

"Give it to me!" Joan snatched the envelope from him and leaned it up between the pale pink light bulbs of the long mirror of her opulent baroque vanity.

Henry said, "It looks important. A ransom note."

She jumped up and washed her hands with two different kinds of soaps, Yardley's and Vinolia Cold Cream, and then used a tissue to turn on the radio. "*News flash! Joseph Stalin dead of a stroke.*"

Joan yelled at it, "Good! He didn't do business with Hollywood! What a cheap bastard!" Then she yelled at her producer, "Speaking of cheap bastards - why does my musical barely have any musical numbers? One, really. Or two!"

"Four."

She huffed. "Repeating a dance number, and singing a two minute ditty don't count, though I did sing it beautifully. I sing from the heart. I trained my voice and sound like a pro."

"Sure."

"Really! In the 30s I sang the alto part in a very good private recording. It was Verdi's *Requiem* and I was good. Rosa Ponselle said so and she's a real opera star. It was good because I'd worked damn hard at it! I always work hard at everything. But give me something to work *with*! Why am I gonna have to work twice as hard as anybody else in this picture just to make sure it doesn't end up a clinker? Why do I always get the rough end of the pineapple in this stupid town! Damn Hollywood! Just kick me around! Why *me*? Why not somebody else for a change?"

"Hush!" Henry pointed to the radio. "I want to hear this!" Joan turned the dial to another station, while he insisted, "This is important news! Stalin *dead*!"

Joan found the brand new hit song, "Doggie in the Window", so she turned it up and tried to sing along, *"Arf! Arf! Arf!"* She danced around the room thinking about how she used to win dance contests at the clubs because her dancing was so wild. She'd been shipped to Hollywood for her dancing. But that was 1920s *flapper* dancing. She silenced the radio, popped another mint, and sat to fiddle with a row of nail polish colors at her vanity.

Henry looked around. "You're cooped up on such a nice day?" He spotted her letter opener on the floor and handed it to her. "You dropped this."

She refused to look up at him as she took it. She went to wash it. "I'm busy making a picture, not lollygagging with the nobody starlets in commissary. I don't need attention. Not that kind."

He asked, "Is this room roomy enough for you?"

"Bless them, bless all the other stars who let MGM knock out their walls for me. I'm sure it was all no thanks to you. You're so cheap. *Lili* looked a little Poverty Row around the edges." She blasted a few puffs of floral perfume on him. "What did you think of that aroma?"

In an instant it was already cloying. He held his breath. "I didn't do *Lili*."

"Oh." Joan darkened and looked away, pretending to need to change her ring again, but she got flustered so tossed the entire perfume bottle in the metal garbage can. He jumped at the noise. Joan continued, "That's right! You're not even listed in the book. Neither is the other producer. A nobody."

"Franklin."

"Great." Her heart sank. "My big touted MGM comeback is produced by two complete nobodies. Who did you have to go south on to get something as prestigious as a Joan Crawford picture? Or was it just blackmail? You better be careful or the mafia will come and get you. They'll dump you in the desert if you mess up." She handed him a small clear plastic box. In it were false eyelashes. "Do you think this set would photograph nicer? Which style would the producer like?"

He looked at the little box in bewilderment. "I don't know."

Joan scoffed. "If you want to produce, you have to be on top of everything. And if you want to produce a Joan Crawford picture, you goddamn always better be on top of Joan Crawford!" She realized she didn't say that right. She snatched the box from him, cracked it open, and proceeded to deftly glue the lush awnings onto her lids.

The producer asked, "Are you really camping out in here for the whole shoot? Your house isn't *that* far and you can have use of our limo."

"I'm staying. The studio is my blood. It helps me concentrate. And I'm using the limo, anyway. I'm a star." Joan winked left and right at herself to check the angle of her lashes. She decided they were correct. "I work hard and that's why I'm living in this dressing room until the last shot's in the can. I have to concentrate!"

Henry joked, "Concentrate anymore and you'll burn a hole in the back wall of the theater."

"Good! My fans want a pro who gives a damn. Not these gum snapping nobodies. They just slouch around the studio these days. *God* this place has gone to the dogs! All the new starlets think this is all a party for them! They just think they can roll out of bed and open a door and we'll all applaud their beer breath! I remember when hard work was in fashion."

Henry blinked a few times. "Is everything alright?"

Joan noisily flipped through the pages of her script. "This script is not believable. The characters are not appealing. None of them. So I'll have to work twice as hard to make it all feel right and make them love me."

"The script is from a story called *Why Should I Cry*. It's all very proper. And don't worry about the costar. Everybody will know it's a one woman show - a Joan Crawford picture, and that's all that should matter to you," he said.

"I never worry when I have Robert Taylor at my side. He's a pro like myself. We understand each other! And I'm also so glad to have Robert Planck photographing me again. He understands my face. I haven't worked with him since my last MGM stinker, ten years ago. But Planck and I go way back. We ruled the 30s. He even did *A Woman's Face* with me where I got to wear a big scar all over half my head. He even lit that beautifully. We did so many pictures in a row. In a *row*! We worked sooo hard back then."

The producer took a full step backwards and when he was up against the wall he timidly informed her, "Michael Wilding is to be your costar."

Joan paused to take a deep breath, and then slowly slid her severe auburn wig off. "I was told that when I get angry, I should count to five." She did so, on her fingers. "Kill! Kill! Kill! Kill! Kill! Kill! *Kill*!"

"Feel better?"

In a threatening tone, Joan asked, "What happened to my Robert Taylor?"

"His plate's very full this year."

"And what about Clark Gable? Get him, then."

"He's completely out of the country."

"BALLS! So who's Michael Wilding?" Joan slumped. "I'm so afraid to ask." She took a moment to place him, taking noisy sips of her vodka. "Oh *him*. Crap! The British actor. He has such pretty lips - and that upturned nose. Is he bent? I know he got married to that very pretty child star, but – you know. If he expects me to flirt with him because he's such a snob, he's gonna go home crying to his nanny!"

"He's a good actor."

"He comes off as a snob! An *utter* snob! How does somebody like me do a scene with something like that? It's as bad as trying to do a scene with somebody who's decided to act like an idiot. It's all to steal the attention from me, and that's what it does."

The producer wearily put his head in his hands and sat down. "Oh boy."

Joan responded, "I didn't say you could sit. Isn't Michael one of *the girls*? Wasn't he larking about on Stewart Granger's boat - they were playing with each other's pee-pees?"

"Everybody knows that those guys are two of the world's greatest womanizers."

Joan poked her finger at him. "It was in Hedda Hopper's column! She made her innuendo quite clear. Michael Wilding and Stewart Granger were playing with each other's pee-pees, and that's that. Hedda said it, so it's now true."

Henry stated, "And Michael is suing her for libel."

Joan laughed wickedly. "You can't sue God."

"I thought the head of the studio was God."

Joan took a big sip of her martini and yelled, "Both! It's Hollywood! It's a pagan town!"

"It's a town of something." He rolled his eyes in disdain.

"Are you being a snob to me, too?" Joan's great eyes became radioactive. "Did you just call me some Texan trash? Some washerwoman's dirty *whooore*?" Joan leapt up and threw her glass of vodka at him. "Goddamn you! Don't you *ever* say that to me again! If you do - I'll KILL you!"

"Joan! This isn't a scene from a movie! Calm down!"

"A scene? You want an actress? You got an actress. You want an actress who plays a scene? You got an actress who can play a lousy scene! You want it? You got it! You want it? You got it! Get OUT! Get out before I *throw* you out! Get out before I KILL you!"

He walked out. Joan looked at the broken glass and thought about how fantastic she looked when she threw her drink through the glass door in *Humoresque*. It was an inch shy of getting her another Academy Award. She fixed a new drink. She sipped it with regal finesse, and then grabbed the phone. "Get the maid here, please! And her tip will be in an envelope on the vanity." After the line clicked off, Joan screamed into the phone, "I'm Joan Crawford and

I'll be treated with the utmost respect! There *is* no star of my caliber! I paid for MGM! Goddamn you snotty critics and producers and sluts up in casting! I came back here so you could finally treat me with respect!"

Joan took a deep breath, washed her hands, changed her jewelry, redrew her lipstick, and then refreshed her drink. She started to laugh. "Listen to myself. A *star*! I close my eyes for a minute and I'm back in that filthy laundry. I'm a washerwoman's daughter running scared – feeling small and kicked around." She turned to the mirror. "And I'm gorgeous because I *made* myself gorgeous!"

Her stomach sank. Something was very wrong. She had bailed out of this studio ten years earlier because the scripts got ludicrously bad for her type of act. Her last MGM picture under contract, *Above Suspicion,* squeaked by and only because she was the only woman in it and she got to wear clean clothes. But *Cry Havoc,* a fourth-rate movie from a fifth-rate play, was to be her next assignment. If she'd done that picture like a dutiful contract player was expected to, she'd surely be a has-been by now on TV. Joan stood and defiantly looked in the mirror. This new script was bad but it wasn't like she was playing a sweaty war nurse tossed in with ten other sweaty war nurses. She was now a star who was playing a star with all the glamour of a bright color MGM musical. Still, something didn't feel right. She sat and took a sip of her drink and hoped the feeling would go away. She willed it to go away. There was no time for self-pity. She fixed another drink and then redid her bright melon lipstick again to make it just a tad bigger. She had work to do. Joan finished her drink. "I have to get going! I have to get to work! I can't afford to be lazy!" She took her fancy silver letter opener and slashed open dozens of fan letters and put them all neatly in a pile.

Chapter Two

"Oh my GOD! It was all for nothing! It was all for nothing! Nothing! Balls!" Joan realized she didn't like how her first meeting with the costume designer Helen Rose had gone. It was supposed to have been a "get to know you" praise fete, but now Joan felt hollow about it, and somehow lazy and bad. "I haven't worked hard enough! I haven't worked hard enough to be worthy of the title Joan Crawford!" She slapped the sides of her face three times to keep jowls from sagging, punched herself hard in the gut three times, grabbed a bunch of past costume sketches, slid them into her black alligator portfolio case and loudly zipped it shut. She changed out of a raw silk caftan into a pair of bright yellow pedal pushers, thinking they helped her look intelligent, and then went out into the hall.

She heard woman's heels clicking around the corner. Joan called out, "Hello?" She walked after the sound of them to her dim shadowy New York proscenium theater set. "Hello?" Joan stepped up onto the apron of the stage. "Who's on my set? A fan? Don't be shy. I'm Joan Crawford. This is all for my next picture. Isn't it exciting? Bless you. Don't be shy. Let me give you an autograph. Please? Hello? Don't be afraid. I'm not really thirty-two feet tall. Come out, come out! May I give you a gift?" She reached for her earrings.

With a *kha-phump* all the work lights went out. Joan was left standing in complete darkness. She became frightened. "Hello? Someone?"

She heard footsteps.

"Hello? Who's there?"

The footsteps came closer and faster.

"Hello?"

"Bloody knife! Bloody knife!"

"What?"

"It's *my* face!"

"Hello?" Joan called out. "Who are you?"

"It's mine!"

"*What* is?"

She heard someone fall over a metal folding chair just at the edge of the set. A man said, "Fuck!"

"Hello?"

After a moment of hearing feet scampering around she saw a bright blast of daylight across the back wall as someone ran out of the far exit to the back alley.

Joan called out, "Who's there?"

With a click and a loud clomp the work lights came back on. A gruff man said to himself, "Crazy woman!"

"Who's there?" Joan yelled.

"What?" The gruff man was surprised to see Joan up on the set. "But you was just running out the back door. And you were limping, and holding your shoes in your hands. Like you stubbed your toe real bad or something. You okay?"

Joan walked up to him and smiled warmly. "Yes. I'm right here, darling."

"I saw you. Just now. Over there. You had a big white dress on like you wore in *Love on the Run.* And you looked like you'd just hurt yourself. Limping."

"Bless you, but that dress was in the 30s, with Clark Gable. I haven't worn anything like that in a long while. Adrian designed that dress. It wasn't me you just saw, then, of course, since I somehow got through all the dance rehearsals and I'm not limping – but I probably should be."

"I'm serious Miss Crawford. That sounds dangerous to have two of you running around this place. I'm calling security. Oh wait, you got stand-ins all over this place now for your new picture."

Joan nodded. "Of course, and the best. I have to go now. To wardrobe. And I'm late." She marched out a side door into the narrow studio street, her long legs propelling her like a powerful machine. It wasn't too hot yet and the cloudless California sky was a clean cheery blue. Buzzards were circling high overhead, but Joan didn't see them, she only looked down at the cement path, picking her brain about how she couldn't place where she once knew Helen

Rose from, before Hollywood. In Broadway? Chicago? She hoped it
was *not* in Kansas City where Joan had been at her hootchie cootchie
lowest.

"Hello Miss Crawford," A passing stagehand hailed her, carrying
a larger than life sized Joan Crawford cutout that would be part of
an egotistical scene. "Great legs!" he added, referring to what he
was carrying.

"Bless you," Joan extolled the cutout of her, and then said to the
man, "Now you watch where you put your hands when you handle
me!"

The stagehand laughed. "*All over* a Joan Crawford, that's for
sure!"

"Oh my." Joan pretended to blush.

"You're just the best, Miss Crawford!"

"Bless you."

He looked at the cutout and said to it, "You're the prettiest
woman in the world."

"I hope you don't ever say that where your wife can hear you."
Joan blew another kiss and rushed off. She charged into the wardrobe
building, blowing more kisses in the direction of the secretary at the
lobby, then looked at the two giant 1930s pictures of herself - one in
a gorgeous maid's uniform and the other in a sleek black beaded little
number, both Adrian designs. She ignored all the other framed stars.
"Those were the days." She invited herself into the main studio.

"Miss Crawford!" Helen Rose greeted, stepping back from an
easel. "How lovely for you to come back so soon. My, aren't you
raring to go."

Joan blew a kiss. "What a beautiful dress you have on. But then
you do have the best taste in dresses."

"Thank you."

Joan said, "They say there was just another Joan Crawford out
there. But I think she sounded like a *he*. I'm sure of it."

Helen replied, "Probably your stand-in. And the cold is always
going around."

"Oh, sure. Are you making me a big white dress like Adrian
would have done? Are the 30s back in fashion?"

"No. Not at all."

"No?" Joan grew worried again. "But she was just seen – and that's what she was wearing. That wasn't your dress?"

"God, no."

Joan was flustered. "What do you think of my new shoes? Aren't they adorable?"

Helen said, "Yes. Very cute."

"Are you sure? You like them, really?" Joan pointed her toes out this way and that. "You're not just saying that? I trust your opinion. You have the best taste. I'm so glad this studio has you while I'm here. It's a comfort to me." Joan plopped down the heavy alligator portfolio and loudly unzipped it. "We'll make a great team. Designers always love to work with me because I give one hundred and ten percent back. But I haven't worked hard enough yet for you though and I don't want to look like a frump."

"I'll take care of that," Helen assured her. "You won't look like a frump."

Joan gushed, "I brought ideas! Ideas ideas ideas, I'm so full of them and I can't wait to start working. We gotta ponce me up good. I want miles of taffeta so that I look like I just fell out off a cloud. I want it to swirl around me like a great magical carousel in some fanciful ballet. I want it so great that the department stores can't copy it. Goddam them! I won't look like I came off the rack!"

Helen frowned. "But the department stores have always copied your wardrobe. You've been the biggest fashion influence on America. People certainly weren't running out to wear what Gloria Swanson wore."

"Sure – Adrian and I were the first great fashion team and we used to *make* fashion in the world. But now I'm too big a star for that. If you want the girl next door - go next door. This picture has to look bigger than it is, goddamn it, and it can't be sold in a department store. The script is a bit two-dimensional. I'm a bulldozer on gams. So we'll just distract them by pounding them over the head with dresses. That's how I got through most my past MGM weepies - making them look like a million bucks! Have you seen the script? Ain't it a riot? I just yell at everybody and they call it a Joan Crawford picture. Goddam MGM!"

Helen replied, "Oh? I never pay any attention to the scripts. I just ask the director *what do they wear*? Then I draw it, then …"

"Since we've never worked together, I mean, *have* I ever worn a Helen Rose gown?"

"Night gown," Helen reminded her.

Joan fought to recall. "Huh? A nightgown!"

"Mildred Pierce! Your Academy Award! I did your nightgown for when you accepted it. You got your Academy Award in bed!"

"Oh! I was so nervous I couldn't go out. I'd had so much to drink, I was so nervous. And through it all I wasn't going to wear just any old nightgown off the rack. I'm a star! So thank you very much for putting that little number together for me and putting all the department store nightgowns in their place!"

"You're welcome." Helen smiled. "And I think that for this picture, I'll top that nightgown."

Joan grandly pulled out a few costume sketches from *The Bad and the Beautiful* and the remake of *The Merry Widow.* "It's no wonder you got an academy award for this picture. The gowns are just amazing. Bold! Arresting! But I'm a MUCH bigger star than that poor Lana Turner who really has nothing about her to make you remember her after the credits role. We only remember those gowns." Joan started manically pointing to places on several of them. "And I want *this* and *this* and *this* but more and more of *that*! Especially wide at the shoulders and narrow to the knees, with a big slit all the way to the top - we just HAVE to show off my great legs! And then bunches of loud lace that just SHOOTS off my marvelously delicious caboose to show how trim and tight it all still is!" Joan slapped her own behind.

Helen Rose asked, "Where did you get these drawings of mine?"

"Oh bless you, darling, for noticing how hard I study. But don't you think this one would look so much better on me if the skirt just went out to the walls. I am Joan Crawford and I'm back and I sing and I love - and in color!"

"But, Miss Crawford …"

"Just call me JOAN! And I'll call you DARLING! Because you are the most *darling* designer I've seen at MGM since Adrian. I miss having a star designer make my pictures so distinctive."

"Yes, Joan. And I also want to do something new and different for *Torch Song* that captures the age. And you'll just have to put all those old drawings away and trust me."

Joan frowned, cringed, pouted, and sat down. "I'm just so damn nervous about my new look that I'm gonna have this time around. You have to understand how nervous I am. And I have a scene right within the picture where I go over my costume drawings for the Broadway show – I play a Broadway star- and I make changes. I'm such a take-charge character. A bulldozer with a pencil." Joan pretended to boldly draw on large sheets of cardboard. "I want to do the scene so *brashly* that you just *hear* the sound of my pencil on the paper, *bam, bam* like a drum. I guess I'm already rehearsing that." Joan chuckled at herself again.

"Are you ready to see what I've come up with so far?"

"Taffeta," Joan prayed. "*Please* make it miles of lovely taffeta! Ribbons and bows all over it! Or silk flowers and butterflies! I already have the loveliest butterfly hair combs we could match with something!"

Helen Rose cautioned her, "Now don't panic. It doesn't look like much on paper, but I want you to keep an open mind and realize it's a fresh approach to your look. The girly ribbon-and-bow 30s are over. And no more feathers shooting off of shoulders or sleeve cuffs the size of baby strollers. A woman has to look simple but decisive and strong, and you're the one to pull it off if anybody can." She flashed Joan some drawings. "I'll make you a 50s icon - the quintessence of the 50s! Why not? You've been the look of every decade since the 20s!"

Joan looked at the new drawings in horror. "B-b-bb- they're so - stark. So severe. We need to compete with television! We have color! They don't!"

"Don't worry. On *your* broad shoulders, they'll be powerful.

And smart. A week ago when we first measured you, and you were so athletic, without a stitch of clothing on, I decided right then and there to show off your body as directly as possible." Helen flashed another large drawing at Joan. "And look at your dance rehearsal outfit. Isn't it smart?"

"Oh. Yes." Joan frowned. "There it is, isn't it. But. It's so plain! And GRAY! This picture is to be in *Technicolor*! Are you – are you making fun of me?" Joan fought back tears, feeling like a little girl again when she was always let down and kicked around by her mother and big brother.

Helen was getting excited. "The color accent will be your grand lips – since you paint them so big on your face – which looks just stunning – of course. And the costume's detail is all on the belt with these wonderful decorative chains. And then - *wah-lah* - the skirt rips off and we get a full view of your long wonderful legs. You rip it off to dance and then you later snap it back on when you're done - since the film opens with you rehearsing. Smart?"

At that idea, Joan's eyes widened with glee. "Will the censors allow that much leg to show?"

"All of it."

"Really?"

Helen assured her. "It's no less than a swimsuit."

"I LOVE it! That's the cleverest costume I've ever worn! Measure me now for it."

"We already have your measurements. Tomorrow morning we'll do a fitting."

"But I've been taking more diet pills!"

Helen frowned. "They don't shrink your bones! I hope."

"Bless you!" Joan stood and showed Helen again how high she could kick her legs. Then she quickly sat. *"Woah."*

"Joan! You okay?"

Joan let herself be helped up. "Bless you. I suddenly felt a little dizzy."

"Are those diet pills safe?"

"Who cares? Look at my gorgeous body. I do feel like my brain is melting, though. I need my cigarettes. That'll be good for me.

They say they help the digestion. It says so right on the box."

Helen still worried. "You'll be okay?"

"Sure." Joan kicked her legs high again to show she wasn't some wobbly little old lady.

Helen waved her off, playfully, "Now shoo and let me get to work so we'll have something to fit you with come tomorrow morning. And please remember to wear the bra size we measured you with. That one you have on now won't fit under what I've just sewn."

Joan batted her eyes. "I don't know what you could mean." She gave Helen a big waxy red kiss then traipsed off, happy and confused. She knew she'd have to look modern. She'd always been good at that. In the 20s, F. Scott Fitzgerald had said she was the best example of the flapper. In the 30s, she was the archetypal shop girl and she ended the 40s as the ultimate femme fatale. But Joan worried that the new 50s styles were ugly and harsh compared to the classical looks of cinema's glorious past. "But my legs! We see my legs - *all* of them! As much legs as that Esther Williams and she has bathing suits!" Passing the commissary, she saw Debbie Reynolds.

Debbie greeted Joan, "Hi! Nice day, huh? Hey! Wait a minute. Hold on there. I never noticed before. Must be the light. You have the most beautiful baby blue eyes. I'd always thought they were brown. The movies always made them look so dark. Wow!"

Joan blew a kiss. "Bless you. And what cute sandals you have on."

"Thank you. I got them in Texas while shopping with Mother."

At the sound of the word *Texas*, Joan felt dizzy. "Oh. Texas."

"You okay? You look a little pale. Have you stopped by for some of Mayer's ol' chicken soup? They say the chickens still come from his ranch!"

"You been there?"

"No. I haven't seen it for myself. It's just what they say."

Joan warned her, pointing to the commissary, "And from one friend to another, don't go in there either."

"It's fun to see all the stars chewing."

"It's full of germs," Joan warned. " Everybody with ringworm and gonorrhea sitting on the same seats. And then you put food in your mouth?" Joan put her hand up to block the harsh sun from her face.

Debbie chirped, "Did ya like *Singing in the Rain*? Wasn't it nice to make a movie about the movies?"

Joan shook her head in angst. "What a charming film about this town. I fear people might believe it. I sang the title song first in the movies - me and a hundred other contract players. Oh, those were the days. When sound first came into movies, for real."

Debbie blurted, excited, "People like old things, like you - I mean, I didn't mean it like that. I mean that you're such a star from the very beginning! The silent days!" Debbie gestured wildly to the grounds around them, to the mountainous white steel soundstages and the two story balconied strips of offices and dressing rooms within the high white enclosure of the MGM walled city.

Joan regarded the sight. "Yes, the MGM castle. When you're in you're in. When you're out you're out. When you're in you have the world. When you're out you might as well be dumped dead in the desert. Just dumped."

Debbie smiled big. "We're *in*! You and me both!"

"For *now*. Bless you. You're such a dear." Joan stomped off, fuming, deciding not to eat anything no matter how hungry she felt. "I'm not poor! I can eat and get as fat as I want, but I have a picture to make, goddamn it! Will anyone appreciate my great sacrifice? Will people realize how hungry I was to give them their plate full of glamour?" She popped another diet pill. "I'm going to starve to death until I look as cute as Debbie Reynolds!"

* * * * *

The lady of ill repute clomped down the L.A. street on shoes that were absurdly heeled to help her advertise. From a bar she heard jazz and singing that didn't go together, and it made her think of the year's failures flipping behind her ears like a clanking unlucky roulette wheel. She put her hands up to her head but all the discordance of the sounds of heels and clanking and singing and jazz wouldn't stop.

So she added to it all the soft sound of her own airy voice. "I came to be a star. A star. I can't even make a buck sellin' it." She pushed her fingers into her belly again, being so hungry, wishing she could just push the horrible feeling away. She began to sing her favorite song, an old Joan Crawford number from *The Bride Wore Red*. It was a jaded plaintiff ditty about not needing love - not when what one really needs at the time is food. Nobody could pull off that sort of desperate sentiment better then Joan Crawford, being maudlin yet heroic. She started to sing louder. *"Who needs love?"*

Out of the corner of her eye she saw the flash of the razor, but didn't react and half her nose was cleanly lopped off.

A powerful voice yelled, "Bloody knife! Bloody knife!"

She opened her mouth to say, "Hey! You're Joan Crawford!" But opening her mouth only made her realize she was pouring blood. The razor came at her six more times and she saw herself fall to the side of a building - and then through the bricks into a long white tunnel of brilliant swirling stars and into the warm loving arms of her dear departed grandma.

Joan Crawford heard a man with a throaty voice say, *"Dirty whore"* while she was clomping down the street, lost, confused, having come out of some sort of blackout. She saw a dead body of a starlet-type crumpled against the building with vivid red blood streaming to the gutter. Joan decided it was real because it was in color, so she ran in terror to another street, with the movie music from *Sudden Fear* screaming in her head.

Then Joan saw herself and gasped. She decided it was just a reflection in a shop window across the street, but then doubted that. The Joan Crawford didn't have a fur. "You're not Joan Crawford!"

The Joan Crawford turned, looked shocked, and yelled right back, "I am too! Who are you, you goddamn drag queen!"

"ME? YOU! You're *cheap*! Where's your fur? You're all off the rack! All of you!" Joan pointed to the dead body, her hand shaking. "And - is that fake, too? Am I dreaming?"

The Joan Crawford pulled out a razor that flashed like an explosion in the harsh sun. "Bloody knife! Bloody knife!" Joan's migraine increased when the knife's reflection hit her eyes, lighting them up like pale blue jewels. She staggered backwards against a fence.

Then a limo pulled up. The driver hopped out. "There you are Miss Crawford. I thought I'd lost you, and then I'd lose my head." He made a scissors action with his fingers against his neck.

"Who is that impersonator?" Joan pointed down the street.

"Who? Where?" No extra Joan Crawfords could be seen anywhere. There was only the fading sound of somebody running in tall heels.

"Over *there*!" Joan pointed. "She's gone. *He's* gone - whatever that was! No fur! All the clothes were off the rack! And so old fashioned – like it was still the 30s."

"I don't know."

"I was right there!"

"Maybe you just caught your own reflection in that shop window."

"No! The Joan Crawford wasn't wearing an expensive fur!" Joan quickly glanced down at herself to make sure she hadn't lost hers, not that the heat didn't reminded her that she had it on. "I'm so confused - these diet pills are melting my brain. I think I'm seeing things." She looked back to where she came from. Far up the sidewalk she saw the rivulets of blood. She began to faint but the driver caught her tiny body and tossed her into the open door. Face down on the seat she came to, relieved to feel the air conditioning. As she slipped out of her steaming fur and pushed it onto the floor, she asked, "Did I just murder somebody? I must have. Joan Crawford. That's me. So – it has finally come to this. I tried to be nice but you can only kick a dog so many times before it bites back." She began to weep.

The driver warned her, "You're pushing yourself too hard."

"I have to. I'm a star that wants to stay a star."

"Would you like to stop somewhere for a bite to eat?"

"Nope. On a diet. And stars don't just stop *somewhere*. I just need a cigarette and I'll feel better."

"You sure?"

She put her head down on the seat. "*I'll* take care of everything. I always do. I always have." She began to weep.

"You okay Miss Crawford?"

"I'll have to be. If even one person sees me weak, they'll all pounce."

Chapter Three

Back at her dressing room, Joan Crawford took a quick cold shower and then looked around in her fur pockets but couldn't find the weapon she'd used to kill whoever it was that had been out there. "Did I do it - or didn't I? I saw Joan Crawford do it! But how? Was I so angry at somebody to go that far? Who could it be? No." She washed her hands and arms again with two different strong soaps, Packer's Pine Tar and carbolic smelling Lifebuoy, and changed dresses and shoes two times, then finally fixed a drink and took a long boiling sudsy shower before she felt any better at all. Leaning close to the mirror and putting a special French chamomile lotion around her eyes with a tiny round sponge at the end of a cardboard wand, she finally regarded the unopened envelope she'd left between the light bulbs of the mirror. She sliced it open with her fancy razor sharp *From the Desk of Joan Crawford* letter opener. "What's this?"

In plain type, it read, "The Fountain of Youth will be yours for $50,000. Call this number and ask for The Goat of Osiris. Cash for the holy water of the desert. It will make you look young!"

Joan made a face at the note. "You're rude!"

"What's that say?" Frenchy, her hairdresser asked, walking in with two wigs on mod aquamarine papier-mâché heads. She set them high on a shelf then grabbed a towel and took over drying Joan's hair while Joan popped another diet pill.

Joan watched in the reflection, scowling at what Frenchy wore on her head. "You always are up on the latest jazz – but – is that turban the latest thing?"

"You like?"

"Is that the new look of the 50s?"

Frenchy said, "I just bought it yesterday."

"Oh did you." Joan decided to tear the note up. "Did your son ever finish hair school?"

"Oh Christmas was that expensive. How sweet of you to remember that."

"I'll have to have him do my hair so he can say he did a star. It always helps to have that kind of a credential when you're just starting out. We'll make sure there's a nice picture taken. I'll frame it nice and give it to him when he opens his first shop."

"He'd really appreciate that. It is so hard to get started."

"I've helped a lot of people get started."

Frenchy said, "I suppose it's easy when you're famous. You just show up and smile and they take pictures."

"Smiles aren't cheap - the caps are expensive and hurt like hell. They expect you to have a new outfit in the latest fashion, new shoes, and no freckles. The eyelashes have to be on just so. The whole Joan Crawford has to be on just so. And it can't look cheap and off the rack. It's harder than you think. It'll take me at least four hours to get ready to have your son do my hair."

"Oh sure. Sorry. I didn't mean."

Joan ordered, "Let's try the blonde wig." She could barely hold her tongue, wanting to tell Frenchy that her tan turban with fake rubies looked cheap and dumpy. "Hmmm. Will I be blonde in this picture?"

"Yes, Miss Crawford," Frenchy readily agreed. "There, that makes you look like a million bucks, and quite a different sort of character."

Joan tried to pat the sides down more. "Hmm."

Frenchy questioned the wig. "Maybe this pageboy is too stark. Is it?"

"I have to dance and sing and love and even yell at a few people in very smart hair. It has to be disciplined." Joan ripped off her wig. "I'll be blonde for the big jazz number and then at the end I'll *rip* the wig off like that. Oh wait, I'm playing a mulatto in that scene within the scene. Hmm. It's all very confusing. I know - I'll be blonde and then *rip* off my black wig. Yeah. That's it." Joan popped another diet pill and washed it down with vodka. "This will help me feel better. I hope. How many have I had now today? Was that my first one? I'm so dizzy. Have I done my sit-ups yet today? I can't remember." She punched herself hard in the gut a few times. "I can't tell. I'll do them all again just in case. You can go now, darling, bless you. Take these wigs to Helen Rose at the costume department and have her approve everything - to make sure they really do go with the dresses. Everything has to coordinate. And you can do that now because I have some calls to make and I'd like to be alone when I tell everybody to go to Hell." She gave a warm smile and blew a kiss. "I appreciate all your hard work. Bless you."

"Oh, sure, yes Miss Crawford." Frenchy scrambled to put some brushes and pins away, grabbed the wigs and scuttled out.

Joan downed the rest of her vodka and poured another. After a dainty sip, she changed her bracelets and then called her secretary back at her house in Brentwood. "Darling! Are you still there!"

"Of course I'm still here."

"Oh thank god you're still there!"

"Why wouldn't I be here?"

Joan asked, "Is it all still there?"

"What?"

"The house hasn't gone up in a puff of pink smoke? Has it? Oh it hasn't!"

"Why would it?" her secretary asked. "It's a house. Your house. Why do you talk like that?"

Joan admitted, "Don't you wake up sometimes in the night and nothing seems real? You wonder if you're back in the ditch you started out in? You wonder if everything you've accomplished was nothing? And what was real has just slipped through your fingers? Like a handful of champagne?"

Her secretary chuckled. "You're a poet. And no, I have no idea what you're talking about."

"Bless you. Maybe I am a poet - an artist. Yes, sometimes I think I have nothing in this world but my own Joan Crawford creation, and that's only a giant puff of smoke, a bluff against all the snobs who are out to embarrass me and take away everything that I have. And then they just kick the shit out of you as they laugh and laugh and laugh!"

"Nobody can take anything," her secretary assured her. "Don't worry. Now, why did you call? What can I do for you?"

"I don't remember."

"Think."

"First tell me what you're wearing - you always look so smart," Joan said.

"Just the black dress I always wear."

"But you always look so smart in what you wear, for some reason. I always feel like a shoebox in my clothes - with the most gorgeous gams and Johnny Weissmuller shoulders." Joan laughed.

"I saw a nice big photo of you in the paper. Getting off the plane."

"Did I look as nervous as I was?"

The secretary assured her, "No, like a queen."

Joan said, "I'd still be chugging through Cleveland about now if I'd taken the train."

"You're not going to get your picture taken stepping off a train like you will stepping off an airplane, nowadays. These days everybody likes *modern!*"

"It cost a fortune," Joan said. " I kept my wig on its stand on the seat next to me the whole way and didn't put it on until I was ready to step off, so I'd look fresh and not a single hair would be out of place. Nobody else looks fresh stepping off such a long flight except a Joan goddamn Crawford. And did you notice I wore a dress with horizontal stripes that would hide the wrinkles. The plane doesn't have a nice changing room like trains do. Luckily the dog blows up with this little straw so I didn't have to buy a seat for it, too. I had to reserve the seat for the wig, though, goddamn it, and they actually charged me full price for it!"

"How was New York?"

"The charity work is always nice. The fans are so kind. Some of them even dressed up like me, even the boys. It was so cute. I love seeing me everywhere when I'm in New York. We sold Joan Crawford cookies for a dollar apiece to buy children's books for the hospitals. It was such a joy to see my face everywhere, on cookies, too, and we sold hundreds. It was a lot of work but I loved it. You know how I love hard work. That's how you get things done."

"That's a great charity - books for sick children."

Joan said, "My only regret is that I can't do more for the poor darlings. They should all have books and food and clothes and shoes. In this country at this modern time they should at least have that. I always wish I could have seen a book with pictures when I was little. I saw a catalogue once but it didn't have any pictures so I had no idea what it was about. But I fixed all that now with Joan Crawford cookies."

"That must have been a fright to see them eat your face."

"No, I've always enjoyed bringing pleasure. But once somebody dropped my face - er - a cookie - and it was shocking to see me, my face, on the floor like that. Shattered." Joan suddenly was jolted with an image of a body lying on the sidewalk with blood pouring from it. She wondered where that could have come from. "Cookies don't bleed. Did she step on it? No, she'd tripped over it, or did she? Did I kill her or did the other me do it? The other me? Where was I? The me in the shop window - but I didn't have my fur. Was it me? My mind! I'm having trouble thinking." Joan gulped the last of her drink. "*Oh*, that's better."

"Miss Crawford? You okay?"

"I just needed a little sippy."

The secretary said, "Oh, I got to go. The mailman's chiming me from the front."

Joan got excited. "Then I'll call back in ten minutes to see what came for me today. I have to change my earrings, anyway. I don't think they match anything I have on and the press might just bust in on me any second. If they see me with the wrong earrings they'll think I've slipped and am no longer worthy to be Joan Crawford. Then MGM will give her away to somebody new and I'll have nothing."

"Bye!"

Joan sighed, irritated that she felt like she'd been rudely hung up on, so she washed her hands again and then started to open more fan mail. She accidentally ripped an envelope wrong so the letter was ripped in half. "Balls! I've never done that before! How can

I be so stupid!" She took her letter opener and started to slash the whole letter to ribbons in a furious tantrum. Then she realized what she was doing. She sat and downed a drink. "Now how am I going to read this thing? They may have been trying to tell me that they love me and I killed them like I'm ready for the loony bin!" She washed a pencil, put lotion on her knees, then shoved the pencil in the dial and connected with the deep dark bowels of the MGM CIA. "Get Gangster Al on the line."

"There is no one by that name ..."

"Don't be a shmuck! Don't you recognize my voice? This is Joan Crawford! I'm back and I've lost ten pounds and you're gonna deal with me and I damn well remember who's the goddamn goon squad around here."

"Hold on, Miss Crawford."

After a minute of ringing, a very manly voice came on the line. It was Gangster Al. "Joan? You coming over, baby?"

"Suffer, goddamn it! *Just* suffer. I've got a cookie for you to clean up. I mean a tart. To scrape up."

"What? A stiff?"

Joan nodded. "Just laying there. Horrible! It was so horrible I don't even know if it was real."

After a pause Gangster Al finally spoke, "Oh *god* Joan. I was waiting for this day when you'd go too far."

"How far?"

"I knew it! I knew one of you old timers would crack one day and this would happen. I knew it all along. This town hasn't had a good movie star murder in a long while. Why not a Joan Crawford murder. You're such a hothead, everyone will believe it somehow."

"Hey. Wait a minute. I don't think I actually did it myself. I think it might have been an imposter. I'm not a murderess. I'm the lady who pays for two hospital rooms to always be available for sick people who can't afford to pay for it themselves. So that we don't get things like dead people always laying around in the streets. I'm Joan Crawford, the lady who does great charity all the time on purpose. And don't you forget it!"

"Until you get mad."

Joan said, "A spitfire may throw her glass of vodka at you but she don't plug you full of holes."

Gangster Al asked, "You're not sure?"

"Am I sure? I'm never sure of anything. Those diet pills – I think – I was in a blackout. I couldn't see what I was doing."

"I knew it would come to this."

"I'm a star who has to fight everything and everybody! It's war out there and war means – oh hold on. I feel dizzy again. Where's my cigarettes?"

Gangster Al said, "Do you need to take psycho pills for that - for your aggression? They make them, now."

"What?"

"They tested them on Frances Farmer and they've gotten safer."

"I'm not crazy," Joan said. "I'm only fighting for my life in this sick town. And I help poor people, I don't kill them, I swear. You know that. Who am I telling who Joan Crawford is?"

Gangster Al said, "You made a dead body happen?"

"Joan Crawford did it! I'm sure. The other one. And I was crabby - this picture is driving me crazy - and then Debbie Reynolds talked to me and that put me right over the edge - she looks so *young*! *How* can she look so pretty and young?"

'She's twenty."

Joan said, "And don't question me, I'm not going to waste my life on regrets. I never did. I never will. And I needed a cigarette and I was out and I tripped over a dead girl – and I was there! It was like a dream! I'm so confused! Are these diet pills safe? I felt like I was walking around in front of a big black spot until I saw Joan Crawford flash at me like a nightmare. And the sun flashed at me. Are these diets pills safe at all? You tested enough of them on Judy Garland. Did MGM ever get them right?"

Gangster Al asked, "When did this dead body happen?"

"I saw myself staring at me in the shop window - but - but - I was dressed so cheap and old fashioned. It was like a ghost that was mocking me. A ghost of Hollywood's past telling me I was a nothing! But it could have just been a tacky impersonator out murdering the streetwalkers and I happened to be there making two of us. But how can I know for sure? These diet pills confuse me - or it could just be the diet. I ate three prunes this morning." She finished her vodka and poured another. "Or maybe it was just a ghost of Hollywood's past telling me I'm really a cheap nobody under this expensive dress. Balls!"

"*When* did it happen?" Gangster Al asked.

She took a loud sip of her new drink. "A ghost! A Joan Crawford ghost! My time has come! My time! Oh God!"

"When did the dead body happen?" Gangster Al calmly repeated.

"A while back. I've been on the phone to my house. Important business that couldn't wait. Can you believe it's still there?" Joan let out a loud sob.

"If you start crying like that, for real, I'll hang up. Now get it together, Joan."

"And there was nobody around on the street anyway, except for the dead body. And blood! And Joan Crawford was there. But I don't know who I saw other than it looked like me. I needed cigarettes! Can't you understand? I had to call my secretary! The stress! The stress of this MGM comeback is driving me crazy!"

Gangster Al scolded her, "Chatting to your secretary couldn't wait for a stiff that could get you *the chair*?"

"Screw you! I'm Joan Crawford! And do you have *any* idea how busy that is? And I have a picture to make on top of all of this! A picture that tells the world whether MGM is still on top or not!"

"Where's the stiff before everybody trips over it?"

"I don't remember exactly. The poor dear. I bet she came to this town to be a star. I bet she wanted to take my job."

Gangster Al said, "See? A motive. Jealousy."

"No no no. She was just crumpled there with blood coming out of her from all over the place like she was about to be tossed into a barbecue. That's it! It was near Babby's Grill."

"Where is it, Joan?"

"Oh - and there's a bar across the street. And there was a billboard high up on a hill with a face on it. Somebody new. She was just grinning. I can't believe this town doesn't have real stars anymore. Just children."

"I know where that is. God you woman. There *are* tourists tripping over that stiff by now. I'll have to just wait and pick her up at the morgue."

"You know where it is?" Joan asked. "Well then who's up on the billboard smiling like she owns the whole goddamn city? Somebody just kill her."

"You know who Esther Williams is, she's just down the hall from you, and you can't kill someone MGM has under contract."

"God! You think I'm just out to kill everybody now? Balls! It's an expression everybody says! From what I heard, Helen Rose is trying to kill Esther Williams by sewing her bathing suits so full of beads that she sinks right to the bottom. Now what are you going to do about that? Put Helen Rose in a hole in the desert? Balls!"

Gangster Al said, "Esther could swim in a beaded iron lung."

Joan wondered, "Does the studio still own that funeral parlor? The one where Valentino was."

"Are you asking me does MGM own Hollywood?"

"I should know better then ask that. Take care of everything, bury all bad Joan Crawford press, whoever she is, and I'll make it worth your while." Joan kissed the telephone, thinking it sounded sexy. It just sounded drunk. "Joan Crawford is coming over tonight and you better be hard-up. I gotta go and phone the house back before ..."

Gangster Al hung up.

Joan put her glass down and tried to remember what she had just been talking about. She rubbed some more cream on her elbows and then slapped them so that they'd be just as pink, tight and soft as Debbie Reynolds'. Then she looked around for a gift to send Debbie. "This odd bracelet doesn't match anything I have." She held it up and wiggled it. "Debbie gets it!"

* * * * *

Frenchy marched into wardrobe, with the wigs, and said to Helen Rose, "Would you believe? Last night! They had a big Joan Crawford look-alike contest at some big bar - and all the people competing in it were *men*! Oh, Christmas!"

"Oh really?" Helen smiled. "How very imaginative. And I bet it was all very festive and gay. Does the real Joan know about this?"

Frenchy made a face. "How could I tell her something like that?"

Helen inserted the wig stands on top of the dress dummies. "Yes, she loves good gossip like the rest of us, but it's hard to tell how she would take something like that – since they were all Joan Crawford." Helen slowly walked circles around the dresses and wigs to examine them.

Frenchy continued, "And the winner was some snot from New York. Very arrogant."

"Oh, do tell!"

Frenchy said, "The shameless brat insisted that he *was* Joan Crawford, the true real Joan Crawford, for real, even though when he went to the bathroom he had a ding-a-ling so far out so how could that be so. *And*, he said he was going to destroy anybody who would tell him otherwise. He threatened anybody who would cross him. He threatened with a knife! In the men's room! I say he's ready for the booby hatch."

Helen chuckled. "And how would you know about what's happening in the men's room? I don't even think Luella Parsons could have gotten that kind of a tidbit – or –*er* – ding-a-ling."

Frenchy explained, "My son is a hairdresser, like I am. He said he was there and saw the whole thing."

Helen asked, "The whole ding-a-ling?"

"That too."

"Oh? Was your son a Joan Crawford, too?"

Frenchy frowned and quickly shook her head. "Oh *no*! He's not funny like that. He's such a nice handsome young man. But I wonder why he *was* there? Hmmm. Actually, he did put this hat on for just a minute and he looked just like Joan!"

Helen jumped like she'd been stuck with a pin. "Not in *that* turban!"

"He especially has Joan Crawford's nose and eyebrows. And jaw and eyes. Well, all her face. Except for his teeth. Don't you think Joan has the most glorious teeth? He just has regular ole teeth."

"How can one turban make a man look like Joan Crawford?"

Frenchy reached up and gently touched the fake rubies. "It's a lovely hat. And he's just - well - how does a mother say this about her only son. I don't want him to get hurt. He might get picked on. But he's *short*. And he doesn't look *exactly* like Joan Crawford. As I said, his teeth are very different so he doesn't have her fantastic celebrity smile. And he doesn't have her strong shoulders, either."

Helen asked, "So how do you know he didn't pad them, like most men, and wasn't part of the Joan Crawford contest?"

Frenchy insisted, "I just don't think that kind of thing would interest him. He's not funny that way, I'm sure. And he has nothing in his closets that he could wear. He just has nice men's clothes."

"How would you know?"

"I know every inch of his closets. I do his laundry."

Helen said, "Maybe he was at the contest as a hairdresser. Somebody hired him to improve their wig. That's all. I hope he had fun."

Frenchy smiled. "That could be so – that he just did somebody's hair. I'm sure of it. Yes. That must be it, since he's a good boy, really. So, Helen, what do you think of my new turban? Do you like it?"

The costume lady honestly said, "No."

* * * * *

Joan washed her hands and then picked up the phone to dial her secretary to find out how much fan mail had arrived.

Henry Rogers, Joan's publicist, stepped in the door. Mad at him for not getting enough newspaper coverage, she decided to make him wait and listen to her phone call, hanging up and redialing to get someone else, instead. "Marilyn, sweetheart, wake up. It's me. Joanie. I know you have nothing to wear, are you naked now? Are you laying on top of your bed naked? Are your breasts covered with your sheet? Tell me! I have some pink pantyhose you can have. Are you awake? Hello?"

"What?" Marilyn Monroe asked.

"You can have 'em!" Joan offered, winking at Henry. "Hey! They're all the wrong color for me and I didn't even pay for them. MGM did. I was going to wear them for my *Two Faced Woman* number, but we decided I'm going to play a black woman - just to make it exotic. Pink is all wrong. And it's a bright pink. It'll go with your coloring quite beautifully."

"Pantyhose?"

"Yes."

Marilyn asked, "Have you worn them already?"

"What?"

"Did you put them all the way on – all the way up?"

"Of course," Joan assured her. "I thought it would be very *very* exciting for you to have a few pairs of pantyhose I've already worn, for good luck, you see, since I'm such a big star and you're just hoping to get established."

"No, thank you, Miss Crawford, but I really don't want any pantyhose that have already been worn by somebody else. That's just ... "

Joan imperially insisted, "I am NOT just any ol' somebody else. I am Joan Crawford and I am offering you Joan Crawford pantyhose. I thought that would be exciting for you - being that you're so disadvantaged right now and I understand how that is. When *I* came to Hollywood I had *nothing* but the few clothes I stole from some friends in Kansas City, which is neither here nor there right now, I needed *something*! I was winning all those dance contests and had to wear a dress! Nobody was kind to me! Everybody was waiting their turn to kick me back down. I had to scratch and claw for everything I have now!"

"No thank you Miss Crawford. That's so very sweet of you to think of me, but I don't know ... "

Joan slammed the phone down, gulped her drink, and turned to Henry. "I try to help. You just heard me try. I know what it's

like to be just starting out in this town and not have much. Can you
believe the little starlets today? Back when I was just beginning I'd
have taken a pair of silk stockings if they were offered to me and I
wouldn't dream of asking if they'd been used, I'd just look for the
run! What is it with people today, the *young* people - they're so damn
SPOILED! They won't even take a perfectly perfect pair of pink
pantyhose that goes well with their coloring. How does she know
she won't need them someday? Why doesn't she just let me help her
get started? I know I sure needed help when I first came to town.
I was grateful! If it wasn't for Bill I'm sure I'd be a blah housewife
somewhere right now." Joan squinted at the publicist. "And why are
you here? What is it that you do?"

He started to talk but Joan didn't hear him because she was
stomping over to a dresser. She loudly tore through it, and when
she found two pairs of pink pantyhose she cut them into ribbons
with a gleaming pair of scissors, and then put them into the garbage
can. "SCREW the pantyhose, then! NOBODY will have them, if
Marilyn won't have them! Goddamn it! Hollywood nowadays is all
waste waste waste *waste* WAAASTE!"

Henry put up his hands. "Joan. Listen! I got a good table for
you at the Crystal Room in the Beverly Hills Hotel."

Joan paused, thought, and then perked. "Oh? Oh! OH! That
means I'll be voted favorite actress by *Photoplay*!"

"Again. So calm down."

"Again is never enough," Joan reminded him. "Yesterday
is nothing. The people out there in the movie theaters have *no
memory*!"

"They do too. They're fans."

Joan said, "They're like me, they only ask *what's next*? Never look
back on your life or what you see might turn you into stone. You
gotta keep running in that one direction. Fast. And yes, I'm the
most popular but that's only because I make myself that way. I'm
better because I work harder!"

He warned her, "At the Photoplay Awards you're not supposed
to know how popular you are."

Joan winked. "I know how to act grateful and grovel and squirm on the floor and kiss everybody on the ankles as they're walking away from me. I'm an old pro at working this shitty town by now. I know how to act anything, *anything,* but especially how to act as grateful as a dog that's just been kicked real hard in the caboose. Now, darling, is Hopper or Parsons sitting close to me? I want any little gold nugget that falls out of my mouth to be in the next day's papers. That is your job. Do you even remember what your job is?"

Henry nodded, victoriously. "Hopper *and* a reporter from Associated Press will be at your table. You'll be a queen in her element. I can't stay, I have pictures of you I want to drop off at a few places and the wire service."

"Let me see them first." Joan grabbed the dozen black and white glossies and quickly flipped through them. They were all *Torch Song* rehearsal shots of her and her dance partner, also her choreographer, Charles Walters, kicking up his legs with her. "Not this one, please." Joan set it aside. "If I don't look like a startled frog in real life then I shouldn't in a photo. Yes, that one has a very nice leg line, doesn't it? Doesn't it?"

"Yes."

"Tell me how much you like it."

"Yes."

"Tell me! I pay you enough – tell me I look young and exciting!"

"You look like Heidi trying to get laid."

"Bless you. I *do* look so young and fit. And so sultry." She growled like a tiger.

He nodded, "I'll push this one on them, Joan."

She stabbed the others furiously with her letter opener, finding it strangely compelling that she was stabbing herself. "Of course. If I don't have a new award, I'm dead. I can't rest on past laurels. That sounds so sad, and it's been awhile now that I won that Oscar! We have to work harder! Much harder!"

"The wire services will be pleased with that new photo, I'm sure."

"Tell me something." Joan tossed the ruined photos away, then pounded and lit a cigarette. "When I said I could act anything, I have to confess, I still find a challenge here and there. And I need some advice."

"Shoot."

"I know you know acting these days as good as anybody else. I know that you know how things are done in the craft."

Henry offered, "What do you want to know?"

"I don't know how to act when I'm in a scene with black people."

"What?"

Joan said, "I can't leave my scenes to chance. I can't afford to take a chance."

Henry said, "You just act like you would in a scene with anyone else."

Joan shook her head, angrily, and then pulled a tiny piece of tobacco off the tip of her tongue. "No, I know that. What I mean is, that it's like they don't give those people a part. A real *part*. The scripts don't have them acting like *people.*"

Henry asked, "How do you mean?"

"You meet them and they act normal and you think you'll know how you'll do the scene, but then once they're delivering their lines they act like they're mentally deficient."

Henry dismissed her concern, saying, "You're just still confused with acting with Butterfly in *Mildred Pierce*."

"Henry, I tell you, I *didn't* know what to do. That voice of hers is up there so high only dogs can hear her! I just didn't know how to talk to her. I didn't know what she was doing. She wasn't an idiot like that when we met. She was a real person. She was nice. I gave her a watch and her thank you was so beautiful that I started to weep. Then we're on the set and she went bonkers. What *was* she doing?"

"Joan, didn't you see *Gone with the Wind*? She brought down the house when she ran around weeping, not knowing how to *birth a baby*."

"What I want to ask is, well, I have this scene with a new black actress I've never heard of before and she plays my secretary in this picture, but I do a whole long scene with her where she helps my character rehearse. She can't play a cartoon character. If she does it like Butterfly I'll be out to sea, again. I don't know if MGM knows how to give a black person a real part *anybody* can actually act along side with."

"Who is it?"

Joan asked, "Have you heard of Maidie Norman?"

Henry smiled in assurance. "Oh sure. She just did a picture here with Dorothy Dandridge and a brand new guy with promise, Bellefonte. It was done all very naturally - a little second feature about a teacher, called *Bright Road.* Nobody played a cartoon character like Butterfly."

"Oh, I'm still so nervous!" Joan cringed. "You tell me I'm gonna play a scene with Robert Taylor and I know just what to do. Same with Gig Young - or any guy who might play my vain gigolo. We've all had a hundred of those. But how do I do a scene with a black woman who acts like she just fell out of a Warner Brothers cartoon?"

"She won't. Really. What's the scene?" Henry asked.

"I'm rehearsing in my apartment. She makes some notations. I say *goodnight.* She says she'll type up the changes for tomorrow. That kind of stuff."

Henry suggested, "Why don't you invite her in and rehearse it with her."

"Rehearse a scene where I rehearse a scene with a starlet?"

"Sure."

"But I'm Joan Crawford. The only thing stars and the new kids on the block do in their dressing rooms with each other is a little boffing between takes. This picture, I think it'll just be me and Gig Young, and he ain't even that young, not that I'm that old."

"Joan! Listen to yourself. Just do it. Just rehearse it a little until you get a handle on it. You had to rehearse your dance steps."

"That's different. But the drama stuff I can do in my sleep, especially if it's with a strong Clark Gable type. I've been around too long to fuss with such a thing as going over lines with starlets. I don't rehearse like I'm some hayseed who's brand new to summer stock. I'll stand for eight hours being fitted for a costume and test it under the lights for another eight, but darling, this Maidie Norman woman is a nobody so far – she just hasn't paid her dues. Sorry to say it like that, but that's life, and life ain't nice. Life is not nice at all!"

Henry frowned at Joan. "Is it important to the movie?"

She nodded. "You're right. Call her in and we'll meet each other and I'll get a sense of how her voice is, and how she looks at a person. I just hope and pray she isn't all normal but then when they say *action* she becomes a flighty Butterfly type. MGM always throws the worse casting at me to try and trip me up. And MGM always treats black people like cartoons. Those FANGS. Call her and get her over here!"

"I'm the publicist," Henry reminded Joan. "I don't do that."

"Balls! Give me the damn phone and I'll call, myself, goddamn you!" Joan washed a pencil and dialed with it. "Central office? Find that Maidie Norman and tell her to report to my dressing room on the double!" She hung up.

Henry said, "You didn't tell them who you were."

"If they don't know by now, you're fired."

He laughed.

She didn't, but added, "And this movie is gonna be in color. BIG color. I want color pictures in the magazines. Big pictures. Big color! JOAN IN COLOR should be a giant caption. Do we want everybody in Ohio going off to wild crap like *The Band Wagon* because they want a color picture? Certainly they'll choose a Joan Crawford picture over any picture, anyway, they always have - but remind them of the color to help them along in these confusing times."

"Yes, Joan."

"Go now and leave me to do my work and I'll leave you to do your work. We both have so much work to do to keep from getting buried alive. The more they bury you, the harder it gets to dig yourself out. I've been buried a few times too many, so far. Go! Hurry!" She blew kisses. "Bless you!"

He left. She changed her underwear, washed her hands and dialed Gangster Al again. "Do you have anything to do with who wins the Academy Awards?"

"It's democratic, Joan."

"So. People vote. What really matters is who *counts* the votes?"

Gangster Al said, "If I counted them, myself, Joan, I wouldn't stack them toward you. I have a whole town to run, a whole studio. I have to keep my eye on the big picture. On tomorrow."

"There is no bigger picture than Joan Crawford. And talent improves with experience. If I can handle the crap MGM has thrown at me, then just think what I'd do with a good script?"

"There's new talent for the new generation of films that I have to protect and promote," Gangster Al said. " You know that; don't be a pain in the neck."

"But the new nobody stars aren't groomed," Joan argued. "They just pop out of nowhere and don't know how to behave so they behave badly and will be gone tomorrow. Who'll remember Esther Williams or Grace Kelly in five years? Poof! Gone for all time."

"I have to go Joan. I'll see you tonight." He hung up in her ear, which made her mad, so she rearranged her broaches, scrubbed under her nails, changed wigs, finished another drink, and dialed her secretary again. "Any mail for me?"

"So you *are* there."

"Of course I am."

The secretary said, "I thought you were spying on me. I went to the door to get your mail and there you were across the street just staring at the house. You looked so angry. You gave me the creeps. Did you ever go to the prom?"

Joan said, "No, but I scrubbed their floor afterwards. Why?"

"Well, the Joan Crawford I saw was wearing a 40s style prom dress. But you were before that time, now weren't you."

"I'm before my time? I'm here and now. I have no idea what you're talking about. But bless you. It was probably just a fan."

The secretary asked, "It was eerie. Should I call the cops?"

Joan said, " Of course not. Fans always come by to have their picture taken with me. All kinds of fans."

"Even somebody creepy like that? I really got the creeps!"

"The Joan Crawford impersonators are my more intense and most loyal fans. Really. The papers won't mention them, with there being such complete censorship on those kinds of people. America is only supposed to have the Doris Day type people," Joan winked at the phone, "but *you know*. Just leave it be or you'll attract the F.B.I."

The secretary asked if she felt safe.

"At MGM? You crazy? They're only trying to kick me into a hole and then bury me good. But leave the fans alone."

"You really only think the best of people."

Joan laughed. "Of course not! People will all stab you in the back! I only think the best of my fans. They can never let you down if you suffer enough for them. What was that noise?"

"Oh my GOD! Somebody just put a brick through the window. I'm calling the police." The secretary hung up.

Waiting for her to call back, Joan finished her drink and nodded off.

There was a tap on the door.

"What?"

The door knocked louder.

"Go to hell! *I'm* Joan Crawford, not you!"

"It's Miss Norman, Miss Crawford," a woman said through the door. "Have I caught you at a bad time?"

Joan cracked a smile. She liked the woman's voice. "Come in." Maidie Norman stepped in. Joan beheld her face and burst into tears of relief, "You're gorgeous! You're *gorgeous*! What a marvelous face."

"Why, thank you, Miss Crawford." Maidie wasn't gorgeous in a way that would compete with Joan's energetic flashiness, but was sensibly handsome, motionless and stern.

"Come in and sit down," Joan invited, smiling ear to ear. "I can see we'll photograph beautifully together. And what a pretty dress. That color is so pretty."

"Thank you, Miss Crawford."

With utter finesse, Joan fixed Maidie a cocktail, tossed in an olive, set it on a napkin, and then pounded a cigarette on the arm of her chair and lit it with a loud metal snap. "Oh, don't be nervous. No, don't sit there. Sit *there*. Scoot your chair away from me a little to your left. Away. There. No. Scoot. Scoot. Scoot. There! Ah – that's it. Look a bit to your right. AH! The light is so wonderful on your face. You will light nicely. Wonderful! Now tell me about your credentials."

"Thank you for the refreshment." Maidie took a cautious sip of her drink and then began, "Just finished a picture here … "

"Yes, dear, I know all about that one about a teacher. I know all about what goes on at the studio."

"Of course, Miss Crawford."

"Call me Joan. We're going to be friends. It sounds like you have experience in pictures and you won't confuse me while I'm doing a scene, talking to me like that Butterfly woman did. I had no idea what she was saying so I just waited until she stopped doing her Butterfly thing. And then I resumed with my lines as if nothing had happened. It was horrible. Just as I wouldn't want somebody in a scene acting like a snob around me, acting like an idiot is just as bad. If you're going to act with Joan Crawford, then you should act *with* Joan Crawford – gracious and kind and in a pleasing tone of voice."

Maidie smiled with a red face. "When Butterfly came out in *Gone with the Wind* and she did her Butterfly thing, I wanted to crawl under my seat."

"What?"

"Everybody laughed," Maidie explained. "And it was like they were laughing at all black folk. I could have died with embarrassment."

"At that point I doubt anybody cared anything about *that*." Joan waved her cigarette around. "They were far too distracted with Miss Vivian Lee's forced performance, and thinking bad things of the British because of it. I should have played the part of Scarlett O'Hara. Then you would have believed it when Joan Crawford came down the stairs to blow the Nazi away with that gun. That was a Joan Crawford scene if I ever saw one, but, casting was asleep, or they just snub me. I don't know why MGM always gave me such a bad time at their own expense. If I'd been in charge we'd all be a lot happier today - the South would have won the war and Canada would be a part of America, now - er, or, however it went back then. History is all so goddamn confusing. I spent my days at school scrubbing their floors! That's why I'm a tough cookie."

"Yes, Miss Crawford. History is confusing sometimes, isn't it?"

Joan nodded. "History has been very rude to not make itself clear. But I *admit* that I don't know everything. I admit I was scrubbing floors while everybody else was sleeping through the lectures. I now make a point of learning all I can, now that I'm an adult. I'll make a point of learning new things for the rest of my life – not like everybody else who runs around acting like they know everything, and all just because their parents paid a ton of money on their tuition."

"Yes."

Joan laughed at herself and took a big drink of vodka. "I spent all my time cleaning the damn place. But look what I've made of myself. When the talkies came in, MGM taught me how to speak correctly. I sounded like some pretty sorry lowdown Texan trash when I came here. But I worked my goddamn caboose off, day and night, to learn all I could! So, now, I have the best goddam voice in all Hollywood."

"Yes you do have a fine voice, Miss Crawford," Maidie said.

"Call me Joan since we're gonna be the best of friends. Now if you work hard enough, you'll be a big star too! It's really all about hard work and outsmarting the sharks up in casting. Don't ever blame anybody else for anything. Nobody wants to hear you cry. Just work harder than your costars. Don't look directly at the camera. Know where your marks are on the floor. Be alert. Don't let your costume wrinkle. Don't wear makeup louder than mine – no lipstick for you. Make sure they powder that shine off your nose before each and every take. No false eyelashes for you – I am the star. Know where the microphone is. Speak clearly. And most important, don't go through the roof like Butterfly when they say *action*. It's a Joan Crawford picture. It's an MGM Joan Crawford picture. That means the character is cardboard and the plot could fill a fortune cookie.

The whole movie is on my wide shoulders, again, and I'm the only actress who could pull a part like this off. If we take the attention away from Joan Crawford for a second the picture goes up in a puff of smoke. I am the only reason the picture is. Period."

"Yes, Miss Crawford. I'll take your advice. And I understand your great responsibility."

"Oh, bless you!" Joan jumped up and lunged for her dresser drawer. "Let's see if any of these gloves will fit you. You are going to be a lovely new star and a new star needs lovely gloves for waving and blowing kisses. Here, try these ones on. Do they fit? I have such tremendous hands."

"They fit fine. Thank you Miss Crawford. Thank you!"

Joan dug through a jewelry drawer until she pulled out a matching set of tiny black hair combs with bright silk butterflies across the top. "These should set off your black hair. You have groomed it so nicely. I'm so impressed to see a woman well groomed these days. Did you ever see Frances Farmer's head? A mess! Oh – that was before your time."

Maidie Norman flustered at the exquisite combs. "Miss Crawford! Joan! But that's just too much!"

"Nonsense. They get lost in my hair. I can't stand them. And they're much too lovely and expensive to go completely to waste. I can't stand waste. Please take them and wear them when you feel light and gay."

"That's so very kind. They're so lovely! And thank you for the advice!"

Joan shook her finger at her. "And one last nugget. When it comes time for the casting couch, don't be a brat about it. It's so much nicer than the cold hard floor." Joan dismissed her with an imperial wave of her hand. "There. You may go now and I hope to work with you again someday. It was truly lovely. Bless you. *Bless* you!"

Maidie paused; she was perplexed. "But. Joan. I thought you wanted me here to rehearse our scene together."

Joan said, "I do hope you have it memorized."

"Yes. Of course. To the word."

At that, Joan smiled and shooed her away again. "You have experience. Your voice is lovely and you act like a real person. Just talk to me in the scene like you were talking to me, just now, no different, and I'll be fine, and you won't make me feel lost and out to sea while the camera rolls. And if anybody up in management tells you to play the scene like a retard because you're black, tell them you've already had this little chat with me and you know better, and you know how to behave in a Joan Crawford picture. They'll tell you I'm trash and don't deserve any respect. They'll tell you to give me a good swift kick in the ass as soon as my back is turned. But please don't listen to them. They're all fangs."

"Yes, Joan. Thank you."

"Bless you." Joan lunged at her and gave her a big red greasy kiss on the lips, and then grabbed a tissue and wiped her off. "No lipstick for you. I'm the star."

When Maidie Norman left, Joan whooped with delight.

Chapter Four

In the backseat of the limo, Joan glanced out occasionally to see the dark steep Hollywood Hills pass by as she quickly signed piles of autographs. "Slow down, I'm writing my damn name and it doesn't have camel humps!"

"Yes, Miss Crawford."

"I have three hundred more to go so don't get there before I'm done!"

"Yes, Miss Crawford."

"I have to sign these nicely. Each and every fan must think I signed this with love in my heart just for them alone. And I do love them. I love my fans."

"Yes."

"And I love them far more than I can express. Just try being a star without fans. Just try it. You'll end up like Bette Davis. She hasn't had a picture all year and so they say that's it for her. Her last picture was a sick attempt to make fun of me and it backfired. She's through."

"Yes."

"And these hills are dangerous! I saw what happened in *Sudden Fear*! A car can go right over the edge and fall quite a distance! Fire everywhere! There's nothing even left for the coffin!"

"Yes, Miss Crawford. I'm the best driver in Hollywood."

She leered at him naughtily. "The *best* driver I've ever had? I've had a lot of drivers in my stable." She winked at him.

"I don't know ma-am." He blushed and finally came to the end of a path carved into the side of a steep wall of crumbling rocks and scraggly weeds. After she finished her flask, she slipped out and walked with a swagger across a fussy multi-colored stone veranda to Gangster Al's front door. She rang the grand chime, then smiled at the kitschy Laurel and Hardy statue lamp holders on each side of the portal. "So Hollywood."

The thick door whooshed open. "Joan!"

"What stops a rock from falling on your head when you're in your driveway?" she asked Gangster Al.

"Nothing."

Joan stepped inside and shoved her wrist under his nose. "Do tell me I smell divine? Do you like my new smell? It smells *rich,* doesn't it!"

Gangster Al agreed, "Yes, Joan. Very nice."

"Are you sure? Do you like it? Really? Are you sure it smells rich enough to be worn by a Joan Crawford?"

"How many of them are there?"

She clicked opened her handbag and slipped her silver cigarette case out from under her gun. She looked around and darkened. "I should kill you."

"Why?"

Joan struck a pose from her movie *Possessed.* "You should be *shot!*"

"But, why?"

"What happened to the painting of me above your mantle?"

Gangster Al smiled in embarrassment "It's in the rec room."

Joan said, "You're rude. Before we go to bed, make me a martini. And not one with one of those dead salted olives. I want a real olive. A fresh olive just plucked from a tree. And the pit *will* be removed."

"Yes, Joan the Ripper."

"*What* did you call me?"

Gangster Al wagged his finger. "You killed a lady of ill repute."

"I don't know if I did it. I shouldn't even think about it. A person like me can't afford to have regrets for a second. I gotta keep moving. I don't know. After all I've been through in my life it could just be a mafia trick on me just to get somebody like you all excited. Hell if I know. It disturbs me. I don't like being used."

"How can you not know?"

"I *don't know!* I was all very confusing."

Gangster Al raised his grey eyebrows. "*It* was confusing?"

"And *I* was, too. I couldn't have done it. How can I kill somebody if I don't have a weapon. A lethal slap?"

"You have that letter opener than could bring down a pit bull."

Joan nodded. "I do. But I don't remember ever taking it with me. I don't think it ever leaves my desk, but why would I think about something like that? I have lines to think about this week. I haven't messed up a line in over twenty years."

Gangster Al repeated, "But - how can you not know what you did for sure?"

"So I had a temper tantrum, maybe." Joan packed the end of a cigarette on his wall, and then waited for him to light it. "I don't know, now. I was blacked out from hunger. I may have just seen a ghost that appeared to make fun of me - to belittle me. Or maybe it was really another me – the me that is still being kicked around. I don't know. I'm not a scientist."

"Then I'll call you Joan Jekyll and Joan Hyde."

"Balls!"

"All you stars get all split up in your personality after a few pictures. It's amazing I don't see this more often. I've been waiting for it to happen, that's for sure. And with your famous temper, I'm not surprised."

"You think you got me pegged?" She swept her cigarette through the air. "I don't know what you mean."

Gangster Al closed his eyes. "You're not going to hypnotize me with your cigarette antics. I'm not so impressionable with your fancy baton tricks, like you've got a magic wand, there."

Joan pulled a piece of tobacco from the tip of her tongue. "You think you're clever to not be spellbound by a movie star? I'm not so dumb to think you're so dumb. But goddamn! Jekyll and Hyde! Balls! If you want a new monster movie out of all of this, Lugosi with shoulder pads could play a Joan Crawford better. I'm far too big a star to ever play a horror movie. And he really needs the work. The poor dear. Bless him."

"You *are* a horror movie."

"I will *never* make a horror movie. But I will *be* one if I stay thirsty!" After he left the room, her great blue eyes quickly spotted a gun behind a lamp. She grabbed it, dumped out the bullets and replaced them with the bullets in her own gun. "Goddamn it!" She laughed. "I pray his aren't as fake as mine. Why Hollywood can't make real bullets to blow a few real holes in the saloon wall. My ass."

"What'd you say?" Gangster Al asked, returning with ice.

"Your ass - I mean your gun over there." Joan pointed. "Are there real bullets in it? I mean, *real* ones?"

He chuckled. "I got them from Vegas. Yeah they're real. They're not intended for any cowboy movie. Did you touch it?"

"Of course not."

Gangster Al was accusing. "But it's not exactly where I left it. It's pointing a hair north more than it was before."

Joan chuckled. "So, I spun it around for luck, so what. I guess I'm pretty lucky I didn't shoot myself, huh? If those were real bullets."

"Stars are like children," Gangster Al stated. "We must keep them far from the real bullets."

"And we can trust *you* with them? What keeps you from ever being found out? Wouldn't it be a scandal for the studio, and Hollywood, to know that a Gangster Al works for them, doing his dirty deeds, running around with real bullets in his gun?"

"Everybody knows there's gangsters all over the country, running it. That's how it works. That's our economic system so don't be a lousy commie trying to pull down all the good money. And if my gorgeous mug should ever hit the front page, they'd all say *so what?* That's America! Land of the free!" He tipped his gun open, saw bullets in it, aimed it at a few invisible foes, and pretended to shoot, "BAM! There goes a labor leader! Unionize the prop department and I'll plug you full of holes and throw you in the desert!" He chuckled, the prop department had been unionized decades ago and that leader long dead, so he locked the gun in a drawer and went to mix the drinks.

Very self satisfied with her quick switcheroo, she wanted to laugh, but played it cool and started to hum *Tenderly*, the main song from the new movie, while she kicked her pumps across the room, then shimmied and slipped out of her fishnets. She draped them over his head. He smiled and pretended it was a sexy move. It just looked drunk. "Would you believe I tried to give a few pairs of pink pantyhose to Marilyn Monroe but she was too good for them? Can you believe how spoiled and wasteful the young are nowadays. Can you arrange to have somebody teach her a lesson? And I want a really good hit on her. Have some thug push her into a fountain where there just so happens to be a lot of cameras. Let her ruin a good dress and then she'll appreciate the value of it."

Gangster Al chuckled. "We old timers just think different - we lived through the Depression and two big wars. We know hunger. We know hard labor. They have a new America that's never *ever* been richer."

Joan didn't like his excusing wastefulness or calling her an old timer. "I see *you* aren't afraid of my hose."

"But *you* would never wear something somebody else has worn. Lighten up, Joan."

"I'm a clean woman, though. I've been working hard *all* day and you could still eat off of my lap!"

"Yes Joan, you are utterly remarkable that way."

"And look at these legs - better than any of the children at MGM today." She leered at him and slid her hand in his pocket. She frowned. She was on the wrong side. So she asked," Can we dump Michael Wilding on Senator McCarthy? I hear he's deporting commies and fairies to save America from an evil takeover. Boy is he full of himself."

"Wilding isn't either."

"Well just whisper something in Elia Kazan's ear. He likes to tattle on the stars that don't vote Republican. Tell him a thing or two about Michael. He's *not* an American. The House of UnAmerican Activities should hear about this - and show him what a real American is - by kicking his snobby scones back across the sea to his nanny!"

Wilding is true blue. Americans love the English."

Joan stuck out her lower lip. "Screw him - screw you."

"Have you screwed the cameraman yet?"

"Robert? *Pfff.* I had him years ago."

"He's really a peace of the MGM furniture, isn't he?"

Joan said, "I haven't even seen him yet, this time around. The assistant DP has been doing the tests. I hope Robert looks well. Gosh, it's been so long since I've been at MGM. It's such a shock to see some of my old pals looking ten years older. How could they have allowed that to happen? Everything has to look good all the time or we're no better than the animals. And I'm worried about the costumes - I'm concerned about how stark they are. The 50s is ugly. But my singing is gorgeous; you can always count on me. My recordings are finished for playback." She reprised *Tenderly* triumphantly in his ear, again, her hand slowly entering his other pocket. Gangster Al smiled blandly, not wanting to wince at the unsubtle presentation. He finally took the hose off his head and tied them around her throat. "Watch it! You'll stretch them out in all the wrong places!" She tried to slap him but his elbows were in the way.

He laughed. "Now it's my turn to be on top."

Joan finally got him. "That slap was a Joan Crawford slap and that wasn't made in a day! And I'm tired of talking about it. Let's just play a little game of casting couch. I'm gonna win a big part."

* * * * *

When Joan returned to her dressing room she took a shower, poured a glass, chewed on some ice, and then began to bawl. She took out her special tan leather diary, for moments of special enlightenment, and then scrawled quickly so she wouldn't lose the intense feeling of the moment, "*Poor Joan, poor Joan, broken feet work so hard. Work so hard and all laugh at you.*" Tears began to pour down her cheeks. She allowed a few to drip on the paper to prove her depth of feeling. She ended with a bit of a Shakespeare sonnet, "*Should I compare myself to a summer's day? I am more lovely and more temperate. Rough winds do shake the darling buds of May.*" Rough winds reminded her of Gangster Al.

She jolted from her reverie when she heard a slight paper scrape. She noticed that from under the door was coming another envelope. She gently dabbed her tears away with a tissue, re-powdered her foundation until she couldn't see any freckles, and then promptly ripped the envelope open with her fancy razor sharp *From the Desk of Joan Crawford* letter opener. It said the same thing about the Fountain of Youth and the Goat of Osiris. She knew the studio was buttoned down at this late hour, if not always, so she figured it was a sick rude joke from a jealous nobody starlet who had no memorable face. She shredded the note.

She downed her drink, fixed another, and then she dialed up her old friend from the silent days, Bill Haines. She said, "How's my favorite fairy dust?"

"Cranberry! Do you know what time it is?"

"Who cares!"

Bill asked, "Who rattled your cage?"

Joan said, "Bless you! Thank you for understanding. I was just writing poetry. I'd read it to you now but I might want to change a word in the morning."

"You'll bless me woman, after what Jimmy and I've just thought up about an hour ago – when we were still wide awake."

"What. Do tell. I adore you two boys when you think of me. Were you two in the middle of doing it when you thought of me? I always think of things when I'm in the middle of doing it. It's funny how that works. What have you thought up?"

Bill said, "You've got such balls, you're pure moxie."

"Bless you. But I knew that. My fans won't let me forget."

Bill said, "Jimmy and I have just decided that you're a total dyke."

She roared with laugher. "Don't give me any flak. I can still slap you from here, you know I can."

"No! Serious! No horse feathers."

Joan still decided it was a joke and so bellowed out an even bigger masculine guffaw. "Damn you, you two gadflies, I should have never said what I did about Garbo." Thinking about how many years ago that was, Joan grabbed her stomach muscles and pinched hard to punish them into greater firmness, then she firmly pounded a cigarette against her desk. With a decisive loud snap of her silver lighter she lit it. "I said I sounded like a man," Joan admitted. "I didn't mean I thought like one."

"You do."

"You're not funny. You are rude." She flicked her ash into a tiny glass tray with complete finesse. "You think everybody is bent. I suppose the world would be a better place if it was. You and Jimmy are the happiest married couple in Hollywood."

"I wish we could marry for real."

"Ha! Two men walking down the aisle? Which one would wear the veil?"

"Both of us," Bill answered.

"Then that would be two women getting married and we all know that doesn't happen."

"Why can't two women get married?"

Joan explained, "It's the nature of women. I know. Believe me. They'd scratch each other's eyes out in no time. Women hate each other. When you see us hug and kiss at restaurants it's really the same difference as two prizefighters shaking hands before the bell rings. Now that was so sweet of you to call me. Bless you." She slammed down the phone, took a big gulp of vodka, and when she felt it warm her heart and fill the void inside, she bolted the door, deciding no more flowers and presents would come marching in. She stripped off her makeup with cold cream and tissues, added a new thick layer of lanolin cream over her heavily freckled skin, slipped on her tight elastic chin/jowl/neck thong, and then strapped herself into her gray canvas corset that buckled onto her cold uncovered sanitary blue plastic mattress. Now she wouldn't be able to toss and turn at night, scrunching up her cheeks against the mattress that would put lines up and down her face, or even worse yet, allowing her lay on her side where her spine would bend so she might wake up a hunched dowager.

To relax, she practiced her lines. *"I don't need anything or anybody. Don't worry about me."*

Chapter Five

Early the next morning, after Joan poured herself an eye opener and had a swim in the Esther Williams pool, she scampered back to her own area to steam and ice her face and neck, and methodically arrange jars on the table in preparation for imposing an even grander face upon her grand face. Her phone rang.

"Good morning. You're interrupting a star - Joan Crawford, who made money for this place so you could all indulge in that Garbo who did not make money like I did. So you should thank me."

"This is Mr. Hammer from *Life*."

"Oh? Oh! The press! Bless you, darling!"

Mr. Hammer said, "I'm sorry to call so early but I was told that you'd be well up by now, and we're already humming over here."

"Of course. I'm Joan Crawford. I've been up. I had my swim." She looked at her image in the mirror and was irritated, then rummaged through her lipsticks. "I'm just not Joan Crawford *yet*. Who is this? Bill? Bless you! How's Jimmy? You sound funny. Are you having sex with Jimmy right now while you're on the phone? You dirty bugger!" Joan breathed heavy into the receiver and started to guffaw.

"No! This is Mr. Hammer from *Life*. We'd like to run some comments by you, under a new picture of you that we got from your publicist."

"Who is this? This isn't Bill?"

"No, It's Mr. Hammer from *Life* magazine."

"Oh. Then you can't be having sex with Jimmy right now."

"No ma-am."

Joan took a sip of vodka to clear her mind. "A magazine! Oh! And - is the photo you have of me a glorious image?"

"Of course."

"Tell me about how glorious it is. How old do you think I look? *Young* I look."

"It's great. It's a big closeup of you so ... "

"No it is not," Joan argued.

"Yes it is. I'm looking at it right now."

Joan insisted. "It is not!"

"But ... "

"My publicist did not send out a closeup!"

Mr. Hammer said, "Well then it came from somebody else. It's a closeup all right."

"God! He can't even lay an egg right!" Her heart sank and she felt like throwing up. "Do I look just divine? What photo is it? Do you see freckles?" Joan swallowed hard to try and calm her stomach, really worrying about the lines around her eyes. "Oh GOD! Tell me you don't see any freckles! Balls!"

"You look like a marble statue, your skin is so smooth. And you have your hand up to your face. You're wearing a big round ring."

Joan was relieved. She knew the picture and it was heavily retouched. "Bless you. That is a picture of me you'll see up on the wall in my dressing room set of *Torch Song*. I play a star who is surrounded with images of herself. Of course you don't have the very same one. You have a copy. Thousands and thousands of copies of Joan Crawford have been sent out. The one for the set is still there."

Mr. Hammer asked, "Now can I interview you, for a moment, for something to go with the photo?"

"Oh? Now? On the phone?"

"Sure."

"How very modern." Joan thought about it for a second. Then the idea of it made her very angry.

He asked, "So - w*ho* is Joan Crawford?"

Joan looked in the mirror. Without her Joan Crawford lips carefully drawn on, with only normal thin lips like any other housewife, she was stymied. She suddenly didn't recognize herself without her gorgeous half melon mouth. She thought she looked like a poached frog without her eye makeup. She thought her freckles made her look like rotting fruit. She hated who she was looking at. She took a gulp of her vodka, hoping it would make the bad feeling go away. "Joan Crawford is a *star*! A *star* shits diamonds and pearls!"

"I can't use that copy."

"Balls!"

"What's that mean?"

"You want a goddamn celebrity bon mot? Get your goddamn ass down here like any other gentleman with balls and ask me whatever you goddamn like, you rude goddamn ass!" She violently slammed the phone, but kept yelling, "You lazy bastards spending all your day on the phone! You lazy slob! Who the hell do you think you are that you can just ring-a-ling any ole Joanie up on the phone and think I'll be so lazy with you and be dragged down to your tacky level of slop to just lay around all morning on some cushy couch just talkin' and talkin' like some crappy, lazy, ole … Oh crap, shut up Joan!" She took a deep breath, fixed a new drink, washed her hands several times with several different fragrant flower and shell shaped soaps. Then she returned to her vanity and took a sponge wedge to wipe a heavy dead pale pancake coat over her face, ears and neck, proceeding to create a vacant canvas on which to build a work of commercial art. She plastered on a thick glowing warm copper Max Factor foundation. Her tin of translucent powder set the two layers. Then she drew a bold orangy-red mouth above and below her own natural lip line, improving the proportions between her jaw, chin and cheeks. Finally, in the most expert calligraphy with a long thin brush, she painted a protracted bold black line above each eyelid, making the arch a tad perkier than her actual eyelash line, to paint her eyes to appear wider and more open then they really were. Happy with the results, the left side matching the right, seeing a striking gorgeous Joan Crawford looking back at her from the mirror, she poured another cocktail to wash down another diet pill, lit another cigarette, and phoned Bill again. "It's Joan Crawford. Sorry I had to hang up on you but I was just too busy for your silliness. Now as I was saying, I'm gonna sing duets with Judy Garland."

"What? Cranberry? Cranberry! Do you know what time it is? Good GOD woman! Don't you sleep?"

"My voice is much better of course. Her's sounds like Minnie Mouse on the old ration MGM pills. My voice is just more sensible, like a woman you want to sleep with time and time again."

"You told me you thought you sounded like a man," he said.

"Oh *poof*, fairy dust on you and Jimmy! You both make things up. But you're right, maybe I shouldn't actually sing *with* her. Not at the very same time. Judy goes too fast and it would make me sound slow even though my tone is more pleasant. But I do have to admit, it's all in phrasing, and her phrasing is divine so she has a way of making you feel sorry for her. But beyond all that technical egghead stuff, I just sound better. Of course. I'm Joan Crawford. If I'm not going to be better then I might as well go jump in the sea."

Finally Bill asked, "What are you talking about?"

"I'm going to weep. You cad! How can you be so forgetful? I'm talking about my big backyard party at the house, after *Torch Song* is over. Remember? You're helping me throw the biggest shebang Hollywood has ever seen! To remind them who's still on top!"

"But that's so far away." Bill moaned. "Now let me sleep."

"No, Billie Burke will be there and it'll be nice to have Judy sing a few songs from that children's movie they made together so long ago, before Judy totally blew out. Now she looks like some old troll who lives under a bridge. The poor dear. MGM did that to her. All by itself. She was a pretty girl and MGM made her into a drug fiend. I've said so many prayers for Judy Garland. And I pray that Tinseltown pays for what it has done to all of us!"

"*The Wizard of Oz* is great!" Bill said.

"For humbling the toddlers with a great witch, I suppose. And did you know that Billie Burke made more movies with me than she did with that hunchback."

"Hunchback?" Bill gasped.

"That's what L.B. Mayer called Judy, not me. He called her a gerbil, too, but that was way back when he was calling all us girls, monkeys, and all the men, gorillas. So Judy was the gerbil. We were all called names to keep us in our place and poor Judy got the worse of it. But my point is, Judy's gotta sing for my party. It'll be my last party before I go and MGM takes me away and puts me in a hole in the desert. I guess it's good for a woman to die alone. Then she doesn't have to make sure her hair hasn't slipped, or worry about having to act gracious."

"What? Dead? Desert? You're being poetic again. You'll find more work - another role. Trust me on that."

"Bless you, Bill, but no, they're going to take me away after this movie, I know it. My luck has finally run out in this kiddie town. Oh, wait, what's that in the hall. At my door! Oh Bill! It might be flowers! Presents! I gotta go! I hope I get some new ones, soon, the last flowers wilted. When I get close to things like flowers they just wilt from my energy. I'm radioactive with energy!" Joan slammed down the phone.

The door knocked again. "Hello? Miss Crawford?"

"Who's there?" Joan fixed her smile.

"Mr. Hammer from *Life* magazine."

"Do we have an appointment?"

"Er. Aaah. Yes."

Joan jumped up, slammed her glass of vodka, slipped off her panties, tossed them into the hamper, sat with her long gorgeous legs high up on the counter top and began to rub rose smelling pink lotion all over them. "Come in."

A handsome blond man in his mid thirties stepped in, regarded the sight, then jolted. "I - I can come back later if you're not ready, Miss Cra ... "

"Come *in*. Sit *down*. Have you never seen a woman's legs before?"

"I - I - a - never so vividly, ma'am."

"Call me Joan. Just Joan. And I'll call you Tom. Now sit! There!"

"My first name is Sam."

Joan smiled big. "So, Tom. Did my publicist send you? Henry Rogers?"

"No. My boss sent me."

Joan tried again. "He's sometimes called a *press agent*."

"No."

"Or a *publicity agent*. I know I'm calling him the right name so don't you even try and confuse me to try and prove that you're smarter by making up something in French! You see, I know French.

I was married once to a Fairbanks. He would say, *baiser moi, stupide.*"
She winked at him.

"Kiss me stupid? Funny. No. My boss sent me."

"Damn him. Not your boss, but Henry. Henry isn't sending me
enough reporters. Anyway, have you never seen a more gorgeous
set of gams? Longer than Bette Davis' who only had tree stumps
even when she was nineteen, and now her legs look like two bags of
oranges that have been run over by the props department. I'm more
gorgeous than anyone in this studio, don't you think?"

"Oh, most certainly, ma'am."

"*Joan.*"

He nodded. "Joan."

"Now do you have a few questions for me for your magazine?"
Joan asked his pants, then batted her profuse eyelashes and
looked about the room in mock surprise to add, "Where's your
photographer?"

"We already have a photo."

"I'm *always* ready to be photographed. Always. I am Joan
Crawford."

"Of course."

"Are you homosexual?"

"No ma-am."

"*Joan.* Call me *Joan* - or *Sweetheart.*"

"Joan."

"*Baby!*"

He nodded again. "I'm a regular guy."

"I didn't think you were homosexual. Your voice sounds so
film noir." She slowly and gracefully put her legs down in wide arcs,
flashing him. She could tell he saw because his eyes bugged and
then he looked any place else as his ears turned bright red. Joan
chuckled. "My dance numbers are almost ballet. I am most fit. I
swim everyday. Even now that I'm away from my Brentwood home
I still swim everyday. I just slip over to the Esther Williams pool
across the street in the next soundstage and do a few laps before
anybody else in this studio is awake." She decided not to admit she
also peed in the pool for Esther. "And then I do my leg lifts," Joan

gracefully put her legs back up on the counter top, airing herself out again on the way over. This time he ogled and the rest of his face went red. "And I have never felt more gorgeous in my entire life. Do you swim? I bet you do. You look so fit. You should take ALL your clothes off and I'll see if I have a tidy little suit in my drawer that fits over your your – your - you."

"Do you - do you - um - what do you think about being photographed in Technicolor? It's so vivid. So vivid!" He squirmed a bit in his seat, pulled sideways on his belt and re-crossed his legs.

"Yes vivid head to toe. Have a drink with me." She poured and handed him his glass. "I have been involved in Technicolor before, mind you. One of my many silent films, *Winners of the Wilderness* in 1927 had a few two-strip Technicolor sequences - but that god-awful process just had the poor strip of celluloid looking like it had been dipped in dirty red and green motor oil. You may have missed that picture but I was almost raped by Mohawk Indians who were not wearing any *shirts*. That part was just thrilling! You could see their nipples!"

"1927?" he started to write but he dropped his pen.

"Yes," Joan said, "But I was so terribly young, then - an infant, really. So I'm still very young, now. Don't write down 1927, for heaven's sake! You'll just confuse everybody. People hate old movies. People only want to hear about what's next."

"Of course.

Joan took his drink away from him and pressed her cardboard stiff bosom into his face and breathed heavily. "This next picture is overly serious crap. But I make them work. I have to! You have to take what you have in life and kick the damn thing as far as it'll go, no matter what a piece of shit it is. Just kick the living shit out of it." She stepped back and leered at him. "I see there's a band wagon trying to dance out of your pants. Let's take care of that yummy little musical number before we talk anymore. I'm tired of talking all the time. Talk talk talk, that's all everybody demands of me. Let's not talk for awhile." She squirted an generous amount of pink lotion on her palms and rubbed them together.

"Oh boy!" He nervously pulled on his pants.

She growled like a tiger, turned her back on him, began to rub all the lotion up and down her arms, demurely, and then ordered. "You can go now."

"But!"

"And the next time you come to interview a great star - the *greatest star*, you take a shower first and you bring a gift worthy of the greatest star. If you think I'm going to talk to someone with food hanging out of his teeth and his armpits stinking, you're crazy. So you will come back tomorrow at this time and we'll see if you can try again. And you will *shave* your stinking armpits. Do you understand! Shave them clean!"

He stood up, his eyes stinging, "Yes, Joan."

"Miss Crawford!" Her face was fixed in a smoldering expression.

He hurried out the door. Joan finished rubbing the lotion up her arms, washed her hands, fixed another drink, and then yelled at the mirror as she pounded her cigarette against it to pack the tobacco tight. "Goddamn amateurs! I scrub and work and swim and practice my diction every single goddamn day and they all slob up to me as if I didn't do it well enough and am not worthy! They all think they can come here and screw me all filthy and stinking! As if I was some stuck pig tied up in some dirty barn! And then they write something for their paper that doesn't even try to capture the glory of Joan Crawford! How dare they? How *dare* they treat me SO POORLY! I *am* worthy! I work hard and they should show it! Goddamn it!"

Then Joan had the most horrible humbling realization. She'd just toyed with a member of the press. The press was her life. The press was her heartbeat and pulse. The press was her biggest and best lifeline between herself and her fans. Without her fans, she was not a star but just some woman, and she had no idea how to be just *some* woman. Joan put her cocktail down and slapped her palms to her cheeks. "How could I have slipped? I'll have to *really* show him a good time tomorrow to make up for what I've done. No! I'll run out and catch him before he gets past the gates! No! A star doesn't run after any man, no matter how important, not even a man of the press. I'll just have to wait until tomorrow and then I'll just have to show him such a good time he'll love me and just gush himself out all over the pages of *Life*!"

Joan took a deep breath and smiled, relieved. *Men* was something she knew how to do.

A delivery boy meandered in with a bouquet of two-dozen roses. Before he could open his mouth, Joan said, "You didn't knock." Before he could leave and try again, she pointed. "Put them over there. *There* - where those weeds are. No wait a minute. She hurried over to them and took a cautious sniff. "And you have to make sure they smell right. Once I sent flowers to Bette and she sent them right back and they smelled like pee. You never know when people are trying to make fun of you." She moved to her handbag for a tip. When she saw the gun in it, she decided, "No! Wait! Stop!" She took the gun out and pointed it at the bouquet he brought.

"What!"

"Balls!"

"What?"

"Please kindly remove that ugly bud right *there* and take it out with you. That one. I don't know why you can't pay attention to the flowers you deliver. You're not getting a very big tip for crushing my flowers. Just a dollar and that's all. Good DAY!" He took the large tip and smiled down at it. She looked at her gun oddly, put it away, snapped her purse shut with such an angry flair that the boy ran.

She stood to glare at the flowers. A petal fell. "Oooh. Everything's falling apart! Nothing is nice anymore! Now what? I can't bear to wait and see what'll fall apart next. Everything is just junk! Why can't things be nice like they once were? Flowers used to look so pretty!"

She pulled on a few petals so hard that they came loose. Furious, she pulled more and more until hundreds of petals were all over the floor. Then she pricked her finger on a thorn and that made her even angrier, so much so that she grabbed the whole bunch of stems and ran out of the room with them. At the first delivery boy she saw in the street, who was not the same one, she screamed, "These flowers are not fresh! I will not be made a joke of!" She shoved the roses at him. "You take these back from whence they came!"

She turned and stomped back to her air conditioning. Now dripping in sweat, she tore off her bracelets, earrings, dress and stuffed bra, turned on an osculating fan, took another big stiff drink and sat again at her writing desk and bawled for a few minutes. "I've worked too hard for too many years just to be made fun of!"

She jumped up, washed her hands, put lotion on her palms and slapped her cheeks to tighten the skin, re-powdered her face, then sat again and took a *From the Desk of Joan Crawford* card and carefully wrote, "*Dear Chadwicks, since I am not able to pay my kids' tuition this year (unless this musical leads to another) please be a dear and put my kids on a work scholarship.* Balls!" She dialed Bill. "You got a dictionary handy? Spell scholarship. Thought so. Kisses. Thank you." She hung up. *"Or hell, better yet, put them on a dam pirate ship. Maybe working hard will help them appreciate the value of money (better) if they do, and all my hard work to make money. But you know kids these days. If you don't teach them otherwise, kids just think money grows on trees. And hard work makes a person happy – giving them a sense of pride and purpose. Bless you for working so hard to try and make all the Hollywood kids not be so spoiled, feeling entitled, becoming angry at the world, bless you, Joan Crawford."*

She read it a few more times and couldn't find any mistakes, so she finally decided, "It's good. They can't make fun of me."

She felt humiliation that she didn't have the money to pay the school, like her own mother couldn't pay for hers and had made her, likewise, work it off. But she knew her kids weren't being beaten senseless by the head master, like she'd been, so she tried to tell herself things were different. After she wiped away an uncontrollable gush of tears, she decided she didn't deserve any flowers. She threw the whole collection of them into the studio street, not caring who might see her naked since she was moving so fast. Back inside, she stood directly in front of her air conditioning, gasping. "I can't breathe!" So she lit a cigarette and sucked desperately on it. After a minute she was calmed again with another crystalline splash of vodka poured to the rim. She drank it all down in one gulp. She made another drink and then picked up the phone and dialed her secretary. "Hello!"

"Hello?"

"God! So *many* things to do!" She took big sip and then the lights went out and she fell to the floor as if dead. Her wig prevented a concussion.

* * * * *

When she came to, with her cheek to the floor, she was utterly confused as to what happened. "I've been attacked! Oh my GOD!" She called security to have them find and execute the criminals, though there was no sign of break-in or robbery. She took a shower and then poured herself a stiff drink to try and balm a bad headache. When she finally felt like the world had some small hope of order, she picked up a new clean pencil to dial the phone. "Bill! Goddamn it! Goddamn *goddamn* it!"

Bill asked, "Who rattled your cage?"

"Something happened! I was gonna call you but I was attacked! I woke up on the floor."

"Were you raped?"

"Can't tell."

"Robbed?"

"I ain't got nothin' real."

Bill asked, "Why were you trying to call me?"

"Oh that. Something important!"

"The party?"

Joan said, "Oh that's not until the movie's over. This is big. This is now. Right now! I need a new director! This movie is gonna be silly squirt if I don't take the driver's seat! Give me some great names! One of the top three. What's Vincent Minelli doing right now?"

Bill said. "I read in the trades that Minelli is doing *The Band Wagon* right now."

Joan took a deep breath and continued, carefully pushing the eraser end of her pencil into the big bright sequins she was gluing onto her high arched eyebrow, "Who else is - oh that's right, Stanley Donan is up there at the top. What's he up to?"

"Hmm," Bill Haines thought, "He's doing something called *Give a Girl a Break* and is working up *Seven Brides for Seven Brothers* for next year. They say that one is gonna be big."

"That all sounds like monkey crap. Trivial. MGM has always been good at that. As long as we smile real big like idiot hayseeds they think any audience in Kansas will eat it up." Joan slipped her feet in and out of a few different pairs of shoes as she went on, "I had Charles Walters doing my choreography with me. I just love him. He looks so cute in tights. I wish he could do my whole picture. He understands it. He understands me. He said he had to go work on some other picture - as the *director*. I forgot what it was - it was obviously some nothing movie with a nobody actress who has no face, and no talent, and no future in pictures."

"*Dangerous When Wet*," Bill stated.

Joan said, "But Esther Williams is in a teensy weensy tiny little dressing room just down the Hell from me - I mean hall. *She* has *my* director? But who does she think she is? I have the giant dressing room! I should have him!"

"Don't ask me, Cranberry. And he's not *your* director. MGM decides these things."

Joan sniffed a pair of shiny mauve shoes, winched and threw them across the room so they crashed pell-mell with a few other items she'd tossed. "Not this time! Hell no. Now I'm a free agent and I'm on top without them. This is not a *comeback*! I'm here for payment, revenge, burying the dead. And I'll do the head bashing! I'm gonna leave this place stomped on, pushed over, and going up in goddamn flames! How dare they think I was happy with leftovers!" Joan slammed the phone down, made a drink, changed her shoes, put on a costume and headdress and marched down the hall to Esther Williams' dressing room. "Daaarling!" Joan flung open the door and stepped in, her tall turquoise feathers crunching in the top of the frame.

Esther Williams jolted in fright, then got her bearings at what she was looking at. "Joan! I mean Miss Crawford! You're all - so - so - *so!*"

"Dressed up!" Joan waved her arms about for a moment in great drama. "Yes, I've been doing color tests. I've been so busy. Slave slave slave for MGM, but you know all about that, dear, now don't you, having such a tiny room and undemanding pictures."

Esther thought Joan looked like a bird of paradise who'd been dragged by Woody Wood Pecker through the animation paint factory. She wanted to say, "Oooh don't kiss me with those greasy lips." She prudently pointed out, "You look so fit!"

"Yes!" Joan smiled, looking down at what she had on - a gossamer see-through low-cut leotard that had obvious fake cone breasts in them. "Not like the younger actresses that are so – you know. Yuck. *You* swim, so I suppose that's why you're nice and fit. But enough about how many diet pills this place makes you swallow before they even take out the tape measure, I've come to ask a favor of you." She raised her bright sequin covered eyebrows.

"What," Esther Williams wondered, and with some worry.

Joan asked, sweet as pie, "Esther, bless you, please let me have your most darling director."

"Who? You want Mr. Walters?"

"Oh darling, I have such a mad mad mad crush on him and just *haaave* to have him tight in my arms."

Esther wanted to say, "But Chuck is so very *very* homosexual." But she calmly said, "Yes."

"Oh *please please pleeeeease* be a dear. I just *haaave* to have him!"

"Take him, he's yours."

"I want him! I *want* him!"

Esther shrugged. "I suppose Busby can finish my picture. I can even do it myself. It's just a clown number in a big awful set that we've been having trouble with and Chuck can't fix it. The set broke. It sunk. It has some big ... "

"Oh darling, please!"

"I said YES! Just take YES for an answer! You can *have* Charles Walters! YES!"

"What? Oh? Oh darling! Bless you!" Joan grabbed a tensed-up Esther and kissed her on the lips, smearing bright greasy red all over.

Esther lunged for a tissue and before Joan could attack her with more giant red kisses, she jumped up and said, "Why don't I show you my set where the big broken-down clown number is to take place! Mr. Wilding showed me one of your sets. I'd love to be the one to show you mine."

Joan squinted. "*He* showed you a set of *mine*?"

"Yes, he was the perfect English gentleman."

"A snob. But he's no Robert Taylor. He doesn't fill his pants."

"Come on. It's just across the street." Esther ran out so fast Joan had no choice but to follow.

Once across the narrow studio street and inside the next giant soundstage, Joan looked at the big pool of water, unimpressed, and commented, "Oh yes. I swim here every morning."

"You swim here in my pool?" Esther Williams asked, shocked.

"Just along that edge," Joan pointed to the side of the pool where there wasn't any set. "The rest of your pool is a goddamn mess."

Esther brought Joan right up to the edge of it and nodded to agree. "Look down in there! It won't come up! Not for anything! It's stuck!"

"Your set won't work?"

Esther smiled. "The set won't work." She pointed her toes at giant pale blue rings far under the water. "They *were* supposed to go up and down."

"It don't?"

"No." Esther laughed. "It's supposed to go up filled with grinning sprites. It went up only once and then we heard the most horrible loud groan, and then a giant *crack*, and all the sprites slipped off of it, screaming bloody murder, and then it all slowly sank. The saddest sight I ever saw."

Joan warned her, "Be careful your career doesn't do just that."

"The water is so clear, isn't it?" Esther smiled. "They just drained it to try and fix the set. They gave up. But that means it's all fresh water as of today."

"Oh really." Joan slipped out of her costume. "Do they keep your commode in that rowboat?"

"No, silly! That's for the makeup man to touch me up so I don't have to keep getting in and out. What are you doing?"

"Take off your clothes."

"Why?"

Joan ordered, with a big impish grin, "Take your clothes off."

"Here?"

"I bet I can swim all the way across that pool, underwater," Joan said by way of a challenge.

"That's a bit of a way if you're not a professional swimmer," Esther warned Joan. "You have to know how to ignore your lungs when they hurt really bad for air."

"I don't give a damn about pain. I know all about lungs hurting for air and I love it! I have a pool in my backyard and I do laps underwater without coming up. It's always been a big part of my singing lessons - to learn to sing and not want to breathe very other idiot note like some heaving slob. Now do you want to race me or are you afraid of a woman who is older and more fit than you are, trouncing you, and making you feel a little silly. Not that I'm old."

Esther shrugged. "I'm game if you're game. But *if* you're going to swim that direction, you'll have to swim completely under those rings."

"Or else?"

"Or else you'll certainly get snagged up in any of the cables holding the rings up. You could get stuck. You could die down there."

"But I thought the set sunk."

Esther explained, "It did, but the cables keep it from sinking *all* the way down so it don't cover the drain. So just stay between the bottom side of the rings and the pool floor and there won't be anything in your way. It's a clear path."

"What a mess of a set they built you. Poor Esther."

She cringed. "A clown crash. I can't wait until they drain it all again after we're done for good so they can take chainsaws to the whole thing to get it all out of here. Or just burn it. I'd love to be here to see that. My poor pool."

"Are you ready?" Joan asked.

Esther smiled big. "Let's just hope we don't see Tom and Jerry down there."

"Huh?"

"In my last picture *Dangerous When Wet*. I'm going to be swimming with cartoon characters. They're still working on it. It takes a long time. I'm sure they're being drawn right now, as we speak, over in the animation department. It's being done by William Hanna and Joseph Barbera. You met them? They're real nice."

"Oh. I wouldn't know. I don't watch your movies. One, two … " Joan leapt in and expertly dived. She went deep to slip under the rings.

Esther followed, smiling pleasantly out of habit, watching how Joan was far more graceful underwater than when she was tap dancing in her old movies. Joan kept a cautious eye on the sunken set, but Esther had been down too many times to worry, so kept watching Joan.

When Joan's lungs began to hurt, she became excited and even stronger with confidence - seeing that the end wall was not too far, now, and she knew there was still plenty of oxygen in her bloodstream to get her there alive. When they erupted at the surface they tried not to act as desperate as a whale exploding its blowhole. They smiled at each other, nostrils flaring, and beaming. "Did I win?" Joan said while drawing a breath.

"Of course you won, Joan," Esther fibbed to be nice, as she was amazed how Joan's heavy copper makeup and sequined eyebrows were still in place, the foundation now only needing a good re-powdering. "And you look flawless!"

Joan smiled arrogantly, the swim making her feel horribly sober. She grabbed her gossamer leotard and headdress and left.

<u>Chapter Six</u>

The clock said seven in the morning – that was time to see Helen Rose again for costume fittings. "And she can share my breakfast," Joan decided, grabbing a basket. "If I eat it all, I'll get so fat they'll give my part away to Debbie Reynolds, I just know it. Time marches on and she's the new big star. The writing is on the wall."

Crossing the streets, she worried again about working with someone she hadn't worked with before for something as critical as costumes. "Hey Joan!" a stagehand waved. "You're gorgeous!"

"How's the wife and kid!" she asked him.

"Great!"

"Bless you! Bless you so much! I bet Bobby has grown like a weed."

The stagehand nodded. "So much so that he only goes by Bob, now. Wow. You remembered the name of my kid?"

Joan blew a kiss. "I remember everything I can about the people who make me look gorgeous in my pictures. Because they're so professional and caring. Bless you. Bless you so much for your good work."

"But I haven't worked on a Joan Crawford picture in at least ten years!"

"You will again darling. We're both not going away any time soon. This is MGM." They both heard a big crash from the front gate, and then a car horn, and then somebody loudly screaming, "Bloody knife! Bloody knife!"

Joan asked, "What's that? Are the fans trying to bash their way into the castle again?"

"This looks serious!" He ran toward the gate.

Joan wondered where she'd heard the phrase "Bloody knife" before. "Oh, I know I shouldn't have watched that Lugosi film." She walked in the wardrobe studio with a carton of skim milk, a box of Wheaties, and a jar of cooked prunes. Joan screamed, "Balls! That *bitch*!"

Helen Rose gasped. A Joan Crawford stand-in was on a pedestal before her getting the hem of a saffron colored dress sewn up. Helen dropped her needle in alarm. "Haven't you two met?"

"Who is that – *that* – JOAN?"

The stand-in stammered, "M - Miss Joan - Miss Crawford. I've been doing some of your light tests, remember?"

"No!" Joan didn't remember.

She continued, "I guess you hadn't arrived yet on the set before I'd finished. But I'm your stand-in. Don't you think we look alike?"

"Yes!" Joan agreed. "It scared the goddamn hell out of me! You looked so much like me that I thought the studio had moved to a homosexual bar - which might be an improvement."

The stand-in added, "I suppose you'll see a lot more of me when we film the dramatic scenes."

"Oh. Bless you. How nice. Pleased to meet you." Joan put out her trembling hand to shake.

Helen spoke up. "We'll take a break now. I dropped my needle and that's a sign that I need to take a break." The stand-in was shooed off and out of the room.

"You poor dear," Joan agreed. "Yes, if you've dropped your needle then it's most certainly time for a wee break. *Here.* I've brought some sustenance. Eat something before you diet yourself into the grave. Isn't this yummy? But we get only a drop. The Wheaties and prunes have to last us two weeks, we don't want a fat fanny, goddam it. I suppose I should eat all the prunes I like. They say the more you shit the skinnier you get. Is it true Marlene Dietrich drinks gallons of epsom salts to shit off all her weight just before a picture? No wonder she sings like she's fighting a mouthful of frozen brussels sprouts. I've lost ten pounds and if the dance rehearsals keep up, I'm sure to lose a few more pounds. So I hope all these costumes come in many sizes, and I don't mean Judy Garland costumes where they get bigger and bigger until you can only film her hiding behind a tractor. Why didn't MGM just tie her down and give her a big enema? MGM did everything else to that poor girl to humiliate her. Why not something that works?"

"*Skim* milk?" Helen Rose asked, trying to get her mind off the stuff of enemas before she ate. "What's that?"

Joan smiled big, loving to be so smart. "It's a brand new way of making milk so it doesn't make you fat."

"It does?" Helen puzzled. "Is skim *safe?*"

Joan assumed, "The government approved it, I'm sure."

"Is that good enough?"

"Don't be a commie. We'd hate to lose you. And who knows where they'll send people who question milk." Joan lit up a cigarette. "I have to have one of these while I eat. They say it's good for the digestion, so I'll blow some smoke your way for good health."

"That'll be alright," Helen said. "My digestion is fine. So – that's the secret to your diet? Prunes?"

Joan shook her head. "No. The secret of a good diet, one that really works is only one thing. Fear. Fear of being made fun of. That's the only diet secret you need."

"Fear?"

Joan nodded. "It's hard to have an appetite when you're running scared for your life."

"How have the color tests been going?" Helen asked. "That's so important for what I'm doing with your costumes. We have to test and test. I'm really pushing the envelope on using a monochrome palate for some of these scenes, with Technicolor."

"Oh of course," Joan agreed, waving her cigarette grandly about herself, as if even an intimate breakfast required star poses. "I'm Joan Crawford and everybody expects it all to sizzle! I have to sizzle or they just take you out back and bury you in the desert – like an old mule. Now let's start talking about me and what the hell I'm wearing. I want to look just fabulous!"

"That, you will."

Joan fought from weeping. "MGM gives me the worst crap! I'm the greatest artist of motion picture acting and they give me a bitch script like *Torch Song*. My character is just a bulldozer with lips!"

"Dresses."

"Dresses!" Joan agreed. "But it's still so unworthy of me! Why don't I get better parts? I'm like Mozart only having a kazoo to work with!"

Helen Rose did a skilled impromptu impersonation of a kazoo doing the *Magic Flute*. Joan looked on in amazement.

* * * * *

A few hours later, Esther Williams tapped on Joan's dressing room door. There was no answer. Esther went further down the hall to the sound stage that held Joan's New York proscenium theater set. She heard Joan's voice, so cautiously peeked in. All the lights were out except the warm orange glow from the light board panel faintly illuminating glistening tears streaming down Joan's copper makeup.

"Why have you left me? Why have you abandoned me? I never left you? I've always worked so hard for you! Why don't you come to my movies? Why do you stay away? What did I do? What did I say? What didn't I wear for you? I've jogged and scrubbed and brushed my hair a thousand times a day! You don't even say THANK YOU!"

"Oh. She's talking to herself, who doesn't. She should try it underwater." Esther left, crossing paths with a nice looking blond man. She looked at him like he should speak.

So he did. "Oh, hey - you're that dame in the swimsuit. Sweet. Ah - Miss Crawford's not in her room."

Esther asked, "You a fan?"

"From *Life* magazine. I was hoping to get an interview before I'm fired. I took a bath."

Esther smiled and pointed to the set. "She's blowing off steam."

He stepped into the tremendously dark space. "Hello?"

"Who's there?" Joan called out. She made a fist. "If you're that psycho Joan coming back for me, I'll punch you all the way to Paramount!"

"Miss Crawford? It's Mr. Hammer from *Life* magazine. I took a bath."

"Are you wearing a dress?"

"No."

"Dave? Is that you?"

"Sam."

"Did my publicists send you?"

"No."

"Damn him. What does he do with all my money? And why did you take a bath? I hate baths, Dave! When you take a bath you just sit in your own boiling filth. Think about it. *Shower* all the time and just let it go down the drain! Then it goes away! It just goes away!"

"Can I interview you for the magazine?"

Joan didn't move from where she stood on the edge of the stage set. "Oh, of course darling, bless you, so you're a news man. What's the news today? I haven't had the radio on all day. I've been much too busy. What's going on out there?"

"Did you hear? A woman, a prostitute, was killed in the middle of the street with an axe and the killer got away. But they got a good look at her - the killer. It was terrible. And they say it was you - well, a person who looked and was dressed just like a Joan Crawford."

"How can you say that? An axe? How ridiculous! I would never kill with an axe. That is utterly unladylike, like some lumberjack going at a tree. How dare Joan Crawford kill a goddamn anybody with anything other than a sensible gun pulled out of a smart handbag! With opera gloves – and a bracelet that dangles and catches the light. Naturally!"

"But it wasn't you of course. Nobody insinuated that it was you."

"A real Joan Crawford doesn't just roll off the assembly line! This Joan Crawford takes a lot of work to be who she is to make everybody happy and take a piece of her home. I'm the biggest star and some clown in a Halloween costume ain't gonna ruin my reputation by going at a tree with an axe! But it wasn't an axe. I was there and saw the whole thing. Of course, since I'm Joan Crawford!"

"They'll find the killer, I'm sure. Don't worry."

Joan asked, "So why are you here?"

Mr. Hammer said, "To interview you."

"Then shoot."

"Um - what do you like best about being back at MGM?"

Joan fiddled with one of her corpulent earrings for a moment.

"The closeup. There's nothing like an MGM closeup for making your face look fat. Warner Brothers has the best close-ups. Screw MGM to goddamn Hell. And Warner Brothers can jump in after. I have fans and that's all that matters and the fans follow me to whatever dump I'm making a picture in, next. And then when they think there is no more *next* for you, the mob just takes you out back and dumps you in a hole in the desert."

"I can't write that."

"Why not. It came from my heart."

"We have a policy. We can't accuse the mob of anything without proof beyond a doubt, and with the mob there's no such thing."

"Oh, good, you don't have a commie paper." Joan stepped down off the stage. " I'm getting thirsty just talking and talking and nobody appreciates how hard a star has to work all the time giving interviews and - and let's go have a little drinkie, shall we?" Joan swished off to her dressing room on her tall elegant heels, and Mr. Hammer obediently followed.

Once inside her room, with a light on, Joan took in the sight of the blond man with his hair freshly fluffed from shampoo. She smiled wickedly. "Why didn't you tell me you took a shower? You darling man. Bert is it? It's time for you to ante up. And I mean *up*. Now!" She slipped his belt off so expertly he hardly noticed it going until it had been noisily tossed aside. After she yanked all his clothes off and she bounced him off the walls, and he was done and gone, Joan washed her hands and lunged for the phone. "Bill! What is this about a somebody looking like me killing with an axe?"

"Oh Cranberry. That. That was just a two bit Joan Crawford. Don't worry."

"Oh Bill, bless you. You and Jimmy ... " Then Joan stopped talking, having an odd memory of seeing this Joan Crawford without a fur and somebody else in a street with blood. Or was it a Lauren Bacall movie she was thinking of. She couldn't remember much of it, anymore, so she decided she needed another drink.

Bill added, "God knows there's two Joan Crawford's for every one Bette Davis at the drag shows."

She loudly sipped. "Oh that *bitch*! I wonder now if the impersonators are doing Bette Davis impersonating Joan Crawford like she thought she was doing in *The Star*? How can you impersonate her without hurting yourself, and others - without putting an eye out? Without having to glue two ping-pong balls to the front of your face! Balls!"

"I have no idea," Bill played along. "But it would be just twisted enough to impersonated her impersonating you."

"Well they can't impersonate me or my *voice*! I'm an original. She doesn't act, she just flounces. Flounces and screeches!"

Bill said, "You don't act. You just get yourself into fighting form."

"If that was some of your wit, I fail to see the wit in it! I'll hang up on you."

"Why'd you call me?"

Joan thought a moment. "I can't remember. Oh. I thought you'd want to know, because I know your mind. And tell Jimmy, too, because he's so cute. I just squeezed the stupid juice out of a reporter. He'd just taken a shower so I didn't want to waste him. *Him*. What was his name? I'm slipping, Bill. I used to remember everything, especially names. Especially the names of reporters and their wives and kids and anything else important. I was once so good at being on top of everything and that's how I stayed there. Everyday I polished the whole goddam caboose. Oh Bill, it's getting so hard to keep clawing my way, again and again, to the same top of the same sinking pile of studio crap."

Bill was amused. "You're doing *it* again in your dressing room?"

"Yep, bless you. Just like the good ole days."

"I remember those days, well, Cranberry. Sometimes I miss them. Sometimes I don't know how you still take it. I'm looking at my scrapbook right now. So many Joans, page after page, and there still isn't enough. I don't know how you manage to look so different over the years. God, are you ponced up in this one - from *Sadie McKee*. You're a real drag queen, yourself."

"Screw you! I don't look all *that* different." Joan turned toward the mirror. "Not *old*! Did you put the last clipping in from the newspaper - the one of me getting off the big plane? Don't I look smart in front of such a modern thing?" Ignoring the burning heat on her fingertips, Joan proceeded to unscrew every other light bulb around the mirror.

"Yes." Bill asked, "And who's that Joan Crawford still inside in the airplane window?"

"Who?"

"Still inside. It looks like you're looking out the window at yourself getting off the plane. It's a total hoot. Is that you inside or outside? Who's getting off that looks like you? What were you up to in New York?"

"There's two of me?"

"Two."

Joan said, "I'm the one who got off the plane. Really. Because here I am. I'm the one with the inflatable pet. I blew him up with a straw so I wouldn't have to buy him a seat. That was for my hair."

"Then who's still inside?"

"I didn't notice."

Bill chuckled. "Because when you look at a photo you only look at yourself?"

"And *you* don't do that?"

"Of course I do. Who was the other Joan Crawford following you in from New York?"

"I didn't notice such nonsense," Joan admitted. "I couldn't fidget around in my seat and look around all over the place and dare wrinkle my expensive dress. Besides, a big star doesn't work to look at everybody. Everybody works to look at a big star. I didn't move a muscle the entire flight to keep everything fresh."

"I almost believe that." Bill added, "The Joan Crawford looking out the window at you looks rather angry with you."

"You *do* appreciate all my hard work. Bless you. I've got to go now. I feel a little creaky. I really bounced that poor guy of the wall - the one to Esther Williams' room, *hee hee hee*. I hope I didn't break anything - I mean on him - damn her wall. And *I* don't break, of course. I can screw all day, knowing how good it is for the complexion. Love is good, too, for a rosy glow, but you can't count on it to be there, so just screw anything in clean socks. Oh crap, the only thing you can really count on for a rosy glow is Max Factor blush. I need a little splash of something. My drink is empty and the glass looks so sad for it."

"You're so ... "

Joan resolutely hung up, poured a drink to the brim, slurped heavily, and then started signing a pile of recent studio issue Joan Crawford photographs. Regarding all the Joans, Joans as many as a big box of nails, regarding them all with wide glassy eyes, Joan kept saying, "She's gorgeous. She's just goddamn gorgeous! Somebody send her a fan letter and goddamn tell her that! Just *tell her*, she ain't got a crystal ball, she ain't psychic! You gotta *tell* her you love her or she don't know!"

She signed faster and faster and then decided to run lines with herself, to do two things at once since she suddenly felt a great panic that she was falling behind in her work, falling behind from the herd like an old sick buffalo. *"That's a wilted summer stock line if I've ever heard one! Who are you to always meddle and pick at and rip and torture and dig and claw ... "* Joan took a peek at her script to make sure she hadn't missed anything. She realized she'd added a few works, instead, "oops," and then went on, *"What is it with you? Is that how you get your kicks or something?"* Joan looked in the mirror. "And then I look deranged for a moment and then I look around the room and recompose myself, and my fans are just *feeling* for poor suffering angry Joan, and then I yell at the bastard, but much kinder now, and I blow his damn pants off with my stunning logic, *I'll tell you why you should go on the road with me. We'll have to rework some of the numbers, we always do. It happens all the time.* No, I should say that kinder. *Philadelphia is just a trial, and if you don't hate me, you sure just gave a good parody of it. You're not the star. I am the star. You're just a rehearsal pianist, and a second choice fill-in at that. I'm up on the set and you're down there in the pit but you have me feeling the other way around! You have me feeling like I'm in a stinking outhouse hole!"* She grabbed her script. "Oh no, it doesn't say that. I went too far again. *Don't try and make me feel small. It won't work. I'm the star!"*

Joan threw the script across the room and quickly lit a cigarette. "What utter goddamn horse feather crap. Only Joan Crawford can play such a clinker and make it work. I bet the writer tapped away at his goddamn typewriter thinking, *Let's see how much CRAP we can make Joan Crawford say in this picture. Let's make it a CRAP record!* Well it won't work. I can make any crap work - even crap aimed at Michael Wilding who has to pretend he's blind. I can say any hackneyed crap and make it sound real because I work damn hard and will look like a million bucks, baby! Boy this story is damn stupid! And people will wonder why Joan Crawford is in a movie with a blind guy. How can he look adoringly upon me if he is blind? When they cut to his point of view of me will they just show black leader instead of a fabulous Joan Crawford closeup – since that's what a blind man sees? What a *crap* record for MGM!"

She washed her hands, fixed another tall drink, then leaving the script splayed on the floor in the corner, Joan went on to recite another scene by memory, pretending she was saying her lines to Clark Gable.

* * * * *

It was decided by the fangs that the theme song *Tenderly* had to be re-recorded again. Joan had her wig fixed for the occasion. "More curls to the side and none on top," Joan ordered Frenchy, her hairdresser. "This is the 50s. Sleek. Controlled. *Far* too sure of itself for tacky overdone fuss."

"That doesn't look too stark?"

"I want stark. This is the 50s! Helen Rose says so and I think she's on to something."

Frenchy shrugged in acceptance, brushed down the top, while she asked, "Did you hear about that Joan Crawford out there? Oh, Christmas!"

Joan winked at herself to make sure her false eyelashes were glued in at the right angle. "What are you talking about? Make yourself clear. It's not Christmas."

Frenchy explained, "Just an expression."

"And it was not done with an axe."

"I know I shouldn't tell you things that might upset you, but this one is sort of funny. Maybe."

Joan said, "I always trust you for the gossip. That's what a hair dresser is for."

"Well - the Joan Crawford was stolen from the wax museum in Pasadena!" Frenchy said, pushing down on the top of the wig with her hand.

"Oh?" Joan shuddered. "I hope they get a new one. I'll offer to pose - if they have their own artist. I certainly hope I just didn't come out of some mold - the same mold all the starlets come from. Get me their number and I'll call them as soon as I can. And if you think you can break my neck with your smashing down on my wig like that, forget it. I walk with bricks on my head for strength. I've balanced up to four big bricks and went several times around commissary to show them all how lazy they are as they eat chicken soup all day like they're special."

"Sorry."

Joan smiled and absolved, "Bless you. Don't worry about me – smash that wig into shape - I'm not a wilting daisy. And bless *them* at the wax museum. Remind me to send them a thank you card for being so grateful and kind."

Frenchy asked, "Kind about what?"

"For having Joan Crawford in their wax museum. I'm not some callous brat who doesn't appreciate being included. I appreciate my fans. I do realize I'm the biggest star so it would be rather absurd to not have me standing at the center of it all, but still I want people to know how grateful I always am. And I'll donate one of my gowns for the new Joan Crawford so they can say it's the best and most beautiful figure in all the museum. I do love Pasadena. I do love the little people. Yes - that's it." Joan inspected her hair in her myriad of mirrors. She stood. She removed her black silk beauty cape, smoothed her magenta satin dress as if it had wrinkles, changed shoes a few times until she was happy, changed her bracelet, finished her drink, and then skipped off.

Parked outside was Bing Crosby's golf cart. She pulled on the fancy brown leather driving gloves on the front seat, hopped in, lit a cigarette and zipped off towards the recording studio. As people leapt out of her way, since she was still seeing double from her last few sips, she wished she could sip some more and maybe see triple and then all she'd have to do is watch the movie in the middle.

She looked desperately for a newsreel camera in the streets that might be pointed her way, or a studio tour. "Damn, nobody cares about me!"

"Watch it, lady! Use your break sometimes!"

Joan blew kisses.

"Watch it! Use your steering wheel, too!'

"Balls! Oh - *sooooorry* - you'd better put some ice on that!" she shouted over her shoulder and then almost hit the wall of soundstage 10, but she was stopped by a petunia bush. Having no idea how to go in reverse in a golf cart, she left the wheels spinning as she walked the rest of the block to the embossed silver wallpaper of the art deco lobby.

A reporter was waiting from the Los Angeles Associated Press. "May I have a few words with you Miss Crawford?"

"Bless you." She realized she was still wearing the driving gloves, became flustered at the faux pas, tore them off and whipped them into the corner. "I think these gloves have a spot. They'll have to go." She checked her nails.

He asked, "Do movie stars do their own laundry?"

"What?" Joan frowned. "What kind of a cracker jack question is that?"

He pressed, "People like to read about things like that."

"Ooooh." Joan walked down the hall to the studio. She glanced back to make sure he was on her heels, then continued, "I suppose they do. Well - of course I don't do my own laundry. If you want the girl next door, go next door. I have the most loyal fans that come to my home everyday. I'm too busy being Joan Crawford to do the laundry. Mom moved us to Kansas City where I lived in the backroom of the hot stinking Gate City Laundry for a few years until she could pawn me. She pawned me off to few boarding schools to let them feed me a few crumbs, but only if I scrubbed their floors all day. I can't bear the memories of that horrible place. I wanted to die. I thought of suicide every day because a child is stupid and has no idea how they can grow up and be a star. My mother told me that if I didn't behave and earn my feed, then she'd sell me to a Mexican Circus. I believed her. I was too young to know that would be silly. If she was joking at the time, I didn't get the joke. I was terrified. And then the instant I'm making any money, my mother moves herself and my lazy brother to Hollywood and she spent all my money at the most expensive department stores as if it was her money. I had to smile about it because this is MGM and they're full of happy family propaganda crap. They want you to think mothers are nice. Well mine wasn't nice! My mother thought that giving birth to a girl was getting her own free slave for life. Balls! Now, how's that for a Joan Crawford story? Bless you. You may go now." She spotted the microphone that she would use and gave it an evil glare, as if to tame it. She had him light her cigarette as she posed with nonchalance.

"We've already had enough rage to riches stories - or *rags* to riches. I was looking for a new angle."

"What? Did my publicist send you?"

"Who?"

Joan pulled a tiny piece of tobacco off the tip of her tongue, and then stated, "Henry Rogers."

"No."

"He's sometimes called *a press agent.*"

"No," the reporter insisted. "He didn't send me."

"A publicity agent."

"No, Miss Crawford."

She blew smoke in his face like it was sexy. She just looked drunk. "Bless you. You poor dear. As you can see, they're ready to record me now. I'm singing all the gorgeous songs in this picture. Report on that."

"Are they new?"

"No. Classics. *I'm* back and my fans will be able to see a JOAN

CRAWFORD musical again! It's been so long since I did a musical and those old ones were in black and white. Those were the best, don't you think? Except for my new one?"

"Sure."

"Miss Crawford," the sound technician said as he escorted her to the microphone, with an effort to muster enthusiasm. "You're gorgeous."

"Of course I am and where's the studio photographer?"

"What? We're just doing some sound retakes since I'm sure we can get some better cuts. The director will be by soon."

"*Just* sound? This is important! I don't give a spaghetti noodle about the director right now. I want photos for the press releases. This is monumental! Joan Crawford is back at MGM dancing, loving - and she sings in color! Every step of the way should be documented. The fans will eat up every bit of it! They put me where I am and they'll not be denied! The studio screwed up the press on every one of my last pictures. Not this time. I'm not some spring chicken you can shoo around anymore, and then shoo away. I'll not be worked to death and then dismissed like some nobody. MGM is *not* branded on my ass! I'm not going to work myself ragged for Norma Shearer to take all the glory, anymore, when my pictures did *much* better box office even though most my scripts were all second rate crumbs that fell off the table all the other stars sat at." She took a few deep breaths and then sucked on her cigarette like an angry truck driver. "Those days of humiliation are over! Now Joan Crawford is on top! Now it's my turn and I worked for it, and I'm really really *really* damn tired of being last on everybody's goddamn list!"

"Yes, Miss Crawford."

Joan turned to the reporter. "I dance in this picture, too. When I was a very little girl I stepped on a piece of broken glass and it cut my foot nearly in half. They said I'd never walk without a bad limp, again. I walked and walked until I walked like JOAN CRAWFORD! My ankles are still weak. I used to break them all the time when I tap danced. I discovered Fred Astaire. Now he thinks *he* can dance but he just skips around a lot. I dance like *I mean it*, not just playing around!" Joan kicked her legs high into the air. "And I've made the *fuck-me* pumps famous, and I wear them because the nice big tight strap helps support my ankle. We'll just wait here now until a camera comes to take a picture of how gorgeous it all is. And then if you'd like, when we're done, we can go back to my dressing room together and I'll let you take my shoes off and we can talk about what else they mean."

"Sorry," the reporter said, "I can't stay around. I have to go find Michael Wilding and interview him."

Joan blinked her tremendous Nylon eyelashes a few times at him. "You'll find him on his hands and knees in commissary, sniffing up some nobody starlet dresses, and you can *go find* him NOW!" Joan threw her cigarette down in a wide metal ashtray.

As the reporter left, a studio photographer walked in and Joan was suddenly in the correct spirits to sing. She couldn't do enough takes to satisfy herself. She sang in perfect diction and modulation - the needle didn't waver very from the center of the dial with every stage of the note. Joan could at least make sure that nothing would go to waste for technical reasons from her end.

"We got it, Joan!"

"Balls! It was good, wasn't it? I always meter perfect. I studied singing to a meter back when microphones were as big and subtle as refrigerators, so I had to be perfect. I'm a pro. I need a drink."

"Here, take my flask. MGM still don't allow any real drinking on the lot."

"Right." She laughed, then asked the photographer, "Does my mouth make funny shapes when I sing? I don't want any funny shaped mouth shots in the photos. I want to look like I'm singing, not howling at the moon."

Joan walked outside, blowing kisses to anyone she saw along the way. "Bing! Bing Crosby! You look lost. Aren't you supposed to be at Paramount on the *Road to Bali*? You're just visiting? Bless you, come to my dressing room sometime and we'll have a drink and I'll show you how the gorgeous stars do things at MGM!" She kicked her leg high and then took a few wrong turns on purpose to hope to see more people. When she got back to her dressing room she kicked out of her pumps. She took off her earrings, tossed them onto her desk, and grabbed the phone, "Bill! Did I tell you I have Chuck?"

"Who? What?"

"Chuck! Charles Walters! He's my director, now. He did *Lili*! Now he has a real star to work with. And he *will* be in my arms. He *will* be in me so fast he'll be wrapped around my little finger the entire shoot. I have the very same man for director, choreographer, dance partner and Joan Crawford comfort, now! How's that? How's that for finally stomping all over MGM and finally getting my way, all the way, all the time?"

Bill fought from laughing. "Cranberry. Honey. Listen. Mr. Walter is one of us *special* people. And he's married, even. Like Jimmy and I. He's been shacked up forever now with some real estate agent who is a man like Jimmy is a - well never mind that - he's not your flavor. Really."

"We're going to roll in the hay until he's mine *all mine* and that's that!"

"He's homosexual, honey."

Joan persisted, "But I've just *got* to have him! When we were dancing he just drove me *mad* with desire! He must want me because I just couldn't take my eyes off his gorgeous thighs."

"That's not his problem where your eyes were."

"He made me do it!"

"Take a deep breath, dear."

Joan slammed the phone, made a drink, then grabbed her mineral oil and a sponge, but changed her mind and decided only to re-powder her Max Factor that was still safely so thick that not a freckle showed. She put on a different pair of faux diamond earrings and stomped out the door. Down at the studio gates she waved to fans and got her picture taken with them. Though it was eighty-six degrees she wore an ankle-length fur to make sure there was no mistaking which one was the star. "Bless you! Bless you! I love you all more than you can know!" She wondered why the studio gate looked like it had recently been repaired, and then she remembered the crashing sound of the accident when she was on her way to wardrobe. Somebody had yelled out some kind of threat about a bloody knife. She looked around nervously for a monster or villain but only saw fans. "Bless you!"

A young woman pushed up to Joan and gushed, "I'm such a fan! I want to be an actress just because I grew up on all your pictures! I saw them since I was a little girl and I thought you were the most wonderful woman in all the world!"

"Bless you! What picture did you like the best?"

"Oh, I just loved *Possessed* when you were a nurse that went into that mad murder fit! Oh there's so many great Joan Crawford pictures - and they're all so wonderful! I just love it when you take out your gun and blow somebody away!"

"Oh really? Why?"

"I don't know – but the look on your face is so very – somehow - satisfying. Even if you don't really do it on purpose, like the end of *Flamingo Road*. Wow what an ending!"

"Bless you. Yes, I've made hundreds of pictures by now. And so many of them right here in this sausage factory – I mean – dream factory."

"Being an actress is my biggest dream! How can I make my dreams come true?"

"Don't sleep," Joan answered. "Don't dream."

"What?"

"It's hard work. Damn hard. Sleep and dreams just waste time. WORK! And then when you're done - work some *more*! Remember, there's a lot of goddamn bastards out there ready to take you down hard if you don't outrun them! And they run fast! So goddam run for your sorry life! And if you're a lady you have to do it all in goddam heals with not a hair out of place. And you have to get kicked around with a happy smile! Because there's cameras."

The fan asked, "Can you put in a good word for me? You must know everybody. You must have such power."

"NO! Don't you *get* it? I can't work hard enough for the both of us! I'm working as hard as I can and I'm sinking in stinking

Hollywood quicksand, pulled down by horse feathers and slop and lazy tacky crap! And if you don't say *thank you* while they pull you under, they bad mouth you in the press for it, the lousy bastards."

"But - you're a big star! And MGM is such a dream factory!"

"The BIGGEST star! Not because it came to me on a silver platter but because I decided it, and then worked night and day to make it so. But this is still Hollywood. Tinsel covered quicksand – a thin sprinkling over a deep pile of rotten junk! And believe me, when you go down in that, you go down fast! That's all I can give you now, for professional advice." She turned to the others in the crowd, and smiled for their cameras, photographing as radiantly as new fallen snow. "Bless you!"

"Joan! Joan!" the fans cheered. "We love you Joan!" Joan wept for joy and stayed to sign autographs for over four hours until she couldn't find anyone else around to sign for.

* * * * *

Frenchy, the hairdresser, went home and saw that her new tan turban with fake rubies was not on her hat stand. Only her grown son who lived in her garage could have taken it. "Oh *no*! Oh Christmas!"

<u>Chapter Seven</u>

After interrupting, and then signing autographs for some carpenters who were starting a set for *Kiss Me Kate* of a sea of rooftops, Joan trudged back to her dressing room. She thought about how shooting would begin soon for her own picture and her jaw and neck was looking heavier than she wanted. "Crap on forty nine! I'm not old! Frenchy!" She finally realized her hairdresser wasn't in the room. "You've all left me! Everybody is plotting to make me fail!"

She finally saw that another envelope had been slipped under her door. She ripped it open, feeling her heart pound, and read, "In the dry wasteland of the desert, the Fountain of Youth springs forth. It is the original waters of the Nile, when Osiris is summoned by the great Oracle, the Goat of Osiris. Why can't you believe? Why can't you have faith? Why can't you trust those who would give you a second chance of stardom renewed? Restore your fertility and the movies will be reborn in a new fresh era of Joan, a Joan as fresh as the waters of Osiris. You'll look younger."

She called security. "Darling. Have you been thinking about me?"

"Miss Crawford! Why'd you call?"

"Oh! Who's been slipping envelopes under my dressing room door? Why hasn't my hall been better patrolled? I might be murdered for all you know!"

"We'll get right on it, Miss Crawford."

"Too late!"

The doorknob wiggled.

"Too late!"

The door busted open.

"It's just too damn late! Oh my BALLS, I've just been attacked! Attacked! And now soon to be buried in fairy dust!"

"Cranberry!"

"Balls!"

Bill did a two second tap dance. "Yep! Balls! And we've brought 'em! Two apiece, and all for you!"

"Bless you!" Joan clasped her hands like in prayer. "Bill! Jimmy!"

Bill Haines and his husband Jimmy Shields were with a mob of very dapper men. Jimmy said, "I was hoping to catch you right in the middle of breaking in some new stud. Which wall back there goes to Esther Williams' room?"

Joan laughed. "You're terrible! But bless you for thinking the best for me. I'm working too hard to dilly dally, of course, just too damn hard. I've only had time for one reporter and I think his butt prints are right there on the wall next to the drinks cart." Joan struck a pose. "They don't make dry wall like they used to. Especially when you get it all wet."

The men roared.

She passed a bowl of mints around and everybody took one. "I hate bad breath in my dressing room. I work hard and have to concentrate." She saw a dandy lad with very beautiful lips. "You take two. Who knows where that cake hole has been?"

Everybody laughed.

"Joan Crawford!" He bowed.

Joan smiled regally and held out her hand, "And what have you brought me?" she asked, pretending she didn't see that some held large bouquets of flowers.

"Lovely flowers," he said.

Joan cautiously sniffed at one bouquet and then threatened all the men, "There had better be a bottle of vodka inside there!"

Bill squealed, pulling a bottle out of his jacket. Jimmy followed, with more vodka, and then all the others.

Joan's eyes lit up. "Jackpot!"

Bill said, "We were all hoping *you* would get *us* drunk but now I can see it's the other way around."

They all chanted, "You are so beautiful."

"Really? You really think so. Oooooh, you're all just saying that."

"No! You are so beautiful!"

"Of course I am. I am a star. A *real* star. Not like those bland women running around the studio, today, pretending somebody likes them."

"What's that mysterious note?" Bill asked, pointing to the envelope at the mirror.

"None of your goddamn nosy business, my sweet adorable darling." Joan breezed over to her chrome drinks cart, wheeled it away from the back wall and into their midst, and pulled out glasses. "I don't have enough ice for you all. Bill be a dear and pick up that phone and call anybody who answers and tell them to bring goddamn ice."

"*Goddamn* ice?"

"Yes, and tell them that I'm goddamn mad that it melts so fast and it had better get fixed - I'm a star."

Bill spoke like a gentleman on the phone until Joan grabbed it from him and hollered, "And the ice better be here yesterday or I'll see some big star put your wig through the wall!"

The men roared with laughter. "You're so funny!"

Joan smiled and slid over to one of the men. "Being rude really isn't funny – but my mind is on my script, lately, not clever banter for young fans. Are you really a Joan Crawford fan?"

"Oh *yes*! Yes yes yes *yes*!"

"And what's your favorite Joan Crawford moment?"

"W - what?"

"Bette Davis got your tongue?" she asked. They all laughed too loud. Joan added, "You'll need a shot for that. Rabies! I'll need a shot for that. Vodka." Joan realized they'd laugh too loud at anything she said, so she added, "I should stand on my head!" They laughed.

The man finally spoke, "My favorite Joan moment is at the end of *Mildred Pierce* when you step out of the shadow with that gun and we're sure you're going to blow away that rotten daughter of yours. I was just so nervous."

Joan made a sour face. "Oh that's an *ooold* movie. I don't like old things. *I'm* not old. What about my last picture? Hmmmm? Let's all talk about what we liked best about my last picture! Of course you all liked the gowns by Sheila O'Brien. She knows how to give me the glamour I deserve. But what else did you like? My hair was gorgeous, too, wasn't it?"

Jimmy said, "I *loved* it in *Sudden Fear* when you totally freaked out in bed, knowing your rotten husband was plotting to kill you, and you angst on and on and on imagining all sorts of grand hallucinations!"

"That was so incredible!" Bill agreed, taking Jimmy's arm. "And I loved it when you were imagining that your car is going over the cliff in flames. Only Joan's car would go over the cliff already up in flames. Most people wait until they've crashed into the bottom before blowing up."

Without humor, Joan asked, "Are you accusing the picture of having a *mistake?* Of being RIDICULOUS?"

Bill wouldn't be intimidated and looked sweetly upon her like she was a daft puppy, and repeated, "Only Joan Crawford is so showy to drive over the cliff *already* in flames."

Joan's eyes still looked paranoid, but she uneasily smiled because she thought she should. "What else did we like about my movie?" she asked the other men.

"When you're hiding in the closet!" a man added. "I thought I'd have a heart attack!"

"Oh did you." Joan smiled. "Who here would like to hear how well I've memorized my lines?"

"Which one?" Jimmy questioned.

"You'll do a scene for us from *Torch Song?*" Bill asked. "Please do."

Joan looked around the room with contempt. "It seems the young bucks don't care and would rather look at each other's pants! You goddamn horny *perverts!*"

"Oh we care!"

"We do!"

"Please, please, please!"

"Do a scene for us!"

Joan moaned, "*Oooooh*, I can't remember anything from it now, pour me a drink, and don't be a cheapskate about it, either!"

"Please! Please!"

"Do a scene!"

"Please!"

"Do some lines from your new movie!"

Joan ripped into it, startling a few with her forceful bearing. *"And if you don't HATE me, you sure gave a good parody of it! I'm on the set and you're in the pit, not the other way around!"*

Esther Williams walked in, smiling shyly, totally interrupting the Joan moment. "I brought you something. Happy picture Joan."

Joan squinted so much she finally put on her reading glasses. "What the hell is *that?*"

Esther held out a bottle wrapped in toilet paper. "Since you already have so many gorgeous presents here, that cost a fortune, I thought that you'd like a tacky little present for the start of your movie." Esther wiggled the bottle enough for everyone to hear that it was almost empty. Esther's heart sank as she saw that Joan was apparently not in the mood for a gag gift.

Joan frowned her great waxy swath of orangy red lipstick and regally proclaimed, "I - don't - like - tacky!"

"It's just a silly gag gift."

"I don't like TACKY!"

"I - I - I'm s-sorry - I just thought it'd be - funny."

"How?"

Esther suggested, "An antithesis of Stanley the Florist."

"TAKE your *tacky* present and GO!" Joan commanded, pointing her finger to the door so forcefully that she almost flung off her thick-jeweled bracelet.

The room was dead silent. Esther stumbled out, embarrassed. Joan slugged back the rest of her vodka and handed it out to the dandy next to her. He clamored to pour her more. "Joan, you're not worthy of tacky," he insisted. And they all adamantly agreed.

"I *don't* like tacky!" Joan hollered again. "You all act like I was born in the bottom of an outhouse! Born and raised in filth! Tacky

Joan! Tacky Joan! Tacky Joan without a penny to her name! Damn you all!"

"Oh, Cranberry," Bill tried to sooth her. "Don't let her rattle your cage. She was just trying to be silly."

"Silly?"

"Yes, Cranberry. And all wet."

Joan tipped back the next glass, downing all of it, and slowly creaked an odd smile. Then as she was being refilled and she watched the vodka pour, her eyes seemed to screw off somehow to some other place in the room. Joan looked at everybody as if they were slowly turning sideways. She regained her queenly poise, and bellowed, "*Whoth* that Esss-ther *Wo*wams, anyway." She took a deep breath. "She swims back and forth and back and forth and back and forth and la da da like a trick seal and everybody jumps up and down and goes nuts. I act my face off and dance and sing and fight great dangers outsmarting murderers and Nazis and husbands and cars going over cliffs already on fire, and everybody acts blasé and just wants more more more! They want more like it just happens all by itself. More! A *lot* MORE! But then when somebody else does any ole *little* thing you all just go ape bananas!"

"We love you as you are Joan! We love you! We love you!"

"Oh all you goddamn sycophants and fools! I can tell when you're all laughing at me! You want to drink my vodka and tell all your friends you boffed a movie star - not any old movie star but the *best* - the *very* best! And you're all cowards and dirty lazy horny sycophants."

"You love that word, don't you Cranberry?" Bill said as he looked at Joan but she didn't quite look back. Her eyes were bigger and glossier than usual, and totally unfocused.

"WHO thinks I'm worthy of *tacky*! I'm a big star! The biggest! I have worked my way through tacky in Kansas City where they pay a nickel to watch you dance your brains out on a stage that stinks of old beer, the lousy bum bastards! And if you want another nickel you've gotta suck off the dirty bums. *Take a bath* I kept yelling at 'em, *take a* goddamn *bath*! Everybody was so dirty! So damn dirty! And I danced through tacky *tacky* TACKY on Broadway as the chorus girl!

They always expected you to have all that energy for the show until you're pooped! Just so pooped you know you're gonna die! And then they replace you without even a *thank you, bye, now go! Go get hit by a streetcar*, the lousy greedy bastards! So if you want to eat you gotta go turn a john who don't even take a bath! I'm Joan Crawford and I'll not abide by tacky anymore!" Joan slugged her vodka and was poured some more. She took a big loud indelicate slurp. "You damn right better believe this Joan Crawford isn't going back to dancing for a nickel *oooor* putting laundry on those damn hangers all day long! And you're *alm sssssssycophants* for thinking I'm sayin *ssssthank* you!"

"Oh no Joan, we love you!"

"SHUT MGM UP! You ALL, I'm taking now - er - *talking* how, it's my turn and you can all give me a little respect for once! I'm not in the world of *tacky* anymore! I get flowers from the *nicest* florist in this lousy town because I DESERVE IT! CAKE HOLE! I DESERVE IT!"

Bill was trying to be as nice as possible. "Of course you do, Cranberry," he said.

"Bless you, Bill." She gave him a big fat wet kiss. "My first day back here at this dump and they hung a huge banner - Howard Stricking did it, the cheap bastard - and I got so many gifts for coming back. Clark Gable sent a huge basket of chocolates - oh that's right, he sent them from Italy. They were expensive so they were good. I had to give them all away to the children on a studio tour since I'm on a fucking diet. He was in Italy - that's why he couldn't do the picture with me, but you know he'd wanna! And Ann Blyth brought me a huge bouquet of orchids, since she owes her entire career to me - I put her in *Mildred Pierce*. She appreciates what I've done for her. Her orchids cost a fortune. Few do appreciate what I've done for them. They hate me in casting. They wanted Shirley Temple to play her part, the one Ann Blyth got, and I was so scared they'd do it. Then all the fracas would have been about how amazing it was that a child could have really grown up into a teenager, and Joan Crawford would be just a *who cares* in the corner. Oh it's just *Joan*. Let her work hard. She'll work *real* hard if you throw a nickel at her. But it ain't never hard enough. But *oooooh* look at Shirley Temple just standing there like a lady. *Ooooh* ain't that something! Let's just talk about how amazing it is that Shirley Temple could be so talented that she grew up! What wonder! Thank GOD Ann Blyth got that part! We could work together and say our lines to each other like two normal people.   How do you talk to Shirley Temple when you just know people are only thinking about how tall she got! It just all goes out the window! But I got flowers. This dressing room was *full* of so many flowers there was no room for me, and look how big it is! As big as three dressing rooms! This is all for me!" Joan began to laugh and cry at the same time.

"You deserve bigger," Bill joked. "Let's get some hammers and make this place even bigger!"

Joan grew angry again and bellowed, "Yeah, Esther Williams can live in her goddamn makeup boat. Hammer her out! Knock a hole in the wall. Start with the butt prints!"

Bill pretended to hunt for her wall. "I'll get you a bigger room, baby, don't you worry!"

Joan ordered, "Pour me a drink, baby, you're the only one around this town who understands me. You made me famous." She began to dissolve into tears. "I was a fat nobody when I came to town and you were already a star! You gave me all my advice and all my first breaks - and goddam I love you. I loooove you!" She wiped her tears and wobbled. "Let's goddamn tie one on! Thank you. Thank you! And at the count of three, everybody show me your cute fairy pee-pees." She slurped, dripping on one of her stuffed cone projectiles for breasts, not realizing it. "You and that dead - a, DEAR - deaaar Jimmy of yours who is soooooo cute. He even cuter than you, *if* that's plossiblah. I could just squeeze his things! Commm-eeere Jimmy so I can sqchuueeeze your things!" Jimmy stepped behind Bill.

"Maybe we should order some snacks," Bill offered.

"Snacks! I'm on a fucking MGM diet. Where's my pills?" Joan looked at the drink, sloshing a bit of it onto her wrist, then she looked at them all but she couldn't see anybody. "*Sycophants!* Elephants! TRUNKS! JUBLESHUFF!" Joan teetered. "Who's got a big pee pee? I wanna see it!"

"Cranberry," Bill called out. "You okay?"

"MGM killed the whore! Trucks! Kill them *all!* Kill the *nobody* - thingsssss! Apples! Nuts!"

"Cranberry!"

"That *dirty* shmalmfp!"

"Cranberry! Careful!"

"Damngoddit! Crazy rumpfle*nuff*!" She teetered again, fought it, took an uncoordinated sip of her drink, teetered one last time and then plopped forward as if struck dead. Her glass flew across the room.

"Whoopsie daisy," Jimmy remarked. "Well. Somebody rattled her cage."

"Show's over boys. Vamoose," Bill ordered and they all left the room, some grabbing their vodka bottles back for their own party elsewhere.

* * * * *

Hours later, Joan sat back up in her chair. She saw her wig on the floor at her toes like a dead brown animal and it made her want to vomit. So she did. Then she asked, "Hello? Where'd everybody go? Is this a trick on ole Joanie?" She looked in one of her mirrors and saw that her makeup was all smeared, some of her face had rubbed off onto her knees, and both false eyelashes had somehow stuck up together high on her forehead. "Who poisoned my drink? This shit's supposed to be healthy! It's clean."

She leaned close to the mirror and saw areas of her skin that were uneven. Thirty years ago it had all been a lot smoother. "You old bitch! How dare you do this to me! I worked my whole life to be Joan Crawford and then you got old just to make it even harder for me! Don't I already have it hard enough? An old woman can't be a star! Go away and leave me alone! Now they're all laughing at me not only because I'm a washerwoman's daughter - but because the damn woman got old! OLD! GODDAMN YOU!"

She threw away her dress, took a shower, popped a Valium and then a diet pill, made a drink, washed her hands, then grabbed the mysterious note and called the number. "Hello? Is this the goat man?" she asked. "What kind of joke is this to suggest I need to youthen up a bit? I'm gorgeous! Didn't you see my last picture? When there was my closeup, the people were thunderstruck! Hello? Anybody there?"

"Do you look young enough?" an old scary voice responded with a weird foreign accent.

"And what business is it of yours? I'm no bobby soxer but I ain't old! I'm coming into my prime. After the wild success of *Sudden Fear* I'm right up on top of this Hollywood crap heap!" She took a sip. "*Tall* heap of crap!"

"We can *help* you."

"Not from a quack rip-off scam like you! If this is a joke from Bette Davis, I'll kill her. I'm tired of tacky! *The Star* was a sick tacky joke that was dumped on the theaters of poor America - the few theaters *dump* enough to play it."

"We will send a car for you. Have fifty thousand dollars in cash."

"I'm broke!" Joan stated. "Fifty thousand dollars? Who has that kind of money nowadays?"

"You do."

"Do *not*, you shmuck!"

"You don't have it?"

Joan repeated, "Damn no. I told you. I'm broke."

"You don't have it?"

"Broke!" Joan insisted. "Flat damn broke! Pretty soon I'm going to have to scrub the commissary floor to pay for my next goddam light bill. It's the story of my life!"

"You can borrow money."

"Sure. I'm Joan Crawford. My name means money will be made by everybody but me. My movies built this town. Everybody got rich and I got a swift kick! I don't have fifty thousand dollars."

"Then twenty five thousand."

"Okay. Who are you?"

"The Coven."

"Coven?" Joan echoed.

"*Coven.*"

"What's that?" Joan asked, getting the bjeebees. She poured

herself another drink to calm her nerves and squelch her mounting headache.

"In the Church of the Wasteland. We summon up the Waters of Life from the dry desert."

"Will you take a check?"

"Nope."

"Goddamn you!" She slammed the phone, slammed her vodka, and then quickly poured another. Her face went numb so she scrubbed it with a loofah, iced it and then completely redid her makeup so that she looked like a pickled bronzed million bucks with billboard eyes and lips. She poured yet another drink, added ice, and carried it clinking with her out to her limo and ordered the snoozing driver, "To Charles Walter's house in Malibu. He's my dance partner in my film. And my choreographer. And *now* my director. He owes me."

* * * * *

When she got there, it was dark. She ran down to the surf and yelled at his house, "Chuck! Chuck! It's Joan! Get down here and *come alone!*" When he ran down, he found her frolicking in the frothy waves, naked, wearing only a stark white swimming cap to seal her hair away from the elements. She was also somehow keeping a cigarette dry.

He called out, "Miss Crawford! What the hell are you doing? Careful you don't get bit by a shark!"

"Oh? Is Bette Davis down here?" She yelled down at a wave, "You bitch!"

"No! A real shark!"

"I'm not afraid. They say if you see a shark, just punch it in the nose. No shark would dare tangle with Joan Crawford!"

Chuck warned, "Careful! You're going to drown!"

"Balls! I don't drown! I swim everyday!" She splashed up out of the ocean and traipsed up to him. "Take me on the beach like I did in *From Here to Eternity.*"

"You're not doing *From Here to Eternity*. Kerr has been signed up to replace you. Why did you let that part go?"

"Nobody is gonna go see that movie when it comes out. It was a nothing part and I was wise to bail out of such a stupid picture. It was indecent! What do you mean people were such sluts during the war! They should be put on trial for treason to make such a filthy movie. I worked hard during the war to boost moral. I danced with that man in *Hollywood Canteen*! Now let's pretend *From Here to Eternity* is a Joan Crawford picture, right now in the sand! Award me my trophy."

"We can pretend we're doing a scene?" Chuck was puzzled. "Then you really don't require me to *do it*?"

"You better *do it* and you'd better do it like you *mean* it! I'm goddamn sick and tired of being made a joke of! I'm tired of phony! If you and MGM want Joan Crawford in your movie to make you all a big pile of money off of me - you'd better not be lazy about it!" Joan sprawled out on the dark glistening sand.

Charles climbed on top of her and tried his best to be Burt Lancaster. "Like this?" he asked.

"You're close. Just lose the shorts, for starters."

"Like *this*?"

"Just let me - yeah, oh yeah, baby."

He questioned, "You mean like *this*?"

"Yeah. What did you think you were supposed to do?"

He feared, "Oh dear."

"*Yeah!* Like *that!* Don't be shy, for chrisakes!"

"Are you sure?"

Joan became angry. "Like *this*!"

"*Aaaah!*"

"Yeah, Boy Scout. Come on. A little more. A *lot* more!"

"Like that?"

"You're not going to fall in and die. Come on!"

"There?"

"There. See. You didn't die."

"Are we done now? Can I go home?"

"Now do something."

"Like that?"

"Yeah. A little faster. I'm not that fragile."

"How romantic."

"If you're gonna be sarcastic, I'm gonna beat the crap outta ya."

"No! Please don't! Like *that*? Are you sure?"

"*Oooh!*"

"You okay?"

"Yeah, baby. "*Ooooooo-o-o-o-oh!* Faster. To the rhythm of my heart."

"Like that?"

"My heart is not a broken down suction pump. In and out to my heart, goddam it!"

"Like that?"

"Yes. You're a dancer, after all. Some rhythm. To my heart! Ooooh."

"Joan you shouldn't smoke so much."

"It's more fun for me this way." She took another puff so that it didn't seem like it was as rude as it was.

"They say dancers shouldn't smoke," he huffed.

She pretended to act surprised. "They did?"

"Don't you read the paper? The scientists are on it, now."

"Oh," Joan scoffed. "Yeah, that's right, I remember. They say that it's now proven, beyond a doubt, that smoking is the leading cause of statistics."

"You're funny." He tried to laugh. Then he thought it might be nice to try and kiss her but, just then, she decided to pull a bit of tobacco off her tongue.

Joan agreed. "Funny and well informed."

"It's a good thing I'm a dancer, and fit," Charles said. "Or I could pull my back out doing this kind of thing."

"I've yet to put anybody into traction."

"And a good heart."

"Now concentrate!" Joan said. "This is supposed to be romantic! Or I'll beat the crap outta ya!"

Charles closed his eyes and pretended he was with Gary Cooper.

She closed her eyes and pretended she was with Clark Gable.

Chapter Eight

The next morning, from her dressing room, Joan dialed. "Charles - er, I'll call you *Chuck* from now on since you were so mad in lust for me - since I showed you a few things - and you were such a dear to stay at it. Anyway, I'm so glad your husband waited as long as he did to come down and we could make the Joan Crawford party an even bigger one - tell him for me that he's such an exciting stud when he's fighting back. I've got bruises on my arms that I'm showing everybody and they're just so jealous, I'm sure. But that's not why I called, you can thank me later, and I know you'll understand because you're such a darling, bless you. But I just can't shoot today."

"What? Joan! We *have* to shoot!"

"Nonsense. My dance numbers are all done. All two of them and they weren't very involved. I didn't use any wig pins to protest that fact but you didn't notice, so I have every right to be mad at you. And it's just the dramatic scenes left and I can do those in my sleep."

"But we …"

Joan cut him off, "I have an important errand to run. Love you! Bless you! Kisses! Thank you so much for showing a lady a good time! And tell your husband he's adorable. But I shouldn't say it - I bet all the starlets are at my door with their ears stuck to it. Everyone is so jealous of all the fun I have."

"But Joan!"

"Sorry stud cakes, I'm just too busy today. But don't worry. I'm professional. I have more costume fittings with Helen Rose."

"But … "

Joan hung up and headed for wardrobe. She brought the food.

"Yum," Helen lied. "I don't think I'll ever get tired of prunes and Wheaties."

"This is the last of it. So for the rest of the week, no breakfast for the ladies, that's the best diet anyway." Joan looked at Helen's breasts in envy and wondered if they were real. She wanted to squeeze them to find out.

"Those prunes have certainly kept me skipping off to the powder room with montezuma's revenge," Helen complained, and then fished for a confession out of Joan, "They say it's very dangerous to put rat poison on your food to make you lose weight. You would never do that, would you? I hope. No?"

Joan looked genuinely horrified. "Rat poison? Then it *is* true that Mae West eats rat poison to keep her waist like that! I heard that! But - it *can't* be true! How can she still be alive? Well, actually, these days we're not sure if she is still alive. Must be the rat poison."

Helen grinned with relief, since it seemed Joan hadn't put rat poison in the prunes - that they were just that caustic to her system all on their own.

Joan asked, "Are you sure my dance skirt isn't going to be too stark?"

"Not when you flap it open and we see your long gorgeous legs. And there's really a lot of heavy fabric under there, so it will all move gorgeously – there's just tons of fabric waiting to be tossed around by you."

Joan frowned. "I suppose."

After Joan had the sleeves adjusted on a gloriously yellow robe that promised to blind the Technicolor film stock, it was such a saturated hue, Joan quickly kissed a dodging Helen, then raced off to the bank and took out a loan for twenty five thousand in cash, putting it in two brand new pink travel suitcases. Her limo driver asked, "What's that? Cash?"

Joan fibbed, "Of course not. I start a picture soon and I took some jewelry out of the safe deposit box."

"That's a lot of jewelry."

"I'm Joan Crawford." As soon as she was back, she grabbed the phone and rang the goat number. "Fountain me *now*! I've got a picture to begin - in hours! I have to look my very best! I need the fountain of youth!"

"Tonight," the scary voice said. "At midnight."

"Now! Mr. Walters won't wait all day. I've made him mad with passion and he's just gone crazy and his adorable boyfriend wants me! Do it NOW!"

"Tonight, at ten. We will have a car for you just past the front gate at the W circle. Have your cash." Before Joan could have the last word, he hung up. That utterly infuriated her. She threw her phone across the room. "Now! I said NOW! Now before they shoot a closeup!"

* * * * *

Joan put her letter opener in the pocket of her big white fur coat in case she needed to slash a few throats for protection, but first went back to Charles Walters' Malibu beach house hoping for a quickie. No one seemed to be home. She pounded on all the windows she could reach. "Come out and play with me!" She thought she saw somebody hiding under the table, but finally gave up pounding and jumped back in her limo and arrived at the W Circle a bit late, just to make sure they'd know that she was still a star. She was also dressed to make sure they knew she was a star. She wore a fat long coat of Siberian tiger. A long black limousine was there waiting, as impressively long as her own, and when the driver opened the door for her, it was empty inside. She'd been expecting some pasty-faced warlock, with a shrunken head cackling on a stick. "Where am I going?" she asked the driver, as she trembled.

"To the wasteland, of course." And that was all the driver would say.

As she was driven, she realized she had no photos with her to sign, no knitting to keep her hands busy, so she nervously smoked nonstop in a jerky unglamorous manner, sucking and puffing like an uncoordinated amateur, making horrible faces because tobacco was sticking to her tongue and she couldn't get it off. All the while she looked out the window and made a mental note of where they were going, in case she had to walk home. They passed an ice cream shop that didn't look very sanitary, a souvenir shop the shape of a plump cactus, then an abandoned gas station from back when cars first came out, that looked like it was ready to fall over, then they were out on the open desert road. "If I have to hoof it home from this far, I'll be screaming at somebody."

* * * * *

In a shallow canyon, Joan stepped out of the car to see a large gathering of people in red robes and cheap paper Halloween red devil masks. At the arrival of the car, the figures slowly moved forward and formed a circle. "What is this?" Joan shuddered. "Are you all cannibals?" Joan's heels sunk in the sand and she was reminded of *Humoresque* when she walked glamorously to the surf to drown herself. Before she went down into the drink, she had the best tight closeup in all movie history. She'd gladly give a million bucks to look like that again.

"Do not fear," a man with the same old voice from the phone said, from behind one of the identical masks. "We're here to help. *If* you brought the cash."

Joan nodded toward the car. "In there." The suitcases were brought out and opened. "It's all there or sue the bank." Joan spotted a white and brown mottled goat meandering amongst the crowd, delicately nibbling here and there at some of the hems of the red robes. "Is that Osiris?"

"No," the old voice said. "It is a goat. And a nanny goat at that. Osiris was a man."

"Oh, yeah. Those are some mighty teats. Balls! If you're going to sacrifice a goat to the Devil, I'm outta here. Goddamn you, take me home."

"You cannot leave. You must stay until we finish the ritual."

"I do what I want, creep. I can leave right now if I want. I've jogged longer distances every morning to keep the fangs in casting calling. Don't ever tell a Joan Crawford what to do. Now answer me, *now*. If the goat is here so you can kill her, I'm going home - with you or without you." She righteously pulled her lush white fur tight and shivered. "I don't approve of hurting animals!"

"No. Her name is Dairy May. She is our source of milk for the Ritual of the Bitters, and of course of other mystical things. She will not be harmed. No one will be harmed. Do not fear."

"Of course I won't be harmed. You'd eat your devil mask, first, if you even tried."

"Do not fear."

"What is this cult?" Joan asked, fumbling for a cigarette. "You're all going to Hell!" She tried to pick it up where it fell in the sand but she accidentally stepped on it. She almost fell, with her heels slipping deep again.

"NOOOO*oooo!*" the old voice argued. "We have the enlightenment of the ages. We have the Fountain of Youth!"

Joan asked, "*Thee* Fountain of Youth? I thought it was in Florida, for awhile."

"NOOO*oooo!* It comes forth from the wasteland when and where we summon it! It springs forth from the dry sand where water has never sprung forth before."

"What do I do?" Joan asked, shaking from her fear of the Devil. She pulled her coat even tighter against the cold night desert air. "What's going on? Just read me the entire script, first, so I know the whole picture, I just can't do things in little bits and pieces. Yeah yeah, that's how pictures are put together, little bits and pieces, but I have to know the whole picture first, to do those little bits and pieces correctly – so they all match. I'm not like Bette Davis who can just walk in drunk and read cue cards and go home and never know what any of it was about, and never even care. I'm a very careful person! I work hard! I have to know the whole script!"

"You must trust us, Joan and DOOO the ritual!"

"I'm not good at trusting."

"Trust."

"I never learned it." Joan said, "You never met my mother."

"You must, just this one time. Trust."

The stolen Joan Crawford wax museum figure was brought forth. Its costume had been removed. Joan gasped, "It's *me*! From Pasadena! Stolen! My hairdresser told me all about it!"

The man ordered her, "Take off what you're wearing and put it on the voodoo doll!"

Joan protested, "But I'll be naked!"

"It won't be the first time."

"Even the fur?" Joan asked. "I'll be cold."

"You may keep the fur for warmth, but put everything else on the voodoo doll!"

She made a sour face then took off her clothes and dressed the wax figure of herself with them. "Damn!" She brushed her fingertips against the letter opener in her pocket and that gave her some assurance that she had a nasty weapon if she should need one. "Somebody hand me a cocktail!"

She was. She downed it, spitting the olive out in the sand. The goat found it immediately. Then Joan was handed a saw. "Now when the animal speaks your name, cut yourself in half!"

"What? Are you *mad*! That's Joan Crawford! Nobody can cut *her* in half! That has to go back. It's been stolen!"

"It is now a voodoo doll! Do as I say!"

Joan asked, "But then what happens?"

"DOOO as I say and you will get an explanation after. You must trust us, Miss Crawford."

"But I'll ruin the gown! That's an expensive fabric! It was all hand made! My shoulders are too wide to just wear anything off the rack so I have two Japanese women in Los Angeles make all my clothes. They're dears. They do just what I say. But they ain't cheap!"

"DOOO! When the goat says your name, DOOO!"

Joan asked how a goat was going to say her name.

"Listen!"

They listened. Joan finally asked again, "How is a goat to say my name?"

"In the moment of greatest truth, the animals speak to us in the purest honesty. Now listen!"

The goat finally went "*ba-a-a-b*".

"*There!* Now you must proceed!"

"That goat did *not* say my name! My name starts with a *J*!"

"The goat said your *name!* Now saw the voodoo doll in half!"

Joan frowned and then ripped into the wax museum figure with the saw, as the red robed figures stood around ringing little hand bells. The goat tried to nibble at the back of her wig. She soon had her voodoo doll cut all the way in half and as its pieces fell from each other, the hooded figures all let out a bark that scared the goat.

"Good thing I'm strong. Now why did I just do something so

horrible as cut that beautiful Joan Crawford in half? I want to weep for her! It's horrible! It's just horrible! What did I do that for?"

The hooded figure explained, "There is an old pagan European ritual called *Sawing The Old Woman*. It originated in Hungary. All good stories originated in Hungary. Hungary is the birthplace of religion and paprika."

"I'm not an old woman, thank you very much, you sick bastard. And I can tell you a story about hunger. I know hunger better than everybody!"

"The Hungarian tradition of *Sawing The Old Woman*, as even spoken of by Brother Grimm, is another form of the ancient custom of *Carrying Out Death*."

"What's that?" Joan asked. "I don't understand. I didn't go to sunday school so I don't know any of this. If I had gone they just would have made me wash their floor, I'm sure. Are you all making fun of me because you know I missed out on everything as a little girl and just don't know this stuff?"

The weird voice explained, "The oldest woman in the village was dragged out and sawed in two, amid great clamor and celebration, and it kept death at bay from the village for a year. Now that the crone of you has been sawed, a year of youth will be yours if you bathe in the font that will soon spring forth from this dry barren wasteland - when the goat says your name again."

Joan darkened. "Only a year?"

"Unless you want to do it again. And then it will be fifty thousand dollars."

"You greedy bastard! Balls! Okay." She looked around. "Where's this water?"

"Wait and pray and wait for the goat to say your name again."

Joan asked, "Pray to who?"

"The Goat of Isis."

"What?"

"Just pray."

Joan appealed to everyone. "How? I never learned to pray like that. I went to Catholic mass and it was never crazy like this. It was pretty and *clean*. The people had kind faces. I can beat the crap out of you all if you're playing with me!"

"We will read from *The Book of the Dead*."

Joan puzzled, "How can the dead write a book?"

"No, it's an ancient Egyptian text, older than the Bible."

"How can dead Egyptians write a book?"

"NOOO! DAMN woman! It's scripture, not a movie script. Now listen and pray with us as we read an ancient hymn to the God Amen and the God Aten, the Supreme God, above all Gods. Both of them, for the mystery of Duality was holy to Egypt, making a Holy Trinity with the supreme God above all Gods, Ra. The hymn was written by twin brothers, Suti and Hor, overseers of the works of Amen. Now let us pray, "*O Amen! O Aten! Beautiful Ra is shining forth on the horizon. O living Aten, beginning of life! Oh Amen the breath of hope. O Ra, with Mother Isis who forgives our transgressions, be kind to us. When you arise on the eastern horizon, you fill the land with beauty. When you go down in the western horizon, the earth is in darkness as if it were dead, and every serpent that bites is frozen. Your waters come forth, and youth drinks forth from it, and the one who is chosen is restored.*"

"That's ME?" Joan burst out in glee. "Me! ME!"

"We must make the sacred well burst forth! All chant, *The waters come forth*."

They chanted again and again, Joan growing more excited and shaken. Then the goat went "*ba-a-a-h*" again.

"Your name! The goat has spoken your name!"

"My name starts with a *J*."

"Listen!"

She heard an odd squishing squirting sound, a hiss, and felt a burst of a warm spray. A torch was lowered to the desert floor and a spray of water was shooting straight up out of the sand. Then it subsided into a fountain the size that might come out of a garden hose. "My water!" Joan cried. "My Fountain of Youth!"

"Bathe your face in it. Carefully! Do not touch any water other than what is at the very top of the fountain!" Joan leaned over it and splashed her face. "Stop! That is enough!"

"I wanna do *more!*" Joan insisted. "Are you sure this is enough?"

"The water is very potent and sacred. *That* is enough!"

"But I want some more on my neck!"

"You have touched it with your hands. That is all that is required. Just a drop on your fingertips and you will be restored head to toe!"

The water dropped away, and as Joan was whisked from the spot, she fought to keep herself from squealing gleefully, like when she was fourteen and stole a neighbor's birthday cake from the window and ate it all in one sitting, or when she was in Kansas City and got a fine watch for going down south on a gent and she thought she was only getting a nickel, or when her name was on the Hollywood movie theater marquees for the very first time and she drove all around town and took pictures of them all with her new Brownie camera.

"I don't feel any younger." Joan pushed into her fur sleeves to rub her elbows. "I don't feel any different!"

"Not yet. You will wake up restored."

"Are you sure?"

The man said, "You will dream that you will hear the goat speak your name and then you will be young again."

"Bless you!" Joan was taken away by the limo as all the red hooded figures waved her off.

"Bye!"

* * * * *

Joan dreamt that, overnight, Tinseltown had turned into a desert wasteland. Everything was so dead that the sand dried into a powdery cloud of white choking dust. The town crumbled away into a cloud. The hot winds blew it into her face and she knew she would die from it. Earth had become an inhospitable planet breaking into an ill-defined shape.

"But I'm a star."

It was all just a set. The planet was a ball on a string. The stars were thousands of winking Christmas lights. She slowly lay down on the cool night sand, wanting all the new male contract players at Universal Studios to see her body. When she looked down at herself, she was horrified. Her breasts were only two dry cardboard egg carton cups. When she touched them, they fell off and she had nothing. As the goat tried to nibble on her hair because it was dry hay, the bottom of the set broke out and the desert sucked her under, and she felt crushed by the weight of the sand piling up around her. Before she went under to the lowest depths of Hell under MGM, she saw a pink pillow pop up out of the ground before a brightly painted backdrop of a red sky. It was Marilyn Monroe and she had goat horns, and she laughed at her, "Bah-ah-ah-ah-ah-ah-ah HA HA HA!"

<u>Chapter Nine</u>

Joan woke up with a start. She was in her bed, all twisted up with her sheets. She had forgotten to strap herself down. She saw that her curtains were glowing eerily.

"It's morning!"

Joan ran to the mirror and saw she didn't look any younger. If anything, she looked tired and ugly with red eyes and sheet crease marks across her cheek. "My name starts with a *J!* The goat was trying to say *Bette!* Oh my BALLS!"

Joan quickly dialed the phone, and after a few dozen rings, Bette Davis answered. "What!"

Joan asked, "Are you still old?"

"What?"

Joan repeated, "Are you still old?"

"Joanie is that you again? Do you know what time it is? Drop dead!"

"Don't hang up!" Too late. So Joan screamed, "GODDAMN! Driver!"

Joan didn't take the time to even wash her hands – she strapped on a jutting padded bra, threw on an aqua dress embroidered in yellow thread of bold angular flowers, strapped herself into aqua high heeled shoes with open toes, grabbed her matching handbag and ran out her door. She paused beside a pot of giant aloe, squinting against the burning climbing fury of another red rising sun that looked like a giant Joan Crawford mouth slowly smooching its way up over Hollywood. "*Driver!*"

"What?"

"Say something like Bela Lugosi."

"Huh?"

"Say it! Do a Bela Lugosi impersonation like it's Halloween!"

"I *vant tooo* suck your *blAAAAAAaad!*"

"That's *it!*"

"What?" The driver was puzzled.

"That was Bela Lugosi in the desert last night talking to me and he tried to hide his accent - but, yeah right."

The driver frowned. "You were in the desert? But I didn't take you anywhere."

"No," Joan clarified, "that other limo did. Where's Bela from? Where was he born?"

"Hungary."

"That's IT!" Joan exclaimed. "He told an old dumb story about cutting an old lady in half, that he said was a *hungry* story. BALLS! The *bastard*!"

"Hungarian."

"Take me to the desert," Joan ordered, jumping in the back of her limo. "I'll show you where to drive." The limo took Joan past the ice cream shop, a souvenir shop the shape of a cactus and the old gas station and then to the road out to the desert to the shallow canyon. The sight where she had been was now a riot of expensive beer bottles, goat berries, a Joan Crawford dummy cut in half and the ashes of a campfire. "What a goddamn mess!"

"What happened here?" the driver asked. "A party?"

"Duh! At my expense. At a very big expense. How'd they do it? How'd they make the waters come forth?"

"Waters?" The driver only saw dry sand.

"A fountain sprang forth," Joan pointed here and there, trying to find a wet spot. "There was a fountain of water."

"Joan! Your wet spot!"

"The bastards!" Joan ran to it and dug into the ground.

"No, let me do it, Miss Crawford. You don't want to ruin your nails."

"Everything else is ruined." Joan wept. Then she gasped, turned red, and in a violent fury pulled the garden hose up through the sand. "BALLS!"

"There's your fountain for you," the driver chuckled, having no idea why she was so furious.

Joan stomped up to the limo, yelling, "Take me to Bela Lugosi's mansion! He'll see me if I have to climb over the gate! I don't care how high it is!"

"Oh - he lives in a tiny bungalow in the outer suburbs. No gate. No fence."

Joan paused, alarmed. "Are you sure?"

"I saw it in the paper. They were making fun of him."

"But he's made so many pictures," Joan argued. "How could he not live like a king by now, with a big gate?"

"Have you seen any of his pictures?"

"Last Halloween *The Devil Bat* was on TV." Joan got in the limo. The driver took her to Dracula's humble abode. "BELA!" Joan screamed out her back window before the car was even in the narrow stub of driveway beside a small patch of dry dead grass. "BELA!"

A thin old man's face stuck up against the inside of his window and he smiled, thinking a limo had come for him, but then when he saw Joan Crawford fly out of it like a bat out of a big budget horror movie, and saw her marching up to his front door, he stopped.

"BELA! I've got a bone to pick with you!"

At the door, Bela hesitantly greeted, "Hell*oooo*?"

"I'm Joan Crawford!"

"I know. I loved your picture, *Sudden Fear.*"

Joan paused. She smiled. "Did you?"

He said, "Yes, you looked so afraid."

Joan smiled bigger. "Did I? Did you like it? Did you? Really?"

Bela nodded. "You are so good at horror."

Joan frowned. "Balls! It wasn't horror! It was suspense!"

"I was trying to flatter."

"Flattery doesn't work today!" Joan pushed past him and made herself at home until she noticed how dirty the house was, so she retreated back to the door, screaming the whole time. "WHERE'S MY GODDAMN MONEY AND YOUTH AND FOUNTAIN AND ... "

"Miss Crawford!" Bela shouted back, trying to get some sense out of her. "What is it?"

"You ripped me off!"

"I have nothing of yours," Bela insisted. "Nothing! What is this about?"

"I know it was you who was there last night!" Joan yelled. "I heard your voice!"

"Everybody can do my voice by now," Bela said. "Everybody makes fun of my voice."

"I'll prove it! Joan stomped into his house again, and into the disheveled bedroom. She threw open his closet door.

"NOOO!"

Joan gasped at what she saw in the closet. From between a vampire cape and an old gorilla suit, Joan pulled out a long red hooded robe. "Ah! Just what you were wearing last night!" She shook sand from a hem that had been nibbled on by a goat. "Now give me back my money!"

"I don't have it," Bela said with a moan. "I wished I had some of it. I'm so broke. So flat broke."

"Who has it?" Joan shook her fist in front of his face, wanting to carve it up with her big glass ring.

He coward. "I don't know. The master."

"And who's that goddamn bastard?"

"I don't know. It's all a very secret cult. The Desert Party Cult. We go to the desert to party but keep our identities hidden from each other."

"GODDAMN IT!" Joan felt left out that something went on in Hollywood without her knowing about it. "What's going on around here?"

"I don't know, Miss Crawford, but I don't have any of your money. In fact, could I have five dollars?"

"What?"

Bela frowned. "I'm out of groceries," he said.

"What?"

"Look in my kitchen. It's bare."

Joan tore into the tiny kitchen and threw open all his cabinet doors. When she saw they were bare, she melted down. "You poor dear. Bless you. You must be *so* hungry!" She opened her handbag. "But - I don't have any money."

"But you're rich!"

Joan laughed. "That money I dragged around last night was borrowed. I'm all debts." She looked sadly in her handbag. "All I have in here is my gun."

"I'll take it," Bela said. "I can take it to the pawn shop and get some money that way. Everybody likes guns."

"No. This one has real bullets. I was hoping on shooting up my next party and really shocking everybody. They usually see me step out of my pool house with a big flower on the top of my head, and I'm pretending that I'm my rotten daughter from *Mildred Pierce*, and I shoot blanks at everything like a brat. I've done that so many times by now that they've all gotten so used to it. It doesn't make everybody laugh like it used to. The next time I'm gonna really blow the gardenias out of the pool, for real!"

Bela put up his hand. "No! Miss Crawford! You can't shoot at the water with real bullets. The bullets can skip off of it and keep going and hit something you don't want to hit."

"Really? They can bounce?"

"Yes! Water is very bouncy."

Joan frowned. "But, I was hoping to scare the shit out of everybody. At least surprise them. I gotta! Everybody's always looking for the next laugh."

Bela suggested, "Shoot the windows out of your pool house. That always makes a lot of noise."

Joan gasped. "That sounds so untidy." She plopped her gun back into her handbag. "I'll think of something good. This gun is gonna shoot something real for a good laugh. Balls!" She pulled off her ring and gave it to Bela. "Here, pawn this for some groceries."

"But that's a ring! I'm not worthy."

"This? It's not real. It's something leftover from *Sudden Fear*. It'll give you something at the pawnshop, though. Make sure you tell them that it's a Joan Crawford ring and was seen in *Sudden Fear*. That'll make it worth more than it would be otherwise. You'll eat for months."

"Oh, Miss Crawford," Bela cried for joy. "Thank you!"

"And if you ever find out who stole my money, please tell him to go to Hell! And then tell me. I'll beat the stuffing out of him and send him there, myself, with both my shoes lodged in his cake hole!"

"Yes, Miss Crawford."

Joan looked hard into Bela's eyes. "You don't look well."

"I'll be fine, I assure you. I was just up all last night and I'm getting too old for that kind of nonsense." He tried to laugh. "We're getting old."

"No," Joan said. "I'm not old. And I don't mean tired and hungover. I mean, a bit too thin and run down. Are you on drugs?"

"I'll take the ring to the pawn shop, today, I promise."

"If you ever need to go to the downtown hospital, ask if the Crawford room is empty. I always pay to keep two rooms open for those who can't pay. Always. But they're in such demand."

Bela looked surprised. "How can you afford such charity?"

"I'm Joan Crawford. I may be broke but I'm never gonna ever be poor again! With my next picture, I'll pay off my bill to the hospital and other places I owe money. Or maybe not. Maybe I'll need another picture after that. But who's counting. This picture just seems to keep me steadily going into more and more debt, to keep up, but there's always a next picture and a next, right?" She frowned. "Say, my flask's empty, do you have any vodka in the house?"

"No, no booze in this house."

Joan started opening cabinet doors again. "Just a drop for the road."

"No, I don't have any."

"Goddamn it! Just a drop!" She turned to him and asked, "Why do you live in such poverty - like a lazy person? You're not lazy - you did *so many* pictures!"

Bela said, "A lot of people work very hard and are very poor. A lot of people are very idle and are very rich."

"True enough! Especially in this sick town. I thought you still made pictures! Are they putting you in dept, too?"

"Last year I had *Bela Lugosi Meets a Brooklyn Gorilla*. Did you see it?"

"What?" Joan took two shocked steps backwards. "Is that *really* the title?"

"Yes. You didn't see it."

Joan looked at him like he was scary. "Well of course I never saw it! I can't be in an audience like that. Who *would* be in an audience like that?"

"Ask your driver for some spirits, he might keep some up front," Bela said to change the subject.

Joan agreed, "My driver knows me better than I know myself." She waved the old vampire actor adieu and hurried out to the car, yelling, "Where's the booze!"

Her driver smiled and pulled a shiny flask out of the glove compartment. "A bit of Smirnoff, Miss Crawford? To help wet your appetite for breakfast?"

"Bless you." She grabbed it from him and headed for the back. "But this *is* breakfast. I can't blimp out before the picture's over." Joan punched herself a few times in the gut. "I still have my health to look after."

"Yes, Miss Crawford."

* * * * *

Later that morning in her dressing room, the director Charles Walters said to Joan, "We've got to start shooting your dramatic scenes. Mr. Wilding is already signed up to play the Pharaoh King in *The Egyptian* and we won't have him forever. They're waiting, and already have the matt paintings done. We only have four weeks for everything."

Joan asked, "Including the dance numbers we already did?"

"Yes."

"If Mr. Wilding tries to act like he has balls around me, I'll scream! And if he thinks he's too good to work with the best Hollywood star there is - then we can replace him! Can't we? Get me Clark! Please! I already know we're a great team! We've done eight pictures together and the fans believe it when he takes me in his arms."

Charles explained, "He's busy this year, doing *Never Let Me Go,* and racing off to do *Mogambo* with Ava Gardner as soon as he's finished."

"Her? She looks exactly like a hippopotamus in an old Gloria Swanson wig. It'll fail. Get Clark in *my* picture."

Charles admitted the obvious, "I can't do that Joan."

"Tell him *my* picture is in Technicolor!"

"So is his."

Joan slapped her hands up to her face in shock. "You can't put Ava Gardner in Technicolor! That face! You'll scare everybody!"

"We just have to get this picture done, Joan. Now comes the easy part. The dance numbers are all finished, so be happy, and let's just fly through these drama scenes that I know you can do with one arm tied behind your back."

"Funny. I'm just damn good."

"Yes you are."

"Hasn't Michael Wilding been on suspension a year now because he wouldn't play a horny Latin lover?" Joan said. " Do you really think you're punishing him now by making him play a blind pianist with me? If you think you're punishing him by making him work with *me*, you're full of clown crap! *I'm* the one being punished! Is that how you treat Joan Crawford for her great comeback to her MGM? I could walk out on this picture, you know. This picture is turning into nothing like what I was promised! I signed on the dotted line assuming I wasn't signing on to total humiliation!"

Charles said, "It's a one woman *Joan Crawford* show - what more do you want?"

Joan agreed, "I'll damn make sure it is! And if that Michael Wilding plays it all snotty, I'll punch his lights out. And then he'll be blind. And then maybe he'll be able to convincingly play the part instead of just trying to upstage me with his tea and scone antics."

* * * * *

Later that afternoon, in front of her dressing room mirror, Joan was so nervous she ripped off her wig. "The curls are all wrong!"

"But Miss Crawford," Frenchy said, "You have to be on in a few minutes. Michael Wilding was ready very early today, they say. That's good luck on the first day."

"*His* first day, not mine. I've been slaving for weeks and he just waltzes in whistling God Save The Queen and has no idea what kind of hard work I've already put in. He doesn't have to look like a million bucks. He can just crawl out of bed, shave, throw on a suit and look like the lazy slob Michael Wilding has always looked like. Did you know he's been on suspension ever since he came to America because he *didn't* like the *role* he was offered! What a *brat!* I have taken *anything* MGM has tossed at me like a dog takes a bone and I've *made* it *work*. I've made every shallow script into a *Joan Crawford Show!* I've never been so lazy as to turn a picture down. Who does this Michael Wilding think he is turning his nose down on us in Hollywood!"

Frenchy said, "He'll have to get up pretty early to outdo you."

"Now I want those curls to look like they have some purpose." Joan pulled up on the skin of her neck and cheeks. "How can I make this behave? If there was just some way to shoot all my close-ups with me and the camera hanging upside-down."

Frenchy offered a suggestion. "We can hide some tapes under your wig, Miss Crawford, if it would please you."

Joan's grand eyes spun to life under her lush black canopies of plastic eyelashes. "You know how?"

"I've pulled Miss Dietrich's face up a few inches."

"That cabbage roll?"

"Yes ma'am," Frenchy said. "I made her a very taunt - cabbage roll."

Joan released a strained laugh. "Just lift me up a little here and here. And can you do something about this? And what about my eyes?"

"Sorry Miss Crawford. The tapes can only lift up from the very edges of your face, so they can hide under the wig. I'll put two here," Frenchy pointed to her temples. "Here," she pointed just above her ears, "and here," she pointed to just under each ear. "And here," she touched her neck at the tops of her jugular veins.

Joan asked, "Does it hurt?"

"Yes, and I think Miss Dietrich likes the pain."

"I'm not weird like she is but I suffer pain like any professional. I broke my ankles so many times tap dancing in my old movies. I didn't care about the pain. I just worked and worked, and tightened the big fat ankle strap on my fuck-me pumps all the more. Not that I'm old."

"Here we are Miss Crawford." Frenchy glued strips of fine lace silk at Joan's hairline with pungent burning spirit gum. "That hurt?"

Joan said, "I've been glued on before. Don't worry about it."

"You okay?"

"Sure. What in Hollywood doesn't hurt like Hell."

After it dried, Frenchy blotted foundation make-up over them, and then powdered it.

"Balls! Oh my God!"

Frenchy tied them off at the back of her wig cap.

"Oh my God!" Joan marveled at her narrowed cheeks, grabbed for her vodka glass in excitement. "Is this as tight as it can go?"

"Yes ma'am."

"Tighter."

"Nope."

"TIGHTER, goddamn it! Pull!"

"Any tighter and the tapes will pop loose from your skin the instant you start to perspire. We can't have that happen in the middle of a shot. I'd be shot."

"Tighter!"

"Like this? Joan! Now look! This tight and you'll have crazy cat eyes and a smile pulled up over your ears. You can't look like that! That's ridiculous!"

"You're correct. We can't overdo things. Bless you. Put the wig back on. Hurry." Joan frowned. "But I can see the front edges of the tapes! Look!" She pushed on them with a Q Tip that had been dipped in tan powder.

"No." Frenchy explained, "The camera film is not as sensitive to texture as your eyes are. Being the same color, the silk lace will just blend with your skin - at least to the camera. Really. I've done it before and seen it. You just don't see it."

"Are you sure?" Joan threw the Q Tip away and grabbing another to dab at the inside of her eye.

Frenchy assured her, "Do you think Miss Dietrich would let herself look taped up?"

"She looks like a mummy that just sucked a bad brussel sprout. She should just break down and buy some lotion." Joan leaned into the mirror. "I see the tapes!"

"The camera will never see that. Really. Believe me."

"You're right. Bless you. Okay. Now shut up and let me bring my lips out a bit more. I want people looking at my lips even when he's talking with that snotty stiff upper lip in the air at me." Joan made a funny expression with her mouth, picked up a brush and globbed on more gooey red grease.

"Did you hear about Mr. Wilding's poor wife?" Frenchy said. "While on *Elephant Walk* a big fan blew a metal sliver into her eye. She had it cut out while she was still awake."

"She was attacked by a psycho fan?"

"A *fan*. The kind with propellers that blows up a big wind."

"Oh. And her eye was cut out?" Joan asked with some repulsion.

"No. Just the sliver was taken out. They saved her eye."

"Oh. Good. Poor dear."

"She couldn't be put under," Frenchy said. "She told the papers that the cutting sounded like somebody eating watermelon. And then when she went home to recover, her new baby poked her right in that very same eye. And now she's in the hospital again and she might go blind!"

Joan frowned. "Do you send flowers to a blind woman in the hospital? Oh! That's a tough one. Let's not talk about that now. I have to think about my scene. I know – I'll send something very fragrant! God I hope her nose is still working – that she doesn't have a cold on top of all this."

"But Mr. Wilding is playing a blind man all the while his wife might go blind! Isn't that just something? It's ironic! It's a weird twist of fate. I bet it worries him greatly."

"Child stars never last. Poor dears. This town can't wait to throw them away. This town can't wait to throw all of us away."

Joan looked at herself in the mirror again with a fierce satisfaction, then stood up and held out her arms, letting the black silk beauty cape fall to the chair. "Now call in wardrobe. I'm ready for my dress.".

The pose embarrassed Frenchy, with Joan being stark naked and looking so solid and fit. She didn't know where to put her eyes as she backed out of the room looking just at Joan's perfectly manicured toenails. "Yes, ma'am."

* * * * *

Frenchy hurried to wardrobe. "Helen! I got here as quickly as I could tear away!"

"Where's the fire?"

"Have you heard? Gossip!"

Helen said, "I heard. I hope poor Liz doesn't go blind in that eye. I sent her some very loud flowers to hopefully make up for it, with the other eye."

Frenchy said, "That, and there's more! Remember the man who dresses up like Joan Crawford, from New York, who thinks he is Joan Crawford? Well, a few days ago, he broke through the gate with a stolen limousine, just crashed through, and he tried to find her. He tried to find Joan Crawford. But he was arrested!"

Helen stopped fussing with boxes of shoes, and jolted. "What?"

"Yep! He tried to find her! And the funny thing was, they say that when he tried to outrun the guards, he ran around a corner and right into some big stucco elephant they were wheeling out back to the dump, and he punched right through it."

Helen gasped.

"It wasn't funny like in the pictures when it happens to Laurel and Hardy. No, when they finally pulled him out he had blood all over his head. He went headlong into a few nails. It was just terrible."

"Did he live?"

"Oh sure, but they had to hold him down until an ambulance took him away to the funny farm. He was so angry. I wasn't there but the guard told me and I just couldn't wait to tell you!"

Helen gasped again. "Well thank you for telling me that. I *thought* something had gone on out there. I'm so glad you always fill me in."

"Wardrobe and hair has to stick together."

Helen laughed. "Does Joan know any of this?"

"No. I don't know how to even tell her. It would just scare her. She doesn't need to know about all that. She's busy being her own Joan Crawford, if you know what I mean."

"She'd beat the crap out of anybody who tried to bother her. Then what happened?"

Frenchy continued, "The man insisted he was Joan Crawford, as I said, but he can't be her, now can he, because he has a tinkle-dinkle, so they put him away into a mental hospital for those kinds of people. You know –" Frenchy winked. *"Those* kinds of people. Can you believe it?"

"The world has certainly gotten modern. Say, speaking of drag shows, what does your son say about all this - about the Joan Crawford man?"

"Him? Why?" Frenchy puzzled.

"You'd mentioned him earlier. Remember? He was at a Joan Crawford look-alike contest, maybe doing their hair, and he'd watched this man win. Didn't you tell me that? Is it the same man who won the contest who's now the psycho Joan Crawford man trying to crash the studio gate? Is it the same one?"

"I'm sure. I always said that that Joan Crawford was ready for the booby hatch! That's a bad Joan Crawford. And I don't know why my son would know anybody like that. He's a good boy. He's a career man. He is a hairdresser. He's so wonderful."

Chapter Ten

An hour later, Joan jumped up from her vanity, grabbed a tiny black moustache comb, and in a left and right flash, as if in an indifferent afterthought following all the hours of such slow meticulous preening, she raked down her eyebrows. She carelessly tossed the comb amongst her other things that had been wiped down with disinfectant and replaced in neurotically precise rows, and stomped off to the set.

"Good morning," she said to Mr. Wilding without looking anywhere near him, and then blew kisses to the cameraman, Robert Plank. "You look handsome, darling, more gorgeous than in 1940. Remember that's when we did *Susan and God* together." Joan turned to the continuity girl and clarified, "And, no. This time I did not play God."

"That was a marvelous picture!"

Joan raised her expressive arched eyebrows even higher. "Oh?"

"Yes," the continuity girl gushed. "I'm so glad Norma Shearer turned it down so you could play the part of Susan. You were so wonderful."

Joan nodded. "*Susan and God* was really the superior picture that year. For it's deep theme. I'm sure it changed some people's lives."

"Oh, yes yes yes of course, Miss Crawford," the continuity girl profusely agreed. "It was the tops. The bee's knees!"

Joan loudly called to the director, for all to hear, "Charles? Have you recovered yet from our night on love beach? Darling? Sweet heart?"

"Yes, Joan."

She tilted her head to the side, and smiled gently. "Bless you. We will do the scene now after I've had a moment to collect myself. Now you must stop all this idle chitchat and get to work."

Charles hurried over to Robert at the camera, and got an okay from him. Before Michael Wilding could ask for an introduction or even a bit of freshening powder on his nose and forehead, Joan yelled, "Okay!"

Charles yelled, "Lights, camera,"

Robert watched the dial crank up on the side of the camera, and when it got to 24 frames a second, he announced, "Speed,"

Charles yelled, "Action!"

Michael Wilding wrapped his arms around Joan, glad he didn't have to look directly at her, feigning blindness. They talked and then he kissed her as if he was passionate.

"Cut!"

Michael Wilding smiled kindly upon Joan, trying to find the human behind the imperial face, and nervously said, "That's the first time I ever kissed a lady without being introduced."

Joan shuddered, wondering if he was trying to call her a washerwoman's peasant whore daughter who didn't fit into polite society where one had to be introduced to even say *hello*. She quickly turned her back to him and stomped over to the camera. She said to Charles Walters, "I don't think that worked and that man over there is most certainly *no* Robert Taylor."

"It was glorious, Joan. You looked radiant. And so young!"

"I feel like I've been made up to look like a clown. Do you think my makeup is too copper colored? These colors!" Joan looked at the set. "Can people even look at this stuff with their eyes? Technicolor might be too much! They're gonna duck behind their theater seat. They're gonna think they've been hit by an avalanche of gumballs! The color! This is all crazy!"

"Take a deep breath, Joan. Our cameraman has done Technicolor before – he worked with me on *Lili*, remember? And believe me this picture will *look* good!"

Joan gritted her big porcelain teeth and wouldn't act impressed. "And I don't think my leading man has any appreciation on how one acts around a true Hollywood star, being a foreigner and all from such a bombed-out country. I might have sympathy, but he comes off like an arrogant prick! Tell him that this is America and not some polo club. Tell him I beat the pants off of Spencer Tracy in polo. Remind him that all Americans aren't stupid. In fact we're on top. We have precision. We don't just do any ole slob thing and think it's good enough. Americans expect hard work and quality."

"Mr. Wilding is very professional and exudes great charm."

"I suppose I can't get his nose out of the air but tell that man to move his shoulder a shade to the right!"

"What? Why? The take was fine, Joan."

"Are *you* blind, now? He was blocking my profile!"

Charles maintained, "Your profile was seen."

Joan insisted, "*Tell* him, *now*. We *will* take the shot again!"

The director walked to a befuddled Michael Wilding, who had his head down, looking at his shoes like some forgotten extra. Charles said to him, "Miss Crawford says could you please move your shoulder a shade to the right, as you were blocking her profile." He returned to the cameraman.

Joan re-powdered in her dressing room, griping to Frenchy the whole while, "Who does that bastard think he is? He's a rude snob! RUDE! He thinks I'm some Texan washerwoman's whore - a nobody! And all because I wasn't born with a silver spoon in my mouth! How *dare* that British snob think he's better than me! I'm not a piece of garbage! I worked hard to be a star. In America hard work means something. Why can't anybody appreciate that for at least a minute? Two seconds! Give me just two seconds in my life where I really feel like I'm the star that I really worked hard to be! How dare he act so indifferent?"

Frenchy warned Joan, "You're working yourself all up. Stop it! You have to be in love with him in the scene so please don't work yourself all up like this. You have to look like you love him."

"I'm mad!"

"You'll pop your tapes."

Joan became alarmed and touched at the edges of her face. "Crap. I'll act." Joan took a few more sips of vodka, then stomped out onto the edge of the set like a Prussian soldier. She ignored her costar, again, who she now decided was making her look tacky in comparison, with his most tasteful suit contrasting his cool colors to her glowing warm copper. She swallowed that thought away, grabbed her courage, reminded herself in a full-length mirror that her stark copper brown dress matched her hair, and was accented smartly by a huge gold necklace of layered multiple gadgets. "They'll only look at me, and Helen Rose did a fine job! These skirts weigh a ton and they move beautifully!" She took her place with her costar, and called out, "Walter, darling - are you ready?"

"Ready when you are, Miss Crawford."

She crumpled again at Michael Wilding's side, both of them on the floor. "Yes, Mr. Walters. Action!"

"Action."

And they did it again, this time with Joan's profile clear of Michael's shoulder. Joan smiled through tears, her powerful voice quivering with emotion, as she said, "I've finally done it. It took me awhile but I've cracked you open, you rotten egg. It took me some time. Some time." Joan bravely laughed as she tenderly cried as she calmly spoke in her typical ability to act several contrasting emotions at once, and make it look easy, "You really smashed up the joint with that cane of yours. I didn't know you had it in you. How about helping me up."

Michael said, "It's the first time I ever heard you ask for help, ask for me, ask for anything."

"I ask ... " Joan fought to remain strong for her man. "I - I do – *need* ... "

"Yes. Darling. You do. We all do."

"Oh - sometimes a woman - needs." Joan smashed her forehead into his face.

"I know." He kissed her big forehead since it was something to do.

Joan said, "I guess I'd better take lessons in being a Seeing Eye Dog."

"What's wrong with my dog?"

"Can she make a martini?"

"No."

"*Sing?*"

"Not very well."

Joan concluded, laughing hopefully through more sparkling tears, "Believe me, a dog has her limitations."

They embraced and Michael realized Joan had just done take two *exactly* like she had done the first one - so much so that it was almost like she'd already long ago been pre-recorded and was just being played back.

"Cut."

Joan leapt up off the floor, quickly walked away, ignoring her costar, again, and said to her director, "Bless you. I think that was *much* better of Mr. Wilding this time, don't you? You have to always keep on top of things and make sure that the brand new contract players know what it is to behave!"

"You do know your shots."

Joan agreed, "I've been studying how the camera works since 1925 when Bill let me watch him work. That was before I even got my first picture. Bill said, *Cranberry, study everything!*" Joan flashed a snide look back to the set where her costar stood, again looking forlorn. "I study the *craft* for the enjoyment of my fans. I slaved to prepare myself for this picture and what did Michael do? He could start by lifting weights and putting a sock in his pants so the audience has something to look at." Joan nodded in satisfaction, then left with Frenchy following her back to the dressing room.

Joan planted herself at her vanity and began to weep as she announced to Frenchy, who was gently removing the wig pins, "I did it! I got through the first scene with a big snob. Didn't he try to leave me out to sea? Do you think his British ways upstaged me? It was just as bad as doing a scene with Butterfly, being just as distracting! What is this Buckingham Palace attitude doing in a New York picture with Joan Crawford? And what did Joan Crawford do, the old pro that she is? She treated it all with the utmost professionalism. And did you notice he was so snobby that he couldn't even look directly at me. I've never had such rude behavior since I did *Rain*. That was *way* back when! All my costars were from Broadway and they thought they were real and I was not real. They all ignored me like something terrible. I was paralyzed with fear, then. I don't think I let fear get the best of me this time. I've toughened up a bit since *Rain*." She laughed. "I've toughed up *a lot*! That was what year, now?"

Frenchy answered, "1932. That was the year I graduated from high school. I saw it, Miss Crawford. You had a lot of pictures out that year but our whole theater class went to see *Rain,* since it had been a notorious play, and our teacher told us you were a very good whore."

"Bless you. Bless him! I'd like to meet him someday! I hope Mr. Wilding learned some manners today. After all, we're not here to make friends. So I won't worry what other snobs on the set think of me. This isn't summer camp. I'll be damn professional. I'll do all this lousy work of putting up with the snobs only for my fans. Unlike most of today's nobody starlets, I have fans! I have fans who *love* me so much that they wanna BE me!"

"Oh for sure!"

"Bless you both. Now please leave me for an hour. I'd like to make a phone call in privacy."

"Very good, Miss Crawford." Frenchy left and closed the door behind her.

Joan downed a drink, then poured another. "Bill."

"Cranberry!"

"Bill!"

"CRANBERRY!"

"BILL!"

"What do you want?"

"You adorable tart, bless you for thinking of me and calling! I've been so busy shooting this picture and trying to keep my head above water. It's amazing you caught me! This studio has gone crazy!"

"You just called *me,*" Bill corrected her.

Joan laughed, "You're so witty!" She was slurring her words.

"No," Bill maintained. "You called me. Now what do you want?"

Joan moaned, "Oh, I'm just so confused."

"I told you to stop wearing men's underwear."

Joan chuckled. "Yes, I called you, didn't I? What was I thinking? My mind has been so scattered. Oh, I know. I was almost killed but I got him right back."

"Who?"

"That Wilding bastard. You'd be so proud of me. I have so much more confidence now than when we did those silent films together. That Wilding was trying to trip me up in my scene. He was being so lofty and that poor Joan Crawford was all out to sea. But I did it anyway! I pulled it off! Oh, Bill, congratulate me! You'd have been so proud of me!"

"Proud of what?"

"I just finished my first dramatic scene with the most arrogant British snob!"

Bill scolded her, "Oh, stop that you bad woman! Wilding is a peach! What is going on in that brain of yours? I can't follow you! Stop it!"

"He looks down his nose at me, I can just tell. I'm afraid to even look his way because all I'll see are two nostrils glaring at me like they know so much more than me. It's just horrible."

"You're just nervous being back at MGM. I don't know why you came back. I don't know why you did that to yourself," he said.

"They want to crush me!"

"You came back to MGM on your own two pumps. You only have yourself to blame."

Joan explained, "I didn't do it for the greedy bastards - or myself. I did it for the fans. They don't know how everybody fights to upstage me. They all buy the sick propaganda about this place. People all over America think *Singing in the Rain* is a documentary. They think that's how Hollywood really was."

"Do I hear ice clinking?"

"No, Bill. I rarely put ice in my vodka. It ruins it. That was my bracelet clinking." She slipped it off then took a big long sip of her drink. "Why am I back at MGM doing a musical? It's such a pile of horse feathers and my male lead acts like an heiress."

Bill asked, "What happened to the spy movie they wrote for you at Paramount? Weren't you supposed to be doing that one now?"

"It had no balls. I said, *write it for Gable and I'll play it*. Not that I'd play it *with* Gable, but I wanted to play it *like* Gable. But it was so dumb they sold *Lisbon* to Republic where the hobo actors work."

Bill said, "Ray Milland isn't a hobo. And it's not like you to let movies slip through your fingers. You once told me you'd even play a gorilla if they told you to."

"Joan Crawford is not slipping! Ray Milland became a hobo when he agreed to take that part for a two-bit B studio like Republic. So I sent his dressing room the biggest and most expensive bouquet of flowers I could find, to teach that dressing room a lesson. I don't work on Poverty Row. Joan Crawford needs a Joan Crawford picture! And I want color, now!"

"They're doing *Lisbon* in color."

"Balls! Screw their crappy Trucolor! It sounds like a *parody* of a color process, doesn't it? Just recently it couldn't even reproduce the colors purple and pink, and I *still* wouldn't trust it to look like anything but dirty motor oil! I'm doing *Torch Song* in *Technicolor*. Now *that's* gorgeous! And that's better than real! Screw Trucolor - I wouldn't trust it for the wallpaper."

Bill asked, "What's really the difference between Technicolor and Trucolor, really? I didn't get past making silent films. Our color back then was only two strip – and that looked pretty glum."

"Technicolor is three strips of film and gorgeous!" Joan took a giant gulp of her cocktail. "One for every color of the colors. It's just gorgeous."

"You know your film."

"I know a Joan Crawford movie. Anyway, gotta go. I want to be early for the Photoplay Awards so I can chat a lot. I have to pretend to be surprised. I can pretend anything. I'm Joan Crawford." She hung up, brushed her hair one hundred and twenty five times, exactly, because she had counted rather loudly, put on a wig, then slipped into a thick black fur coat. She sprinkled some gold glitter on the fur, knowing some would stick, knowing it would look great in a flash picture.

Then she picked up the phone and rang a maid. "Hello? Get somebody in here to vacuum, please. There's hair and glitter all over the carpet. Bless you. Your tip will be in an envelope on the vanity." She put a dollar in the envelope, licked it shut, and slammed it down. The door opened.

Chapter Eleven

Frenchy entered the room and asked, "Are you ready for the Photoplay ceremony?"

"Do I look ready?" Joan turned to her mirror.

"You look so well groomed."

Joan asked, "Are you sure my wig doesn't look like a crash helmet?"

"It's very *now.*"

"Damn the 50s is stark but I have to always be up to date or they'll laugh at me. And how about this fur? I can never tell if I want to go dark or light. Are you sure this wig won't be laughed at? I'm in a crash helmet!"

"Your wig does *not* look like a helmet," Frenchy assured her. "Wear that coat, now. And when you accept your Academy Award for *Sudden Fear*, you can wear the other, later. That will help all the photographers have variety."

"You're so wise. *If* I have the nerve to do the Academy Awards. I do hope it wins it."

Frenchy pointed out, "But you have the nerve to go to *this*?"

Joan chuckled. "Photoplay is a piece of cake! It's practically an orgy all for me." Joan opened her drawer and handed Frenchy a beautifully wrapped gift. "Bless you. For all your service."

"Oh! Joan! What is it? Can I open it now?"

"You'd better! I wanna see your face when you do!" She grinned big.

Frenchy tore open the paper and found a cigarette case. "But - I don't smoke."

Joan laughed. "It doesn't matter. It's a prop from the movie. So it's now worth a fortune - *Joan Crawford* used it!" Joan went to her shoe rack. "And *here* take these." She handed Frenchy two pairs of shoes she'd worn in the scene with Marjorie Rambeau, who played her mother. "I'll never wear them again."

"Thank you, Joan! I *do* wear your shoe size."

"You'll look lovely!" Joan kissed her. "Bless you. And I do love your hair that way. No more cheap dishcloth turbans! This new look is *sooo* cute!"

Frenchy sadly touched the top of her head. "Yes. It's gone."

"Good. Those rubies did *not* look real."

"I thought it was a nice turban. I miss it."

Joan wrinkled up her nose and slammed a martini. "It was cheap-looking and tacky and we don't like that, now do we! We don't like tacky! God has this whole town has gotten cheap. Well - I'm off now to be praised." She laughed and walked out to her waiting limousine. She was whisked away to the Beverly Hills Hotel. She promenaded down a red carpet, to an endless blinding explosion of flashbulbs, and then charged into the lobby and up the six steps into the glorious Crystal Room. There, she was besieged by industry friends who told her how fabulous she looked and how they promised to vote for her to get another best actress award.

"Yes," Joan agreed with a reporter. "*Sudden Fear* was a marvelous picture. It was so suspenseful that popcorn just shot up everywhere. I bet there will be more awards for it to come."

The eminent infamous columnist Hedda Hopper grabbed Joan's arm, and said, "Joan! I'm so glad you're here. I tell you, I don't know why they keep talking about Shirley Booth winning for *Come Back, Little Sheba.*"

"Bless you." Joan made a sorry expression. "She may have given a good performance, but who could tell? That poor woman had *no* face! Nothing! It might as well have been a radio performance. Are we now to give Academy Awards out for radio? That's just terrible! I'm sure I'll get the Academy award. I have a voice *and* a face!"

"Your eyes!"

Joan looked up at her own eyelashes. "Are they on crooked? Oh *balls*! So many pictures have already been snapped back there."

Hedda said, "No. The real part. They're just so beautiful in this light. The camera can never catch how beautiful a blue your eyes are. They're just like jewels."

Joan took her hand "Bless you. Aren't you just the cat's meow. I guess I take my color for granted. Maybe Technicolor will finally capture them in their correct hue."

Hedda smiled. "Then they'll look like candy. Everything in color looks like candy."

Joan laughed.

Hedda remarked, "I hear this new picture of yours is back to the usual Joan Crawford standards."

Joan fanned her long eyelashes at her as if they were to blow her away. "What could you possibly mean?"

"You yell at people a lot."

Joan chuckled. "Scriptwriters like to do that to me, don't they. A few good yell scenes and they think they've done a good job. So you can't shake-a-spear at it. That's how I thought the expression went until my first husband told me all about Shakespeare. It's Shakespeare. Not shake-a-spear. Oh how silly I was in the 20s. I was so ignorant. You don't learn much about literature while winning dance contests."

Hedda said, "This town is most certainly not worthy of the bard's talents. Tell me, how is it to yell at Michael Wilding? Fun?"

"He don't do much yelling back." Joan rolled her eyes in mock angst. "He just doesn't fill his pants."

"You and Wilding make a handsome couple."

Joan made a sour face. "Between us, I'm the handsome one and he's the pretty little thing. Not that I want to talk about how pansy he is. I adore my homosexual friends, and you were right about him and Stewart Granger, I'm sure."

Hedda admitted, "Oh, when I wrote that, I was just laughing out my ass. He's suing me anyway, for saying that. Now I'll lose my ass!" She laughed as if she could utterly care less. "It's all just press, anyway, and who says it has to say anything. People read the paper because they just want dirt. Who are they to know if any of it's true or not. And don't worry about what I write about you. I'll give *Torch Song* ballyhoo - until the box office is boffo! You deserve it, you old battle horse!"

"You are a dear. And so clever with all the *B* words. Especially when describing Bette Davis in your column. Why can't you just say *bitch*!" Joan took her arm and pulled her close. "And I'm not old."

Hedda Hopper sauntered with Joan to their table, adding, "And neither am I. We'll just say that 1890 was a good year for wine."

"You were born in 1890?"

"We'll just say it was a good year for wine." To quickly change the subject, Hedda said, "Boy, Joan, speaking of Joan Crawford, there's sure a lot of you around these days."

"What do you mean, dear," Joan asked as she was pretending she wasn't looking around as much as she was. "I don't see anymore of me."

"Not in *here!*" Hedda pointed her thumb at the door. "Out there! And now even murder. A Joan Crawford dead ringer killed some streetwalker. Can you believe it? How dare someone do that to you, to tarnish your good name."

Joan stated, "It's good press to tarnish a good name."

"It's press, alright, but due to the fact that it's a man in a dress, they don't cover it like they should. The papers are so scared of the very word *homosexual.*"

Joan said, "But they love the word *psychopathic killer.* And one Joan Crawford bad apple hopefully will not ruin the rest of the bunch. It certainly won't ruin *my* Joan Crawford name."

Hedda said, "They say a good name is better than a girdle of gold."

"WHAT? Are you *mad?* For most women, nowadays, there's nothing better than gold *and* a good girdle!" Joan sighed. "Everybody wants to be Joan Crawford. The lovely men don't *ever* want to be Bette Davis."

"I wonder why?"

"It's only natural. Their mothers warned them, I'm sure."

Hedda puzzled, "Warned them of *what?* Putting on a dress?"

"Worse. Didn't your mother always warn you that if you made a face like that, it might stick?" As Joan continued scoping out the room, she spotted an empty chair at the main front dais. Twentieth-Century Fox boss Daryl Zanuck sat near an empty seat, reserved for the Fastest Rising Star. "Isn't Marilyn supposed to be up there?" Joan asked, arched eyebrows raised. "Or is she too drunk to make the awards tonight?"

Hedda sniggered. "Her designer, William Travilla, told me she was too fat for the dress. She's busy right now shitting out two high colonics."

"How high?"

"I can't tell you the recipe! How would I know what that woman has pumped up her backside."

"Are you sure?" Joan was utterly amused.

Hedda nodded. "Travilla doesn't know anything but I trust him."

"Marilyn *is* a bit rounded around the edge, for a star," Joan said. "You'd have thought she would have realized that when she chose her gown for the evening. And she would have picked out something that drapes."

"God. When it comes time for her to climb up those stairs, her ass is still going to be left jiggling behind in the lobby."

Joan busted out into peels of rich joyous laughter. "Oh, we must be kind and love her, I suppose. She is a bit child like."

Hedda said, "Why should I hold my tongue? I have a column to write and tonight I might get something more than the usual cold drool."

"Mark my words," Joan assured her. "By next year's party, Miss Monroe will be forgotten. She'll have gone to television to sell bug spray, or various medical suppositories, in that most ugly fuzzy looking black and white image that only television can produce. That's what always happens to the little starlets they make sit up there, accusing them of being the Fastest Rising Star. How very sad for them."

"They rise too fast, nowadays," Hedda agreed. Then she turned to the waiter and yelled, "I wanna martini! And make it a *picture!*" She asked Joan, "What will you have?"

"Balls!"

"She'll take a bucket of nail polish remover."

"*And* a straw!" They laughed, and then Joan sighed. "In the good ole days, they knew how to groom a star. They even made Judy Garland look glamorous when they wanted to. Now we have poor

Marilyn who has a figure that looks like a barn full of sheep. She has no idea how to be pretty. No goddamn idea how. They have no guidance, and when we veterans try to help, they don't even know to say *yes*. The poor dears. The 50s are really going to be a wasteland."

"Speaking of wasteland." Hedda asked, "So, Joan dear, when are you going to get married again?"

Joan smirked into her drink. "Why should I marry again? I've finally become the man I always wanted to marry."

"What's that?"

"I'm rich. I'm strong. I know what I like."

Hedda reminded her, "You're broke."

For a moment Joan looked utterly lost. "Oh. *Oh!* I forgot!" She put two fingertips to her lips and seemed like she might cry. Then she smirked and winked. "I always feel broke, anyway. So what's the difference? I can't outrun my childhood. I close my eyes and see squalor and Mom looking at me like she don't know how to feed me. But look at me! New dress. New top of the line Peter Pan bra. New shoes. A new picture - a goddamn *musical* in expensive color! And there was enough fans outside to make me feel on top of this dung heap. I just have to do one more picture after this one, and of course I will, and then I'll have all the bills paid up. And then I can go get in debt again!" She paused, remembering what Gangster Al had said to her about being through after this picture – about her becoming too much of a Hollywood liability to continue her life. She tried to shake his remark as her heart went ice cold. She took a drink to forget about him.

"What were you thinking? You look like you've just been told you have cancer."

"Oh nothing."

Hedda laughed, "Thinking about Bette?"

Joan stopped slouching. "*The Star* was pure desperation! She didn't even do a good job of impersonating me, so nobody got her sick joke. I DON'T talk like a squeaky wind-up toy. Balls! *I* cannot be impersonated! Yeah, there's a lot of Joan Crawfords out there, but that's just fans showing their love." Joan chuckled. "But I got her back! Oh did I! After what she'd done to me, doing that sick picture to make fun of me, damn her. I got a great revenge! A grand Joan Crawford revenge!"

"On Bette?"

"No." Joan said, "Have you seen her horrible poodle cut? It looks ridiculous. She said she saw stripper Lili St. Cyr wearing one so she ran out and got one. Those new poodle dos are not for elderly women. They look far better on dogs and teenagers."

"How did you get your revenge on Bette?"

"You haven't heard?"

Hedda shook her head.

"My revenge was not on Bette, even though she was the one trying to impersonate me and make me look bad. My revenge was on the *scriptwriter.*"

"Oh?" Hedda asked, "*Do* tell!"

"Well, the scriptwriters of that piece of slander, Kate and Dale Eunson, used to be friends of mine. For twenty-five wasted years! Their daughter, Joan, was named after me and I'm her godmother. Well, that sweet Joan fell in love with a car salesman, Kirby. At seventeen, Mom and Dad decided she was too young to marry and they begged me to talk some sense into her. They dared ask me to do that for them during the shooting of that piece of Bette Davis filth they wrote for her. What were they thinking? Well. I met with dear Joan and Kirby, both. Then at midnight I called her parents to say, *Congratulations, I want you to be the first to know that your daughter and Kirby have been married at my house, tonight. Goodbye.*"

"No!"

"Yes."

"NO!"

Joan chortled as she sipped. "It's a true story!"

Hedda gasped. "What did they think of your not inviting them to their own daughter's wedding?"

Joan took a gulp of her drink, and then wiped her mouth like John Wayne. "What did I think of their filthy script about me. And written for a tatty bitch like Davis? Screw 'em! Screw 'em all! Screw 'em all to HELL! And Bette read about the wedding in the next day's

paper and told the Eunsons to go scratch my eyes out. Yes, she said
that. A lighting man told me. I told him to light her to look like a
witch. He told me she looked like one no matter what. He said that
since Shirley Temple's close-ups had been photographed through
gauze, then Miss Davis would have to have hers shot through a lead
casket!" Then Joan softened. She smiled. "And those two kids are
still happily married and it's a full long Hollywood year later. It must
be a record. Bless them. The only long term happy marriage I know
in this swamp is Bill and Jimmy. It must be twenty-five years they've
been together by now. Goddamn! I feel old. But I'm not old."

Hedda smiled. "They're the sweetest men, aren't they. And
so damn funny. Did you hear the joke - the drink in Hollywood is:
Marriage on the Rocks."

"I don't get it."

"Joan! You're always so literal."

Joan agreed. "If a drink doesn't say *vodka vodka vodka*, then what
the goddamn hell do I care? And the ice always comes from the
filthiest water they're trying to hide. Vodka straight up is the only
healthy drink, since you can't smell it on the breath."

"It smells like you've been pickled and put in a jar."

"Then drink up," Joan said, "That sounds clean. Speaking of
clean, when I was in the hospital doing research for *Possessed* I saw
a lot of clean things. In there, I saw real shock therapy. It was
frightful!"

Hedda shook her head sadly. "Joan Crawford and psychos. You
really know how to pick them." She poured some of her pitcher into
Joan's glass. "What's going on out there with that Joan Crawford
murder? A sequel to *Possessed*? I wonder how many of you they
have now at the mental ward. Here. Have some of this before I fall
sideways off the table."

"No," Joan assured her. "It's not just you. The room really
is spinning." They laughed, then Joan became serious and added,
"You can't report that last story about the wedding at my house. It's
off the record. If you even try, I'll get *your* scriptwriter. I'll get *you*!
I'll take your typewriter and turn it into your next high colonic."

Hedda looked befuddled. "Joan, why would I report a story that took place last year? Nobody gives a damn about last year. I'm a reporter, not some worthless historian!"

"We never accused anybody in this room of that." Joan looked around the room at the three hundred and fifty guests that had been waiting for two hours, waiting for Miss Monroe. Then loud screams, laughter and clapping erupted. Joan turned to the stairs to see Marilyn being helped into the room by reporters. She was sewn so tight into her dress that she had to hop up each step."

"Oh my God!" Joan gasped. "Is she here? Already?"

"My, my how the time flies when I'm talking," Hedda said, then gasped along with everybody else. "Oh my god! She's naked! No! Almost! Not quite! She has a little bit of fabric painted on where there would probably be a pookie!"

Marilyn wriggled to her spot at the dais as the men in the room hollered out wolf calls. Jerry Lewis, the host, jumped up on his chair to get a better view of Marilyn's cleavage, which could be seen from any angle of the room, and did his horny Japanese man impersonation that he always did in his stand up routines.

"It's just a shame," Hedda grumbled.

"God! She's so *pink*!" Joan was not able to tear her eyes off a very nude pink body glowing through such an invisible dress.

Hedda frowned. "How unprofessional to do that to an industry dinner. Poor Photoplay paid all this money to make this event so nice for respectable actors, and now look at it! Ruined by a cheap back-alley burlesque strip show!"

Joan said, "You'd think we were in Kansas City, not Hollywood. At some stag party!"

"SHOW OFF!" Hedda yelled out. She wasn't heard from all the howling. "SHOW OFF!"

Joan sadly shook her head. "What else could Marilyn do?"

"You're so kind." Hedda marveled. "I would have thrown my drink at her, but I need it."

"You do not. In two minutes you'll be upside-down in the toilet."

Hedda squinted at her. "I do too. I can still see. Damn is everybody in this room ugly."

* * * * *

On the ride home, it violently stormed with lightning and thunder and destructive flash floods. Joan took it for granted. She was very angry, and life was a movie. "Don't you think this is all a little overdone?" she coolly asked her frightened driver, sneering at the blue flashes coming at both sides of the car.

"This? The storm?"

"Overdone!" she yelled over the deafening explosions. "Nobody will believe it."

* * * * *

That night, Joan tossed and turned. She dreamed of big round pink skin coming at her, cooing, and singing, "*I love you Joan.*" Marilyn's breasts pushed up against Joan's until Joan realized that hers were only made of small cardboard cups. They crushed flat and she was ruined. They would never plump back up again. She cried. She wanted to be the one everybody went crazy over. She felt left behind and all dried up and done. Marilyn's boobies puffed up bigger and smashed against Joan's face and she couldn't breath. Her entire body was crushed under heavy wobbling pink monstrous pillows that flattened the entire soundstage. Then for some reason she was back in Kansas City with some other name, and she couldn't make enough money dancing so she went out with the stage door johnnies for a quick meal and then an even quicker tumble.

Joan woke with a fright, feeling trapped. The more she thought about it, the more she became furious that Marilyn would have behaved so badly at an industry event financed by Photoplay, and she felt bad for them. She wondered if Marilyn just didn't know any better, having a bad childhood where important things just weren't explained to her. Joan felt eleven years old again. She thought about how her stepfather who was thirty-four years old was having sex with her again. He said it was love so they did it all the time. She didn't know what to think other than she wanted to keep a man around the house at any cost, not knowing much yet about men or costs. When mother caught them one day, he was tossed out, of course. But Joan was the one who was blamed. "Don't you know how to behave? You should just know!"

Joan woke up with a fright. She felt horrible that her mother would blame her. She wanted to die. She hated her mother. That hate was the only feelings she had about having endured a child molester. Joan suddenly felt like she might be crushed down into her bed by the force of gravity. She gave herself some assurance by telling herself over and over again that she had bent over backwards to protect her own children from such a gutter. She'd tried. She wished her mother had tried just a little harder with her.

Chapter Twelve

By the light of morning, Joan's nightmares seemed like some dissipating bad gas. Strong coffee helped too. To keep busy, Joan happily agreed to meet an Associated Press reporter at the Polo Lounge. Her publicist Henry Rogers was on hand to control the topic - this year's Academy Awards. Back at the very same Beverly Hills Hotel where the Photoplay awards had just been, Joan grandly moaned, "Oooh," trying not to moan, grandly posing with her cigarette, "it'll probably go to Leslie Caron for *Lili*."

"Are you considering television?" the reporter asked, watching her hand, entirely mesmerized by how elegantly she smoked.

"It's the tricky devil," Joan answered, blowing smoke off to the side, enjoying that her mannerisms sometimes hypnotized certain people. "Evil! I'm a great movie star on a great screen, and television is so very tiny. Poor Lucille Ball threw it all away in one last gasp. But don't report what I just said about Lucy. That was off the record. I have nothing against all her many years of hard work over at RKO. I just have a right to want to protect the big screen movies. TV seems to be threatening that, now, for some reason beyond me. And that goes double for Milton Berle, poor fellah. The big screen is my work. I am a star that you can only see in the movie theater. You have to understand that."

"Sure. Off the record."

Joan smiled bright and big. The reporter was dazzled. "TV black and white looks so horrible. People could have dust in their hair and you wouldn't know. TV makes everything look so dusty."

"Sure. Off the record."

"Isn't that just sad for Lucy to have to act mentally deficient because she's playing a housewife. Harriet Craig would slap her. *Harriet Craig* was a great Joan Crawford film. Women are smart, and don't you forget it, especially the housewives who keep the world from falling apart into filth."

"What did you think of Marilyn Monroe last night at the photoplay dinner?"

Her publicist put his hand on Joan's wide shoulder to keep her from shooting off like a rocket. Henry warned him, "That's not on my list of questions."

Joan jumped in anyway. "IT WAS A DISGRACE! It was the most shocking display of bad taste that I've ever seen, EVER! And I've seen a *lot* of bad taste!"

Henry softly said, "Joan!"

"Look - there's nothing wrong with my melons but I don't shove them in people's goddamn faces, throwing them around like some slut!" Joan stood and elegantly flicked her cigarette ash into a metal swan. "And look at my derriere! Firm and trim like a star's should be. Her caboose needs a girdle! She wasn't wearing one! She was sewn into hardly anything at all! A woman with that kind of a caboose needs a girdle! Her pictures won't do business because nobody wants to see sex right in their faces. That's why her career is going nowhere! The wives choose the pictures their family will attend and they want JOAN CRAWFORD elegance and taste and good manners - and gowns that aren't just two pieces of cellophane tape!" Then Joan grew calm, sat back down and squished out her cigarette. "I know you've got a few quotes out of me. But go easy, huh?"

* * * * *

After Frenchy got Joan's hair ready for the shoot, and her face taped up, she slipped away to wardrobe. "Helen? Helen?"

"Right here," Helen came through a door with a bolt of yellow silk.

"The radio had the most chilling news! A psycho killer has escaped the loony bin! They told everybody to be aware. They said he kills dressed up as a *she* and might still be dangerous — I hope it isn't the Joan Crawford one — they say he fell two stories to get out, and went through a picnic table. So, maybe he might be too hurt right now to kill. But you can't be too sure."

Helen measured out some fabric. "That sounds dangerous. I wonder if we should tell Joan, to warn her. Do you think she's in any danger?"

"MGM has guards."

Helen asked, "And why would the news report a broken picnic table? That's odd."

Frenchy explained, "It was an Al Jolson memorial picnic table."

"Oh my. Do you think we should tell Joan about any of this?"

"No. She has enough to worry about trying to look sixteen years old again for the cameras."

Helen moaned. "Poor Joan. She's all alone up there on Mount Olympus, isn't she."

"No. She has more friends than anybody. And more lovers than anybody. And more fans. And more staff. And four kids. She would have had five kids now if the mob didn't come back to take that first one away from her. That was after she'd had it a whole year. And she didn't get any of her money back. I don't know how she does it. She really does try really hard to have it all."

"Yes she tries very hard."

Frenchy nodded. "It just doesn't seem like she's popular because all we hear about is how mean Bette Davis is to her."

Helen asked, "I wonder why Joan gets her goat so much?"

"Joan is far prettier. Joan's acting is better. Joan is so generous. Joan is just a better person all the way around."

Helen started to unwind the fabric from the bolt. "I suppose."

* * * * *

Joan sat in the rear of a New York taxi with costar Gig Young. The front of the car had been sawed off so they could face several lights, a microphone and camera. It was her second car scene for the movie.

"What's taking them so long?" Joan asked. "I'm ready to do my scene and this coat is awkward. When Helen made it for me I wonder if she knew how long I'd be stuck in a taxi in it. I'm glad it's a brief scene. I don't think this is one of Helen's best creations, at least in a taxi. I wish I could walk around and really work it - let the fabric just swoosh around a bit to show it off. Could you imagine how glorious it would look if I was just stomping through the streets of New York on a good tall pair of fuck-me pumps in this coat?

Then the picture would have some excitement without me having to yell at somebody."

Gig grinned. "You look great."

"Bless you. I do look great. That's because I take care of myself and have discipline and just did a hundred sit-ups before the scene. How many did you do?"

Gig mumbled, "I forgot."

Joan shook her finger at him. "You'll remember that it wasn't enough when your career is failing. You'll only be left holding your belly instead of your balls." She elbowed him playfully.

"Yes, Miss Crawford."

"Call me Joan. After what you and I have done to each other on that bearskin rug, I think we can cut the formality."

Sure, Joan."

"Now what's taking so long?"

Gig asked, "You in a hurry?"

She chuckled. "Funny. I'll stand for eight hours to get a hem *just right* to show off my gorgeous ankles, but this seems like utter incompetence and a *waste* of time. Has MGM fallen to the low standards of Republic? Everything in the world has gotten so shoddy. Do you know what's going on?"

Gig answered, "We have to see New York in the back window. For nighttime."

Joan turned to look out the back window, being careful her fur-collared robe didn't wrinkle, or she didn't pop her face tapes that were strung tight under her wig. All she saw behind them was a blank rear-projection screen. "Did the bulb burn out? Did the print scratch? I was once in front of a screen and they had to stop production until a new print could be called up from the lab. Because I was acting in front of a scratch. And I was supposed to be in Paris. I was mortified. All that work ruined by a scratch. I suppose that's better than when all the film prints could not only scratch but also burst into flames, for no reason, and burn everything down. That was the old film. It always burned the theater down. That takes the relaxation out of a person's night out. This new safety film at least doesn't do that. Goddamn are we modern in the 50s!"

Gig said, "You sure know a lot about film."

"It's my life. My blood. I'm nothing if I'm not an image on film! And a lot of copies of it dubbed around for everyone! Just think of how many of me there are. Everybody wants to see a Joan Crawford picture."

The shadow of the microphone on a pole passed over Joan's face while repositioning itself. She reacted to it as fast as a cat ready to bite a bird out of the air. Though no film was rolling through the camera, she was irritated. After slumping back in the seat, she griped, "Soon they'll be doing that in the middle of my lines."

"Do what?" Gig asked.

"Did you see the microphone put a shadow on me, just now? Are you awake over there? At old MGM, there would be screaming by now from the director if that kind of thing happened, at any time. MGM used to have very high standards."

The director, Charles, scampered up to them wiping sweat off the back of his neck. "Sorry! Sorry! Sorry! Sorry kids for the delay! The reels have all been confused. We'll get a city moving behind you if we have to use footage of Saint Louis, and put it into color with a blue gel."

"No, no." Joan put her hand up to calm him. "You're the director, so let's do it right. Just wait and find the New York reel. Calm down. Bless you." She thought he looked sexy being so harried, and had to resist the urge to grab him.

Charles nervously said, "Thank you, Miss Crawford."

"Bless you. For a moment there, I'd thought there was something wrong with how I'd done the first take. I couldn't imagine how I could redo it anyway different. It's such an easy scene to do. I act like a bitch to Gig. Cut. I'm so silly to think everything is about me. Or are you just doing all this to trick me into doing another take?"

"You were great Miss Crawford."

"You really think so?"

"Yes, Miss Crawford."

"Oh, really?"

"Yes, Miss Crawford."

"You can be honest with me, I'm a professional."

Charles waved his arms around. "It was just fine! Better than fine! Marvelous!"

"Bless you. You're so kind to notice how hard I work to make everything right. So - when we did that last take, that take that was so very good, what the goddamn hell *did* you see out my back window?"

"It was all mixed up." Charles slapped his hands on his face and moaned. "The reel said it was the New York street at night, and in color. It was color all right, but it was footage to put behind somebody surfing."

"Surfing? You mean *water*?" Joan's eyes widened.

Charles nodded. "The prettiest Technicolor blue water you'd ever seen."

Joan scowled. "We were driving on water? We could have drowned! Oh how absurd. Well, please keep that first take. Have it printed. You may need to use it if the film bombs as a musical. You can cut in the very blue surf roaring behind me as I'm being a bitch to Gig, and un-spool this piece of MGM as an art film. It can play in some beatnik bar, some basement, where they all smoke dope and don't care about logic and plot, and love to make fun of the classic Hollywood stars - especially a star as big and wonderful and *professional* as Joan Crawford!"

"Don't be upset, Miss Crawford. We'll get the shot going again any moment now."

"I'm only upset for the film. I don't worry about my own comfort. The audience won't worry about me when they sit in the theater. They'll think I really am in a car and won't worry that I sat here all day, all stiff in this getup, for just few lines. They'll just think I'm zipping from New York party to New York party. They'll just see glamour."

Gig said, "Don't worry so much, Joan."

Joan said, "I don't worry about me. I know where I'm at. I worry about my fans. If they think I'm cheating them, if they think I'm trying to pull a pretentious fast one on them, if they think I take them for granted, they'll leave me so fast. I'll be through. Through for all time in one opening week."

The proper reel was found, mislabeled "surf" and the shot was done expertly in a second take. Joan doing it exactly like she had the first take, saying to Gig, "Are you mad at me Darling? I was very rude, I know. Don't say I wasn't."

"Maybe."

"It was stupid. You can waste your whole life listening to people like that who don't say anything, talking the whole while, only talking about themselves. Only waiting for their turn to repeat themselves. *That* was rude."

Gig agreed, "Okay, it was boring. That's what booze is for. And for tonight it was the only party in New York."

"That's a lie," Joan said. "It's a big city. You can get out of the car at your place."

Gig asked, "What do I do?"

"Curl up in some corner with a good book or a bad girl."

Gig gave Joan a pleading hard-up look.

Charles yelled, "Cut! Great! It's a take! Print that!"

"Bless you darling." All during the scene, Joan had also been powdering her face, her purse on her lap. Before she left to go back to her dressing room, she grabbed Gig's sleeve and said, "Darling, sit for one more minute. I have a surprise for you hiding in this purse. That's why I was so impatient to get this scene shot. I just couldn't wait a minute longer to give it to you."

Gig smiled. "A present?"

She handed him a small box. "A gift."

He opened it and smiled in relief, "My wedding ring! Where'd you find it?"

"In my dressing room. After a man curls up with a bad girl, he's supposed to put it back on. She wickedly smiled at him, still in character from the scene, lit a cigarette so fabulously the camera should have still been on, and then she left through the back car door and slammed it, as if it was all real.

* * * * *

In the dressing room, the day's newspapers were already everywhere, and the radio was talking about Joan Crawford. "Good god, I'm about to be burned at the stake!"

The article about Marilyn Monroe had set off a Hollywood tempest in a teapot that was blasting across the entire free world. Readers of many languages, mistaking it all for journalism, were delighted to read about one star attacking another, especially when the woman on the rampage was Joan Crawford. "Tarred and feathered!" Louella Parsons took sides with Marilyn while Hopper sided with Crawford.

"Joan is jealous of a younger star," Louella reported.

"Crawford is the defender of public morality," Hedda countered.

"Joan is about as moral as a starving shark," Louella insisted.

"Joan is about as moral as a starving shark in a crowded kiddie pool," Bette Davis added.

"Crawford stands for decency, respectability and high morals," Hedda decided to push it, cackling and sipping a triple martini while she typed.

"I cried for a whole week," Marilyn's account went, when her press agent decided it was finally her turn to contribute. "I couldn't get out of bed, I was so upset. I always admired her for taking in children and giving them a home. I know what it's like to be a homeless child."

Joan panicked, thinking the tide of public opinion was against her, so she made her publicists release the declaration, "I *had* tried to help Marilyn in private and I thought my comments about Marilyn had been in private - off the record. I am so upset! Will I ever recover? What about *me?*" Then she wailed to her publicists, while carefully inspecting false eyelash sets through clear plastic boxes. "I'm ruined!"

"Joan!" Henry assured, "The scandal, as it is, is fitting both you stars! If you'd *both* just shut up for a minute and listen, you'd see how you're both benefiting from this scandal! Immensely!"

Joan thought about that for a moment, looked around her

dressing room for something to throw. "Henry? Can we fix it so that just Joan Crawford is benefiting?" Without waiting for the answer, she tossed three sets of false eyelashes in the garbage can. "Joan is now a joke - a laughing stock of movie star comedy! They even joke about it on television, as if they just couldn't wait and gloat and try and pull down a real star to their puny little box. I'm a stupid fool to think I'd get respect! I *hate* Joan Crawford! She's become a goddamn ball and chain! I hate Joan Crawford – I hate Joan Crawford! I hate her!"

"It's *not* that *bad*!"

"Is so! This town is full of cannibals waiting to eat us right down the instant we've been around long enough to do something good!"

He left. She finished her drink and then ripped opened a few dozen fan letters and put them in a neat pile. As she ripped open the envelopes, she pretended she was ripping up another Joan Crawford. "You're through. You're over. You're done in this town!" She decided she needed some air. One last nostalgic walk around the back lot would do perfectly. She wanted to set fires along the way, but decided that finding the perfect place to carve her initials would be vandalism enough, and would be making her mark, at that. She put her letter opener in her fur coat pocket and stomped out into the night.

Her limo driver greeted her in the studio street. "Can I take you somewhere?"

"I look gorgeous, don't I – fresh and new?"

"Oh, yes, Miss Crawford! A million bucks! A real killer. As always."

"Bless you. Are you sure you're not just saying that? Do you really think so?"

The driver repeated, "You look like a million! A *billion*! Can I take you somewhere?"

"No. I'm just gonna give myself a tour of the old MGM lot one last time. I want to say goodbye to it all. I may never be back at MGM."

"Do you need me to help show you around, Miss Crawford?"

"No, maybe you can help me with some other things when I get back." She patted his bottom.

"Yes, Miss Crawford! Have a nice tour. And don't worry about all them snakes and alligators and things on back lot seven. That's all fake. From *Tarzan and the She-Devil.*"

"Oh. Fake snakes? Then half of Hollywood must be sitting there. Remember the alligator that chased me in *Strange Cargo?* It took a few takes. It kept crashing into the shore. Clark and I couldn't stop laughing - between that and me running in a swamp in heels. If I see ole Hermy the *Strange Cargo* alligator over there, I'll say goodbye to him, too."

"And don't go down that way." He pointed. "That last big rain put half the Sahara Desert over the road. Deserts never last well in the rain."

"Okeydokey." As Joan left him, she lit a cigarette with almost supernatural elegance, walking by an outdoor set for *Latin Lovers* that was falling over. "Oh! That was the movie Michael Wilding refused to do. I'll give you a little cut, first!" Joan climbed over some falling remains of Brazil. Even as a ruin it still looked garish, painted for the Technicolor camera. At the sagging canvas backdrop of a Brazilian sky that slowly breathed with the night air, she noticed a rip along the bottom. "Huh?" She bent down and peeked through it and saw a speck of the moon, so crawled all the way in, her big fur coat squeezing tight.

"Ah, Alice in Wonderland," Joan hoped. Rather the opposite happened. Continuing under a buckled wooden fence and then between tall bushes, Joan found herself outside the wonderland of MGM's back lot and on the top of a steep forlorn hill. A streetlight shone far below on an empty freeway, illuminating the quiet bus stop like for a sad scene at the end of a Warner Brothers' picture.

As she carefully made her way down the hill through crunchy waist high grass, Joan pretended she was Mildred Pierce, suffering for the sins of the world. "Why did you all leave me? I didn't leave you! I work harder and harder for your love and acceptance and you act like you don't care! You all run off to look at Marilyn! I've got a *face!* I don't get old! I get better! This musical is going to be my best part ever because I'll work harder and *make* it the best! Goddamn it!" She started pulling in her stomach muscles *hard* to tighten them. Then she did a few dance moves and high kicks. At the freeway there was a woman on a bus stop bench who looked like she had been crying, but now she was just staring in stunned awe at the magical image of the shimmering glorious movie goddess.

"Yooooou – you - Joan Crawford?"

Joan loved how the woman was gaping at her, "You want an autograph?"

The woman fought to start her brain up again to open her tan purse and take out a pen. She couldn't find a piece of paper. "Could you – just - just sign the side of my purse?"

"I'll sign anything for anyone. I'm nothing without my fans." Joan grandly autographed the woman's purse. "There. Bless you."

The woman looked around. She was confused that there was no entourage. "But – wa-wa-what are you doing out here in the middle of nowhere - and so late at night?"

"I'm not lazy. I'll go anywhere for my fans."

"Huh?"

Joan looked around and breathed in a deep lung full of cool night air. "I always go meet my fans, wherever I can find them. I'm not a snobby star like most. I'm the people's star. You waiting for the bus?"

"No. I - I - I was just."

"You were hit."

The woman sadly put her hand to her face. "How'd you know?"

Joan asked, "Who? Your pimp?"

"He - he - how'd you know?"

Joan involuntarily shimmied as she belted out a pained laugh. "Honey, I know all about these things. I used to hoof on a wobbly stage in a speakeasy in Kansas City. That was before I made it into the third row of the chorus on Broadway where they expected me to drop dead of exhaustion and be replaced, without anybody even noticing. Me? Replaced? Ha! There was a long line of girls waiting in the wings to replace me. They had the same starry eyes. But that seems like a different lifetime ago, now. A past life. Oh that's right. It was. I hadn't even come to Hollywood yet. I wasn't Joan Crawford yet. I was somebody else. I forgot her name, now. You can leave your life and start over. That's Hollywood." Joan's eyes widened with a realization. "I suppose *that's* why Michael Wilding came to America. He hates himself and needs to make himself over. Hmmm. The poor dear."

"You understand me? Thank you Joan."

"Bless you. Have you seen my last picture? Did you like it? Really? Do tell."

"My life's been so crazy. But I loved *Harriet Craig*. I'd do anything to have a house like that. I cried at the end when you pretended your husband hadn't left and you walked up those stairs, alone, head high. You were so proud. Stubborn and horrible, but proud. I cried and cried and cried."

"Bless you. That was a great part. A bitch, but a great bitch, yes."

"You know everything. What should I do? I wish I could just die. Why can't I just die and be through with it?"

Joan said, "I'll tell you what to do."

"What."

"Not here. Not now."

"Then how?"

"I'll tell you in my next picture. See my next picture, *Torch Song* and therein will lie the key." Joan walked behind her, took out her sharp letter opener and wondered if she should give it away as a souvenir. She thought about all the mail she still had to deal with at the dressing room. She'd have a very large pile of mail to open once she got home. She decided not to give it away. She tossed the blade to her pocket. She missed. There was a bright chime on the cement, but Joan didn't hear it because she was saying, "A nice big autograph dressing up that purse is a gift enough, for now."

"Yes, thank you. I will never forget this night. It was – magic."

Joan turned like an army sergeant and marched back up the dark hill as fast as most would run, loudly singing, *Tenderly*. When she returned to the studio, she was out of breath. She grabbed a quick shower, did an alcohol rub, ice rub, then put lotion on herself, put her old clothes in her hamper for dry cleaning and put on a new gold lame' gown with a halter top strap of faux diamonds. The long skirt had four long slits up the front, back, and sides. With every step Joan was all legs. Wearing her fur coat fallen far off her bare shoulders, shimmering and feeling sexy, she slinked up to her limo.

Her driver rushed out from behind the wheel to greet her. "Did you have a nice walk?"

"Yes." Then Joan remembered that she was going to carve her initials somewhere behind MGM, but hadn't.

"You want a ride now? Where to, Miss Crawford?"

Joan kicked her leg out the side flap of her dress. She decided that wasn't dramatic enough so she yanked it up a bit and opened the front to show him that she wasn't wearing any underwear. Do you think I look fit?"

"Oh my!"

"We'll stay parked as I take you around the back lot right here. Right to seventh heaven." She stepped into the limo and kicked off her shiny gold pumps.

"Yes, Miss Crawford."

"I'm sorry this will be the last time I can reward you like this for your excellent service, but the picture ends tomorrow. Then I won't have you anymore. I go home."

"Oh that's a shame, Miss Crawford."

"Indeed. *Indeed.*"

He took her in his arms and she passionately stroked his jacket, while she wept, "Make the pain go away, just take it away."

"Yes, Miss Crawford," the driver said. "But if you don't mind. Before we go too far. I have a terrible hangnail, here, and it hurts so much - it's such a distraction. Do you have a clippers inside that I can use?"

Joan reached into the pocket of her fur coat, "Never fear, I have a deathly sharp letter opener in my pocket that's as good as a knife. We can just carve your hangnail out with that. Oh let me do it! That would be fun!" Joan carefully slipped her hand in her coat pocket. "Huh?" It wasn't there. Then Joan remembered hearing a tinkling chime at the bus stop – it was certainly the letter opener not quite hitting its mark and falling to the ground. Horrified of such carelessness, furious with herself for making a mistake, Joan jumped up. "Wait right there and don't you even think of anything but ME until I get back!"

"What?"

She ran away.

Chapter Thirteen

Joan hurried to her dressing room, slammed a tall drink, and shouted, "MY NERVES!" then crawled out through the *Latin Lovers* backdrop again, checked to make sure her dangly faux diamond clip earrings hadn't pulled off when she was past the buckled fence and bushes, brushed off her knees, and stomped down the steep hill to the woman who was still sitting there. "Hello?" Joan called out. "Wake up! You'll miss your bus at this rate!" Joan looked everywhere on the ground for her letter opener, but it was gone. "But I need it! I need it! Oh God where is it! Oh my GOD!" Joan finally noticed that the woman's throat was slashed. "Oh my GOD - I need a shower!"

"Get away from there!" a man's voice called out from the other side of the highway from between two tall yellow bushes.

Joan saw herself. But it was plain it was a he behind the flimsy hospital gown. A pillowcase made a turban. Another blood spattered lumpy pillowcase was in one hand, and in the other hand he was holding up her letter opener. It had blood on it.

"Who are you?" Joan demanded, shaking. "And what the hell are you doing!"

"I'm Joan Crawford!" the psycho stated. His bold thick slash of blood red lipstick was, perhaps, blood.

"In *that*?" Joan gasped at the shocking attire.

The Joan nodded proudly, "And this is my costume from my greatest movie, *Possessed*!"

"What the hell are you doing!"

"You're dead!"

Joan shivered. Then some fierce power came over her. 100 proof Vodka, perhaps. "ARE NOT! I'M Joan Crawford! You're a juvenile delinquent! A murderer!"

"She had to die! She said I wasn't Joan Crawford! I am!"

"Are NOT!"

"Am!"

"NOT!"

The psycho Joan Crawford crossed the empty highway. "Am SO!"

"Stay *away* from me!"

"It says right *here* on my letter opener! I'M JOAN CRAWFORD! FROM THE DESK OF JOAN CRAWFORD!"

"You may have the letter opener, but I have all the rest!"

"Just because you're good at impersonating a woman doesn't mean you're a real Joan Crawford!"

Joan yanked up her dress, parted it, and proudly showed off her authenticity. "I'm all *woman*, can't you see! Look! You're a fraud! Look! Look upon a star and accept that you're a fraud! Now turn yourself in - for crying out loud!"

"So you had it chopped off. I'm not impressed. Now the rest of you will be chopped off!"

Joan sadly asked, like Mildred Pierce, "Why are you threatening me like this? What did I do to you? I've worked so hard and this is how you repay me?"

The Joan Crawford circled wide around Joan until he stood righteously up on the side of the steep hill, looking haughtily down on her. "You'll have to pay for trying to be me! Only me is me! You'll have to pay with your life for thinking you really ARE me! Nobody can be more Joan Crawford than Joan Crawford and you have been cheating!"

Joan said, "You're just goddamn crazy! You'll hate me no matter what I say! You don't even give me a chance!"

"Are you saying you want to be me by being crazy?"

"No, I said *you* are crazy!"

"*You* are crazy!"

"You're crazy!"

"No YOU!"

She wished she had her gun but it was back in her handbag in her dressing room. It would have helped her play a very exciting Joan Crawford scene like in *Flamingo Road*. "Come any closer and I'll – I'll -" she ran.

The Joan Crawford came after Joan Crawford, swinging the sharp letter opener. "Bloody knife! Bloody knife!" Joan ran as fast as she could down the highway and up a side street where she heard festive noise. She tore through the doors of a large metal warehouse.

"OH!" A man praised her. "You look *divine*! Come in! Come in!" He took her arm and pulled her off to the side.

"Bless you."

A fierce-faced Joan Crawford pulled out a gun and shot her, with water, crabbing, "I've got rotten lovers!"

"What's the hurry?" Another Joan asked.

The real Joan Crawford whimpered, "There's a horrible man after me!"

"You lucky bitch," said the other Joan.

Her eyes adjusted to the weird lights, she looked around, and then she gasped at all the many Joan Crawfords. "It's Joan Crawford!"

"*Duh.*"

At the other end of the crowd, on a long stage, was a drag queen parade of Joan Crawfords. She gasped. "There's so many Joan Crawfords! You're ALL Joan Crawfords!"

"Not all. There's some rude sailors over there."

"You look pretty **convincing**," a Joan Crawford with a beer belly said to her, trying to look like he was in *Flamingo Road* in a belly-dancing outfit.

"But you've got company," another Joan added, using a long turquoise couch pillow for his stole.

"Smile! You look like Joan Crawford!" Two cameras flashed at her.

"But *I'm* the real Joan Crawford!" she insisted, seeing in one corner of the room a very young Joan Crawford in ghoulish black and white makeup and a black and white beaded gown, doing the Charleston on top of an old beat up piano. A flashing spotlight made it all flicker. Photos of Joan Crawford were all over the walls that were barely perceptible since so many Joan Crawfords had put their autographs on them.

A craggy woman dressed like a man stepped up to her and said, "And I'm the real Clark Gable. You're a looker, though." She took her hand and kissed it like a gentleman.

"Bless you." Joan spotted the psycho Joan Crawford in the

room, and he had spotting her and started to push through some horny men dressed as sailors. They made it difficult to pass, pulling the back of his hospital gown the rest of the way open to squeeze his cheeks, until he swung his pillowcase at them.

"Hey, Joan," a sailor asked the psycho killer. "What's in your bag?"

"Van Heflin's head!"

"Wasn't it enough to just shoot him at the end?"

"No! I'm Joan Crawford!"

The real Joan pushed toward the stage, first swerving over to grab a drink left behind on the bar. Then she crawled up onto the elevated platform. She turned to see that the psycho Joan Crawford seemed lost and confused and still looking for her near the bar. She smiled from behind the wall of parading Joan Crawfords, hoping she'd find shelter in the shadows of the wings. Then she realized she was in the shelter of Joan Crawford. She let out a sigh of relief. "I think they call this camouflage. For now I ain't going nowhere!"

A Joan Crawford was back there, a handsome one, but he was a cheap looking Joan Crawford, wearing a man's yellow raincoat and a tacky tan turban with fake rubies. "Oh GOD!" Joan gasped at him. "Please tell me those damn hats aren't in fashion *everywhere*, now, and they're *not* gonna start showing up *all over* the place!" She gulped down the cocktail, irritated that it had so much ice in it, taking up so much important room.

"Why?" the man said, and without a powerful Joan Crawford voice, but a sweet soft voice.

"I've already seen one hat like that in my life and it was once too many."

The man began to weep. "I just wanted to be in a Joan Crawford contest, but I don't have anything to wear."

"Why not?" Joan asked. "You work hard and you can have anything you want."

"My mother doesn't know that I want to dress up like you more than anything in the world. It might worry her. I don't want to upset her. I love my mother!"

"Bless you. You're so kind. My mother was a disappointment, too. So I understand. You're so blessed. I wish I had those pink panty hose for you, right now. I'd give them to you. I'd have you try them on right now! Goddamn that Marilyn Monroe! She didn't want to appreciate them!"

"What?"

"Here," Joan offered, "I know what I can do to help you. I'll give you my wig in exchange for your hat. And my fur for your raincoat. I'll let you borrow them for just a few minutes, and not a second longer. Just long enough until you win the contest."

"Really?"

"Yes, but hurry. A man is out there who wants to kill Joan Crawford, but at this rate it'll take him all week. Did you see my competition out there? And hurry so you don't put cooties on my things. Hurry!"

The Joan agreed, "Somebody wants to kill Joan Crawford out *there?* He'll be lost."

Joan said, "We hope!"

They changed coats with each other as the man busted into laughter. "I'm glad the fur is so thick - this is so exciting. I've got such a boner. How do you hide yours?"

"I beg your pardon? Oh, and one more thing. If you want to win the contest, don't open your mouth. Your teeth look nothing like mine."

"Yes," he agreed. "And *you* look so much like Joan Crawford I could cry."

"Bless you. And it didn't happen overnight. It's not enough to have talent. I had to work and scrape and claw. And then beg and screw and steal. And then do it all, all over again. Joan Crawford don't come cheap. She just didn't fall out of Kansas City this way. Now go break a leg!" Joan quickly unclipped her long sparkly earrings and added them to his ears. "Don't lose these, they cost a fortune. And keep the fur shut regardless of being so naturally excited to be Joan Crawford. She does not wear that kind of underwear, no matter what Bill says."

"Real diamonds?" he asked of the earrings.

"Of course not! I only dress for the cameras and cameras are damn dumb, they just see the sparkle. But fake jewels are still expensive. Now go sparkle!"

The Joan Crawford stepped out from the shadows of the wings, looking like a perfect dead ringer. Joan watched from the side, beaming with pride that she could help a fan out so easily.

He stood in a line behind a bride that wore red. The next Joan Crawford was dressed like the trollop in *Rain* holding an open umbrella with a Bible skewered to the top. A Harriet Craig promenaded across the stage, to great laughter, wearing a cardboard house. The next Joan Crawford had a crumpled brown paper bag glued to one side of his face, for scars, from *A Woman's Face*. Then the Joan that Joan attired finally stepped forward. More camera flash bulbs went off from the crowd.

"Joan Crawford!" the crowd cheered at a vision so glamorous. When the master of ceremonies in a white tux, came forth, Joan's sharp letter opener sailed through the air and struck the Joan Crawford, burying deep in his neck. He looked around, confused, and then felt the pain. He gasped, growing dizzy, and pulled it out.

As he fell dead, a spray of blood shot head to toe over the white tux. Everybody screamed and stampeded. Bodies crashed in all directions at once.

"Oh my GOD!" Joan gasped. "We're all going to be killed!" She jumped off the stage as the psycho Joan jumped up.

The psycho Joan opened the fur coat and looked at the murdered dead ringer's body. "WHAT?" He pulled down the front of his underwear and the killer shouted, "That's not the *right* Joan!"

Joan Crawford pushed harder against the mob to get away. The killer Joan jumped off the stage down at her, directly, and Joan thought she was a goner. But the killer Joan angrily pushed right past her, sliding across the back of the yellow raincoat she was wearing.

"Watch it!" Joan yelled at him.

The Joan screamed right back in her face, "Where's the fake! She's dead meat!"

Then Joan realized she wasn't even recognized in the tacky

clothes, so she wasn't so much a Joan Crawford anymore. "Oh my GOD!" Joan cried. "I've worked my whole life to become Joan Crawford and now I'm *stuck* in THIS!" She considered going back up onto the stage to get her things back from the poor dead Joan, but walked over to the bar, instead, and gulped down a few more abandoned drinks.

"Oh my! I've completely lost my mind!" Joan put the glass down in horror. Somebody else had not only once touched that glass, but put their lips to it and drank from it. "It's dirty!" She fought nausea at the horrible thought of drinking after somebody else, while she ran out the door and up the hill. She crawled through the backdrop. She staggered down the studio street toward her dressing room where she bumped into her driver who was still waiting for her at the limo.

"Miss Crawford! You took so long to change!"

"A drink! Oh god! A drink!"

He handed her his flask. "Sure – but."

Joan was in a daze. The vodka pouring down her throat didn't help like she wanted it to. "Murder. I changed? Oh, that's right. Damn. MURDER!"

"What?"

"All them are dead. All dead. Joan Crawford. I drank from many dirty glasses. Forgive me. Joan is dead! There was a murder."

"I'll call the police?"

"No! I can't be photographed like this! My career will be ruined. Ruined in one flash pop of one camera. No! Hide me!" She looked around. "MGM hide me!"

"Yes." Her driver urged her, "Come inside and lay down. You're not well. You've had a terrible shock!"

Joan nodded to agree. "A shock!"

"Yes," he agreed. "And where did you get a raincoat - and that hat?"

Joan slipped off her tan turban and looked at it oddly. "And there was a horrible murder! Joan Crawfords getting killed left and right. My fans! Oh my god!"

"You're just exhausted. You've had some shock. Calm down."

Joan wept. "I'll never get a next picture. They'll just go bury me in the desert."

"Miss Crawford. I'll do *anything* for you! But - where were you? You've been gone!"

"Murder? I was down there," she pointed. "I was - where was I? Down that way!"

The driver looked off to where she pointed. "There's nothing down there. It all ends with the Brazilian sky. It doesn't go any further. You're in shock."

"Yes. I am. It was in a bar."

"There's no bar, there. It's just the sky."

"I went through the sky. I think I mixed drinks, and the quality wasn't very good. I don't know why I did that but Joan Crawfords were all around me, many many Joan Crawfords. I was afraid for my life. So I drank a few. Only a few. I can't think. My head feels like it's gonna explode. I need some good vodka. I need a cigarette. I need a pill! I need soap!"

"You've had visions! It's just a sky down there!"

"We were going to make love and find seventh heaven. How odd I just went into the sky."

"I don't think we should make whoopee, now. Not with your shock."

"Maybe later. It's so good for the nerves, but first I have to find my fur and my wig. I lost them somewhere but I can't remember. Oh that's right. I remember. I gave them to Joan Crawford to make him more – you know - Joan Crawford."

"You've had a shock."

Joan dragged herself to her dressing room, sat at her vanity, poured a proper quality vodka, but it didn't help her feel better. So she poured another. Then she fell backwards off her stool and lay lifeless on the floor, barely breathing.

* * * * *

The murderous psycho Joan walked through a glass door in the glass wall. He entered a tiny narrow empty diner, announcing to no one, "Kill you all! I'm a *star*!" Then he grandly plopped on a red stool.

A grizzled waitress shuffled up to him. Her steaming coffee pot was held out in dutiful anticipation. "My. What a treat. A movie star in Hollywood of all places."

"Joan Crawford!"

"Oh. I thought you was Theda Bara."

"I'll kill you! I'm the biggest star! Joan Crawford!"

"What the hell are you wearing *that* for, then," she asked, regarding the flimsy hospital gown.

"It's my costume for *Possessed*! My greatest movie! And I should have gotten an Academy Award for that!" He stood up and twirled.

"Hey mister. Careful your ass is all out."

"It's already been out! Damn sailors!"

"Don't sit there like that. It ain't sanitary on the seat." She pulled a few napkins out and handed it to the psycho. "Sit on these."

He didn't take them. "I'm Joan Crawford."

"Yeah. And would you like some coffee or what?"

In a rage, the psycho Joan reached over the counter and grabbed the waitress soundly by her throat. "Bloody knife! Bloody knife!"

Not able to pull free, the waitress smashed her hot pot into the side of his face so hard that the glass shattered, dropping blood and boiling coffee, badly burning her hand and arm. The Joan Crawford screamed. He ran for the door, missing it a few times. He put a few bloody face prints on the glass wall before escaping into the night.

Chapter Fourteen

"Murder!"

"Who! Huh? WHAT!"

"Murder!"

"Cranberry?"

"Bill! Murder!"

"Who? You?"

Joan corrected, "No. I'm still alive. Barely. But everybody was killed! Everyone who was Joan Crawford! Dead Joan Crawfords everywhere!"

Bill asked, "Did you just have a bad dream?"

Joan was puzzled. "Dream. Could it have been? Maybe it was. Have you ever gone through the sky and then down the hill and down the way to a Joan Crawford bar where a lot of the men there are Joan Crawford?"

"Through the what?"

"Oh no. It was a backdrop of a sky. I went through a hole like Alice in Wonderland. And yes it's very crazy through the hole. A killer and a crazy Joan Crawford bar."

"I was once at a bar where everybody was dressed like Tarzan. One was rather not dressed at all, except for a few leaves to make it into a jungle vine. And then there were some men who had such ugly legs I wished they'd come as apes."

"I'm serious!"

"So am I. Jimmy tried to go dressed as a banana but he looked more like a very *very* yellow man. He still got a lot of laughs."

"Hundreds of Joan Crawfords were killed last night. With my letter opener!"

"And I dressed as Tarzan and looked very authentic, I think. I have the gorgeous long legs for it. I've always been such a handsome man, even at my age I still turn a few heads. But I wore one of those wigs the studios make the Irish stagehands wear when they need a few Indian extras. That is never very convincing."

"Bill?" Joan asked. "Am I losing my mind? Did I just dream it all?"

"Dream what? Me as Tarzan?"

"No! Tarzan was not a homosexual with a banana! Did I dream about the slaughter of the Joan Crawfords? Hundreds? Or just one, maybe. I can't remember now. The blood was so - so – *red*! It was so confusing and I think I mixed vodka with gin and other things like a crazy woman. And tequila! And you just know the ice was made out of the dirtiest water that they were trying to hide." Joan paused to fight herself from gagging.

"Cranberry! Don't puke in my ear!"

"They were all screaming and trying to escape. Joan Crawfords crashing into Joan Crawfords! Joan Crawford running in all directions. They left their drinks behind in the panic. So something came over me. I went to the bar and actually drank from other people's glasses that they'd left behind. I really did. Now you don't think so highly of me, do you."

"The service was pretty poor, huh."

"I'm serious," Joan said. "I just feel *sick*! I saw real murder!"

Bill asked, "What was the name of this place?"

"I don't know," Joan admitted. "I was chased there by a murderer who looked just like me, from *Possessed*, but he was a man."

"Now what pills have you been taking for that diet?"

"I need a man to take care of me. I'm tired of trying to get by on my own. I'm a star but that ain't enough. When I had all those husbands, I didn't need them. Now I need a man the size of King Kong to protect me. I just can't take it all alone in Hollywood, anymore. It's hard on a woman, even a Joan Crawford. Especially a Joan Crawford, it seems."

"Jimmy and I will take care of you."

Joan kissed the phone. "Bless you. But you and Jimmy have each other. I need my own husband to help me out. Goddam I need help!"

"I tell you what. I'll call Gangster Al, myself, and try to get to the bottom of this. You can't be harassed like this while filming."

"Harassed! MURDERED!"

"If you were murdered, you'd be dead. Don't worry Cranberry. It's probably just a fan on too much Carmen Miranda."

"Today is my last day of shooting. Gangster Al probably won't care about what happens to me anymore, other than to remind me that it's my time to go."

"I'll try him and we'll see. You need a big break from all this Hollywood stuff. When you're done shooting today let's shatter the rhythm and - hey, why don't we go to a big supermarket and just look at everything. I love looking at all the new TV dinners! It's just the neatest new thing. Have you ever had one?"

"Don't be ridiculous." Joan ran her finger along her mighty arched eyebrow. "You know I can't go to a place like that."

"Yeah," Bill agreed. "You're too tired today. We can do it tomorrow."

"Don't be ridiculous. I can't go to a grocery store. I'm Joan Crawford."

"Aw, come on, you need to go blow some stink off!"

Joan stated, "Just because I don't take as many showers a day as Katharine Hepburn does doesn't mean I stink. I don't stink. Do you know how many showers I've had today just to prove it to everybody who thinks I'm still some dirty washerwoman's whore daughter?"

"It's an expression, Cranberry, don't be a stinker! Let's go to the grocery store and look at all the new things. There's lots of new things out there!"

Joan repeated, "I don't *do* grocery stores."

"You did during the war."

"Oh. The war."

Bill reminded her. "You did! You took the motorcycle to the grocery store. You posed like you were looking at a can of something, also holding your poodle."

"It was publicity."

Bill suggested, "You can go in disguise. A really good one would be to just go out without makeup. With freckles and no lips, no one would know you from Adam."

"But then I wouldn't be Joan Crawford."

"That's the damn point!"

"But, I don't know what I'd be, then. I *don't* ever want to go back to being Billie Cassin or Lucille Le Sueur, *ever* again, those two girls are dead. I killed them *good!*"

"A name change does not make two dead girls."

"They are dead! Two dead girls! And I was also called Miss MGM. That one was okay. I need *some* past I can find comfort in. But the other two are dead. Not real anymore. Dead."

"Cranberry! You sound like God who just killed off the rest of the trinity."

"Balls!"

Bill maintained, "You're the same person at forty nine that you were back in Texas and Kansas City under different names."

"Thirty nine."

Bill said, "We all know how old we are. I'm fifty-three now. That's an easy one to remember when you're born as the century turned. I just remember what year it is or what age I am by remembering the other."

"I have a headache. I gotta go. Bless you and thank you for calling me. It's so kind of you to worry about me in such horrible times. My hair just walked in." Joan slammed the phone and turned to yell at Frenchy, but the woman started crying. Joan melted. "Honey!"

"I know I'm late. But I'm so worried. My boy didn't come home last night."

"Isn't he an adult?"

Frenchy acknowledged, "Yes, but -"

"Don't become a monster mother. He might have been out being naughty and you shouldn't give it a second thought."

Frenchy frowned. "But he didn't come *at all!*"

"Has it even crossed your mind that he might be waking up right now in somebody else's sheets with such a horrible hangover that he wishes he were dead?"

"Oh."

"When you see him again don't even speak of it. He's a man now so treat him like one. A mother has a daughter forever, but a mother does not have a son forever. An irresistible urge will always call a man away and he'll fly. He'll find his own corner of the world and you won't be a part of it. That's a blessing. It's the law of nature. A woman should never have a daughter unless she wants to be stuck with it forever, because she will be. Now slap that goddamn wig on me and tape me together so I can finish this lousy cheap jack musical."

"I suppose."

Joan said, "It's the law of nature! A man would rather be dead than not be free. They have no good horse sense like us womenfolk. In fact some men go flying off of cliffs in motorcycles, and such, and get killed, just trying to be free."

Frenchy gasped. "Don't say that!"

Joan frowned. "It's just the way it is and all we mothers can do is let them go and do with their life what they may. We can do nothing about it. So just let go and say bye-bye."

"I suppose." Frenchy began to prepare Joan's skin for the tape.

Joan began to weep.

"You can't cry now."

"I saw murder. I can't talk about it. It makes no sense. Maybe I didn't. Maybe I really am cracking up. They say you can only take so much stress and then everything falls apart and becomes unreal. Especially in Hollywood. Especially for a star. I can't go on. I don't know what to do."

"You don't have to know what to do. Just follow your script. Do you sing today?"

"I most certainly don't sing at Anna. She's my secretary. Now if you don't mind, I'm going to be quiet for a while. I need to concentrate. I had a bad night and I don't even know if it was all a dream, what I can remember. I did have a few strange drinks I don't usually have. I can't be sure anymore and it's all probably due to these goddamn MGM diet pills. What happened to my face!"

"What do you mean?"

"The bags! My eyes are puffy and I have *bags*!"

"The lighting will flatten that all out. You know that. Just ask that the scene be shot in medium lenses."

Joan sipped her glass of vodka. "Ah. Quality to calm my stomach." She poked at her head. "Do you think this wig looks too much like black woman's hair? My scene is with Maidie and I want her to look black and me to look white - because we are. This wig looks so - I don't know - like black hair that's been very heavily processed. Won't that confuse the audience?"

"*No*," Frenchy assured her. "It looks just fine."

"Maidie will look sensible and I will look like a clown."

"You look great."

"Goddamn it. It looks *worse* than overly processed hair! It looks like goddamn copper wire! I wish my hair was like Tallulah Bankhead's hair. She had the loveliest hair. I always wanted to run my fingers through it. Have you ever seen a woman where you just wanted to run your fingers through her hair - and without wanting to pull any of it out? Are you sure we shouldn't go with a pale blonde wig? A bright yellow!"

Frenchy reminded her, "Miss Crawford. This is the last day of shooting. It has to look just like all the rest of the picture. Once it's all been edited together, and people are watching you, you can't walk from your living room to your bedroom and have your hair completely change color at the door. But not before you give your continuity girl a good laugh because she'd just think you were pulling a practical joke on her - being the last day and all."

"Oh! Oh." Joan ground her teeth. "Of course. What was I thinking? I'll have bright yellow hair for my next picture. No, wait - damn. If I do that western, that my agent is pushing me to do, then it should be a very natural brown. Goddamn it."

Frenchy wished Joan would hold her face still. "Are you ready for your tapes now?"

"I wish the tapes could pull the skin tighter at the sides of my mouth. My face is just too damn big. The sides of my cheeks are getting that hollow look. Don't you think?"

"That's cheekbones."

"No. Going the wrong direction." Joan slowly rubbed her finger from her eye to the side of her jaw. "Like a hollow-faced hag. A crone. I'm starting to feel so very very dismal. I need to concentrate. I have a scene to do and I have to do it like I mean it. I'm not any ole slob like Bette Davis who just says anything with that witch voice of hers and people applaud with joy over it. She's overrated. It's not fair, I know, but they make me work twice as hard for half the applause. So let's concentrate now. Did you see the morning paper?"

Frenchy nodded. "Sure."

"Was there anything in it about Joan Crawford killing Joan Crawfords but they were all men, except for me, I think? It was at a bar where men go who want to be - you know, more homosexual minded. A place for men to wear dresses. Or did I really imagine it all. I had to have. It was so absurd!" Joan looked suspiciously at her bottle of diet pills.

"Dear me, no," Frenchy said. "The paper would never talk about that. Those kinds of things just can't be talked about in a regular sort of way. We have to pretend those kinds of people and places don't exist. We can't send the wrong message to our young impressionable sons who might become tempted by the serpent in the garden. Hide the serpent. Always hide the serpent."

"What serpent? Is that sunday school?"

"Yes."

Joan said, "Oh. Well anyway, murder is in the paper all the time. And it never before made people go out and kill just to read about it. Not too many of them, anyway."

"Boys in dresses just can't be talked about. The paper has to pretend that kind of a deviant thing doesn't exist."

"But it does. And I don't understand. Bette Davis is a woman in a dress and that has to be the most deviant thing anybody ever came up with."

Frenchy pushed on Joan's forehead. "I know how you feel about folks. You're too kind. But the paper is for regular people who want to think things are all a certain way. If it tells a story about what you just said, a Joan Crawford boy in a dress, and a murderer, it'll probably only come out later - after it's all figured out so they can make a cautionary tale about it. They need to make it into a story about how men in dresses are murderous communists, or something bad like that. They say that to get you to lock your doors all the time and always be afraid of other people. The paper has to be able to make an example of people who are so - so *different* - so people know how to think about it."

"That doesn't sound right, somehow." Joan finished her vodka. "It's kind of like what they teach in the westerns, huh. Shoot the weird one. Maybe that's why I'm imagining so much murder lately – I've been in too many movies about it. If only my fans could appreciate the occupational hazards of a big Hollywood movie star. It can drive you mad! All you see is murder – and yourself."

Frenchy continued, "But such things, bars with boys in dresses, just isn't something you can talk about in polite society. The newspaper is for regular polite people to read in their homes. You can't put something so nasty in nice homes. Not if they're going to pay good money for it."

"Yes, we have to be nice for the poor darling fans." Joan thought about all those many mysterious regular people out there somewhere, reading their clean morning papers in long rows of well-vacuumed ranch style homes. She closed her eyes and quickly fell asleep where she sat, snoring while Frenchy glued and tugged her face as much as the face-tape technique would allow.

Joan had flashes of vivid dreams. She couldn't open her mail. Her opener was gone.

* * * * *

Like leaving death row for *the chair*, Joan slowly walked onto the set to film the last scene of the shooting schedule, which was actually early in the script. It was her living room - a smaller and cheaper looking set than Michael Wilding's, but far more gorgeously streamlined and modern looking, in clean angles of cold steel blues. One wall was all indigo floor-length curtains. They opened to an impressive miniature backdrop of New York. "Bless you. Bless you." Joan didn't look at anybody, but kept her head down and her script hugged tight against her bosom.

"How are you doing?" the director asked while heading toward the camera.

"Charles, I'm a goddamn wreck!" Joan paced angularly across the carpet, her grand ultra yellow Helen Rose house robe flowing around her. "I can't think at all. And I have bags under my eyes. I have no idea where they came from. I'm not old, so don't you dare think it came from that! But, no close-ups *at all!* This picture already has its solid ration of Joan Crawford close-ups. Enough."

"Okay, Joan. Fine. Medium shots."

"You think I look that bad?" Joan tested him.

"No. You're gorgeous! But what you said is correct. We already did your closeup that ends the scene and it looks great. You're crying in your pillow. Great Joan Crawford stuff."

"You really think I look fine, now?"

Charles assured. "A million bucks. A star. Joan Crawford!"

"You sure?"

"Yes! You look gorgeous!"

"Maybe I should go back and put my face in more ice."

"No! *You* are *gorgeous!*"

"Bless you. Yes, I do look wonderful, like a star, but I don't even know if I can think. Goddamn it!"

"Let's just go over the lines once," Maidie Norman suggested, sitting where she would sit for the scene. "It's all very strange, I know, to do a scene where you're rehearsing a scene."

"No, darling, it's not the lines that are bugging me," Joan explained. "I've had the worse nightmares. I had dreams of lots of me. I was in a place where there was Joan Crawford everywhere. It's driving me mad. The headaches! Was it real? Now the only thing that seems real is here and now, in my living room. Somebody fix me a drink! If I'm in my own living room then I can have my own goddamn drink!"

"Oh my." Maidie diverted her eyes.

Joan walked over to the wall and patted it. "I'll miss you silly wall. Another picture done." She turned to the people around her and said, for them all to hear, "I've made so many lousy pictures in this town, but every picture is like a family. The family was once young and it was easy to keep together. I always saw almost the same crew each and every picture, and whether it was *Letty Lynton* or *The Women*, it was safe feeling on the set. It felt like being at home. Now time has gotten old and everything is worn out and fallen apart in the world. And now making a picture at MGM is like a family reunion after everybody has been away for far too long, and you don't recognize each other much. And there's so many new faces you don't want to get to know. You don't care. It's just too much work to always have to keep up with something that'll be gone tomorrow. And the faces you thought you would know are now old faces. And bald! And the average person isn't gonna tape their face up, so everybody looks different and you realize you don't even know each other much. You wonder if you even *should* have known each other much. You wonder if all your hard work in life was just a waste of time. You wonder if you were too busy chopping down the wrong tree and you just didn't know it because you were working so hard at it. Or maybe it isn't so bad the way your life has been, but the family reunion just messed with your feelings. Only your family can judge you in a way that it wounds you that bad. Your family is all strangers. You have nowhere to turn for peace."

The director smiled big at everybody. "Thank you Joan."

Others kindly clapped. "Thank you!"

Joan nodded to them, regarded the set again, then noticed the composition and became annoyed. "Could you move your chair back a bit," Joan ordered Maidie. "I don't want anybody in my shots, and I have to move about, to work this wardrobe. I can't let Rose down. I bet she quilted this by hand."

"Yes, Miss Crawford." Maidie scooted her chair farther back against the wall.

"No, not that far back, dear. Stay in the light where we can see you. No. Over. Over. Back. Too far. Up a bit. Aaaaah. Now the light is so nice on your face and puts a good shadow on your neck. Never sit with the light just blasting on your neck."

"Yes, Miss Crawford."

"*Joan.* We're friends now."

"Yes *Joan*."

"Oh, I think we can do better. Yes ... " Joan looked up and studied all the lights that were clamped and chained to the rafters. She looked back to Maidie. "Scoot. There. There. Right there. Right there! Scoot! Scoot. Stop! Yes! That's even better for you! Now the light is even softer on your neck and you don't want a fat neck."

"No. I don't. Thank you."

"And I need to walk right here and move this robe like I'm a queen or Helen will kick my caboose!"

"Yes, Joan, I understand."

Joan groaned. "My brain may be too tired to make any sense, today, but I can at least still work the wardrobe and find the light for everybody."

Charles asked, from the side of the camera, "Ready, Joan?"

Joan looked at the floor. "Where's my marks?"

"It's a medium wide shot. No marks are needed. Move about. Just don't leave the carpet."

"Do you want to shoot the scene now?" Joan asked, swooshing her robe side to side.

"Please."

"Oh. All right. Does this have playback?"

"Joan!" Charles said. "There's no singing in this scene!"

"Oh. That's right. I don't sing to my secretary." Joan quickly blew Maidie a kiss, instead. Maidie just looked back like Joan was crazy, though she didn't want to.

"Lights. Camera."

"Hold it!" Joan yelled. "Where's my cue cards?"

The director said, "You want them *now*?"

"Yes. I must. I can't think. My brain feels like scrambled eggs. And I'd like an aspirin, please. And where's my drink. No goddamn ice!"

It took half an hour for a calligrapher to come down and paint up a quick set of cue cards. "Bless you," Joan said to him on his way out. Then she yelled down the hall after him, "You are the grease that turns the wheels of this shit studio! You don't know how important you are!" She returned to the carpet area and flung her robe around.

"Lights! Camera!

"Speed," the cameraman cued.

"Action."

In character, Joan counted to five on her fingers, and then began, "Anna, I want to try my lines now, to rehearse them, to see if I can remember them all and if they're going to make any sense."

Maidie said, "Sure, Jenny."

"Okay, I'm walking across over to there. And I have to remember to do it while still in character."

Maidie pretended to read from her copy of the Broadway script, "Page twelve. Door chime."

Joan said, "I'll get it. I get up. I go over to the door. Hello. Would you like - - *oh*, that's a divided speech. I'll have to come in faster. I make sure I get up sooner. I cross the floor to the library. I hope I have a nice robe to work, like this one. I close the door. Anna, will you make a note of my having to come in faster."

Maidie pretended to scribble on her copy of her Broadway script, as she said, "What do you need?"

"I don't need anything or anybody. Who do you think you're talking to? Don't worry about me. I'm a star. I'm a rock - oh it's such a long speech and I'm so tired."

"The line is, I am a woman who will always have a crowd."

"Oh, such a long speech and it's late. What time is it?"

"It's nearly midnight."

Joan stretched out and yawned, making sure she pulled out her robe wide for a grand Helen Rose display. "That'll be enough for now."

Maidie conferred, "Okay, I'll type up the changes and have them ready for you in the morning."

"And then you leave and I go over my lines again, alone, and I say I don't need anybody, and blah blah blah, a crowd, and I lay in bed and I bawl, and - and *god* do I bawl in a goddamn flawless closeup."

"Cut!" Charles said.

"Huh?" Joan jolted as if to consciousness. "Was that a rehearsal? You know I don't like rehearsals. It burns up all my energy. Or. Did we just film that?" She walked wearily over to Charles. "What the hell was that?" A woman from craft service finally handed Joan her requested cocktail. She downed it in one gulp and returned the empty glass. "Refresssss this, dahlink."

Charles said, "That was a take. You did great, Joan. You didn't need the cue cards at all. You just *did* it! It's a wrap."

"What?" Joan asked. "That wasn't a read through? We weren't just rehearsing?"

Charles looked at Joan in worry. "Didn't you hear me yell *action?*"

"I don't remember. I guess I forgot. I thought we were just rehearsing. Weren't we waiting for the cue cards? I thought Maidie needed a rehearsal, she asked to go over the lines. Right? What happened? And she needs to move out of my way so I can work this robe, and the light is too bland on her face. Put her in the corner where the light is more dramatic for her." Joan saw Maidie sitting in the corner. "What? That was fast."

Charles said, "Oh boy are you tired. But don't worry. It's done. The camera was rolling and caught it all and it was great, Joan. I don't think we need to do it again. You were too good, and the focus was set so there's no worry about you falling out of our depth of field."

"Yes. I'm so tired." Joan grabbed his arm. "Did you just shoot that?"

"Yes, Joan. And it was great. But you went on a little too long, but that's okay, I didn't yell cut right away. We will cut after Maidie's last line. The camera wasn't even on her, yet, anyway. We'll get her shots next and then we're done! *Done!* Done with every single shot. Do you want to stay for Maidie's shots? You usually … "

"Of course! I always stay for my costar's lines. Only I can do my part. I can't be replaced!" They did the scene again, this time with the camera on Maidie. When it was over, Joan said, "Thank you for not going through the roof like Butterfly. Bless you. You were so very lovely and I hope to work with you again." Then Joan felt dizzy. "I think – I ... " Joan hurried off the set, feeling faint. She barely got to her dressing room before she collapsed face down on the floor.

"Miss Crawford?" Frenchy called out.

Joan started to snore violently, so Frenchy just pulled her wig off, where she lay, then grabbed a pillow and blanket for her.

Chapter Fifteen

"Welcome back," her secretary greeted her.

Back at her own home on 426 N. Bristol Avenue in Brentwood, Joan wept, kissed the wall, and took a grand tour of the place as if she'd been gone for years in the slammer. After she saw where the window had been replaced from the brick going through it, she went on to gently touch her many things as she walked from room to room. "It's all here. Bless you for keeping it safe for my return. Bless you for holding it all down. I've lived here for twenty four years and I still worry that it might all go up in a puff of smoke the second I turn my back."

"Why do you always say such nonsense? Things don't go *puff.*"

"Yes they do!" Joan shook her head. "Nothing is real. We just put things there for our eyes to see and it stands there for as long as it does, but it's not real. *Nuh-ah.*"

"It's a real home. *Your* home."

Joan walked through the drawing room, making sure every piece of Chinese porcelain was in place. "Maybe so for my precious adopted darlings. But they take everything for granted, being kids. They just think that this is the house they grew up in, so it's inevitable, and it's theirs somehow. But it's not the house I grew up in. I didn't grow up in a house and I still think I'm going to wake up and they'll laugh at me as they take me back to my tiny room behind the laundry."

"Nobody belongs in a laundry. Not as a home."

Joan disagreed. "If you grow up someplace it ends up making you feel like that's where you belong. It doesn't have to make sense. It's just where you see yourself when you close your eyes."

"Poppycock. That was the past. This is now. This is your home! Why can't you accept that?"

Joan said, "I don't own it. The bank owns it. We own nothing. At any moment in our lives the bank can pound on the door and say *GET OUT you washerwoman's whore*, and take it all back! And what do I have to fight it? What do I *really* own to give them? They can take and sell my Joan Crawford for awhile. But how long before she gets old and doesn't look like that same Joan Crawford anymore that the fans wanted from 1935. How long before the only thing that I have, I don't have anymore. Then I really will have nothing. In 1935 I did *I Live My Life* and I was a bored society girl. I don't look like that anymore. Ooooooh," Joan bawled, "I love that plant. It hasn't died. All plants die. It's so sad to see everything come and go as if it was nothing! I love this plant and tomorrow it could be dead!" She pushed the white pot of a large palm a few inches to see the floor under it. The floor was glistening clean. "Bless you. At least the dirt hasn't taken over. I get so mad at the dirt! Dirt just mocks all our hard work."

The secretary followed Joan as she walked through the playroom that had walls lined in the same leather as the built-in couches. She made sure her Oscar was still on the shelf. She regarded the gorgeous Jean Negulesco sketch of her on the wall. She went down the pine-paneled hall to the dining room where Chinese murals were so delicate that they were kept under glass. She fixed a drink then went upstairs and opened all the doors to the big-as-rooms closets of her dressing room. The thick white wool carpet was clean. She got down on her hands and knees to make sure. She made sure the quilted chintz on the walls hadn't ripped. She went to the sleeping porch and opened the long wall of Dorthy Liebes draperies all lined with heavy black fabric to block all light during hangovers. She looked out the windows to survey the backyard. The pool house and theater were still there. She looked at where she used to have her victory garden."

She went to her private second floor sitting room that was usually filled with fresh cut flowers. There were no bouquets now. That was a testament of how long she'd been gone. She sat at the Queen Ann desk where she always answered her mail. She rubbed her hands over the beautiful wood, appreciating it. "Anything important come?"

The secretary said, "Here's some mail that just arrived today."

"Fans! Bless you!" Joan grabbed the handled basket that

had long blue ribbons streaming from it. "So much work to do. Goddamn it." Joan picked up a different letter opener and sliced the envelopes open, reverently, reading each letter slowly, then sorted them by fans, industry people, bills, and then she came to a category she didn't know where to put. "Psycho Joan?"

It read, "You are not Joan. I am Joan and you are not. Pretenders are very bad. You went too far. You are Satan. We play house but then we leave it. The real Joan has a scarred face, from *A Woman's Face*. So you are fake. Stay and be punished."

"This makes no sense." She called for her secretary. "What the goddamn crap does this mean? Why would Joan have a face of fear unless she was in *Sudden Fear*?"

Her secretary pointed out, "That is not *scare*. That reads *scar*. Lousy penmanship."

Joan dropped the letter. "Oh my God!"

"And it means we call the cops."

Joan winced. "But, it's not threatening enough. Is it? It's not like the fan who threatened to **tear** all my clothes off. Or the fan who said that if he didn't marry me he'd jump off the Hollywood sign, or the fan who said that if I didn't pay for their children's college education they'd expose a porno movie they claimed I'd made."

"Did you?"

"The porno movie? Oh no, not this Joan, but there was an imposter who made one, and those prints were taken care of by Gangster Al."

"You two go far back?"

Joan grabbed a tissue and dabbed her eye. "He took care of everybody. He took care of everything."

"Why are you crying?"

Joan laughed at herself. "We were all so young, once. There was once a time when I would have been frightened to have a fan threatened to tear my clothes off. I was so chubby when I first came to Hollywood. I didn't even have a name yet. I was just dumb ole Miss MGM."

"Now, you'd love to be mauled."

"You're right!" Joan pounded on her rock hard waist. "Because I've never been more gorgeous. Go ahead. Take this letter to the police. Tell them it might be from the same psycho who's killing the streetwalkers and female impersonators. Tell them I'm in danger because I really am Joan Crawford. The psycho now knows my address. How do you think that could have happened? How clever is this psycho? It's like he's got supernatural abilities and second sight to find me here! And if the cops come to interrogate me about all this, and they take flash photos, I'll be in my own house where I can look good. I have to for the papers. We'll just pray with all our might that they don't want me to go downtown to talk about it. I would look horrible there. Their lighting is so harsh. I know what I'll do, I'll go to bed and then I'll have to stay in. Yes. I'm tired anyway. If the police want to talk to me, have them visit me in my room where I'll be wearing one of those *Sudden Fear* nightgowns that didn't make it in the film. That should make some press while I'm at it."

"Any star map for a dime will tell you where Joan Crawford lives."

Joan tapped her noggin. "Oh! Sure!"

The secretary asked, "Do you want an officer to come over to stay, now? Should I call somebody now?"

"No, let's wait, come to think of it. I won't be here tonight. I've got a wrap party to attend. At the end of every picture they used to throw a big party right there on the soundstage but MGM is too cheap for that, anymore, and they couldn't wait to haul us all out with the trash! Goddamn fangs! So we're all going out to the hills and party it up in style, in a nice place far from that MGM dump. I have to say my goodbyes to all the dears who lit me so well under those goddamn hot Technicolor lights, and kept me in focus. Oh, I have so much work still to do. I have a few presents to box up, yet."

"I think you should take that nap. You look tired."

"I don't know. I might just get my second wind if I get busy. In fact, now that I think about it, can't we just call the police tomorrow? Let's just do one thing at a time. I don't want the police here while I'm somewhere else. What a waste of their time.

"I suppose a few hours can't hurt. I'll call them first thing in the morning."

"Bless you." Joan went to the kitchen, washed her hands, replenished her drink, washed her hands again, and smiled. "Home. Reality."

* * * * *

The wrap party at *The Sour Cactus* was at a very private posh club in the hills. It was at the end of a canyon of stucco constructions built to look like storybook playhouses for large children. Down one deep lane there was a peeling castle, a balding gingerbread house, and even a medieval cottage with plastic yellow straw thatch stapled over tarpaper.

Bill Haines was Joan's date. In the gleaming limo, he proclaimed, "Cranberry, you're not Joan Crawford anymore."

She gave him a searing glance. "Don't be absurd. I'm gorgeous and have never looked better as Joan Crawford in all my life."

Bill explained, "No, I mean, you're out of MGM again. And Joan Crawford was their creation."

"I can go back there anytime I wish. I don't need a picture there to have my own run of the place, say hello, or have breakfast with Helen Rose the sweet costume lady, or to go pee in Esther Williams' pool. They all love me there and know that I paid for the place. If it wasn't for Joan Crawford there wouldn't be an MGM. God knows Garbo and Shearer didn't bring in any real money to pay any real bills."

"Just the good reviews."

Joan chuckled. "I got some good reviews, but usually it was for being so good in so many pictures that were so second-rate."

"*Grand Hotel* was not second-rate."

Joan shuddered. "Now that this one's over, I'm scared. It used to be, in the 30s, I didn't worry about there being a next picture. I just worried if it would be any good. I finally felt like I had my place in the world. A *real* place. I finally did have my self-esteem. I really did think I'd work at MGM until I was a little old lady and I retired. And then they'd ask me back for those special little old lady parts everybody loves so much. So back in the 30s I didn't worry about the movie I was acting in being sort of corny, and then being done. In fact, I was filled with great hope. I'd learned more and more each time. I always thought they'd give me something better for the next time for my heard work. There was always a next time. I expected to work my way up big *A* pictures like *Gone With the Wind* or *Marie Antoinette*."

"You were in some classics, Cranberry."

"Bless you. But I finally had to leave the MGM dump, to do a class act like *Mildred Pierce* and *Humoresque*. But even then, they were Bette Davis leftovers."

"Yes! Those were classics!"

Joan put her head on his shoulder for a moment, careful not to cause her bright yellow wig to slip. "Baby, if you'd stayed with me at MGM then things could have been different. Maybe everything at the studio wouldn't have fallen apart so bad for everybody."

Bill reminded her, "I stayed as long as I could. But the day I knew would come. It came like a stake through my poor heart. I wasn't young enough anymore to be their happy bachelor. They told me I had to get married. To a girl. Jimmy didn't count."

Joan smiled sadly. "I don't know why they were so mean to you. You were a wonderful leading man. We were so good together."

"Gable and you were the real MGM team."

"Gable and I always looked like we were about to fornicate until we went blind and it drove the shop girls wild. You and I just looked like we were having too much fun, and it made them so happy. We were so *so* gorgeous together in *West Point*. What year was that?"

"1928."

"Holy shit!"

Bill smiled at the old memory. "We were gorgeous and fun. And you drove the homosexuals wild, too, but your fan papers couldn't say that."

"*I* knew."

Bill chuckled. "I know. You had a true supernatural sense when it came to smelling out fans. Damn I miss it. The movies let you sit out front and clap for yourself."

Joan moaned. "You stole that joke from Will Rogers and he said that so many years ago. Ooooh! We can't be that old, can we baby?"

"No," Bill assured. "Fifty is not old."

"*Forty nine!*"

"I was making an average out of it. I'm fifty three, you know."

"How does it feel?" Joan asked.

"You mean, does it feel ooold?"

"Yes."

Bill smirked at the cigarette Joan gave him. "I think *these* make me feel old if anything. That's why the kids like them so much. They don't know that you really begin to *feel* old. Huffing and puffing."

Joan elbowed him. "I don't huff and puff. I'm a musical star. And I got a new picture lined up so I shouldn't be nervous about anything. But I feel dread. I hope having a new picture lined up lets me make another picture after that - and then another after that!"

Bill said, "Of course it will."

"The fangs at MGM say my days are numbered and they mean it. They think the world belongs to the young nobodies. They think I'm in the way, a liability, an embarrassment. Gangster Al scares me now these days. He scares me bad."

Bill nodded. "Like the Hollywood Boogie Man."

"Somebody should put a hit out on him! He's the one who'll go on and make the studio - make all of Hollywood - look bad if people ever find out he really existed. The people in Peoria want to think the movies are magic. They don't want to hear about some hit man helping to make the magic happen. Nobody wants to know that Hollywood is crawling with mafia."

"I hope the party has some security to keep the psycho killers out."

Joan elbowed him. "Don't remind me of that. It was all a dream, I'm sure. I heard about the psycho taken to the asylum and then my imagination took over. It was really all an Alice in Wonderland dream, for sure. How absurd." Joan chuckled at herself.

"Okay."

* * * * *

At the party, when Joan crossed paths with Michael Wilding, she handed him a present of gold cufflinks some other man had once left in her bedroom. Then she made a sad face and said to him, "I'm so sorry the picture is over. I'm sure it was so wonderful for you to have a chance to work again."

He smiled too politely. "It's nice to be home again with wife and the kids. And all her damn pets." Then he smiled even bigger, sheepishly, and went on to thank Joan for all the acting lessons, not saying what he wanted to say, while Joan wept for being appreciated. "Bless you," she said as if there was no tomorrow.

Gig Young stepped up and teased Michael, "Is it true you're going to play an Egyptian Pharaoh? You better watch the eye makeup. They may go crazy and paint you up bigger than Kathryn Grayson if you don't watch it."

Joan loudly chimed up, "I'm going to be in a marvelous western. The deal is almost struck with my agent, it's as good as done. It'll be a much better western than *High Noon* because mine will be done in that marvelous new color process Trucolor they have at Republic, which is such a clever studio. A year ago, Trucolor couldn't create certain colors. Purple and pink. But they've improved it! I'll make sure I wear a pink shirt to show it off! My western will also be so much better than that pretentious *Shane* because I'm the *people's* star, and my fans, alone, will fill the seats. So I don't know how the theaters will accommodate the fans of westerns who will also be so interested in seeing a western of such dramatic interest as *Johnny Guitar*. And I'm singing the title song. They had mention that Peggy Lee might do it but I told them that she sounds just a little too lazy. I sing from the heart, and they couldn't disagree. Peggy Lee sounds like she's laying on a couch when she sings. I bet I'll have a best selling record out, soon, and Judy Garland will find she has a bit of competition in the record stores. Joan turned in the direction of Michael Wilding and asked, "Do you have any fans here in America? And are there any fans of Egyptian movies to fill seats?"

He and Gig Young slipped off toward the bar.

Joan turned to Marjorie Rambeau who stepped up to her side, and said, "You look lovely tonight. That is such a lovely dress. Did you read Hedda's article about how Mr. Wilder and Mr. Granger like to play with each other's pee-pee's?"

"Hedda's a lying bitch!"

Joan gasped. "You can't say that about God!"

Marjorie said, "Well then - God is a lying bitch!"

"You're not drinking beer," Joan noticed. "Why? Not enough hops?"

Marjorie answered, "I never drink beer."

"But - but you said you liked beer so much and you wished you could taste the hops."

Marjorie paused a moment, swallowing hard. "Joan, dear. That was in the picture. In real life, I loath beer."

"Oh?"

"It's just a picture, Joan. I'm in real life now and I really *don't* like beer!"

Joan got it. She winked. "How fascinating. Bless you. And I want to thank you for doing that scene with me. It was the only time in the entire picture that I felt like I was a real character with feelings and a real life. The rest of the movie I was just me being a bulldozer with lines. Not lines on my face. Dialogue."

Marjorie agreed, "Of course. It was a part of the picture that had the most reality - and I played your mother! I must have given birth to you when I was - ten?"

"You never complimented me on my singing."

"I never heard much of it except you crooning along with the record player."

"Oh. That's right. *Tenderly* will be put over the scene in editing. But I assure you *I* heard it in my head the entire time we filmed the scene."

Marjorie said, "But India Adams is re-recording all the songs."

Joan blinked at her. "No dear, that must be a mistake. I prerecorded everything myself before a single scrap of film was shot. During playback I heard my own lovely voice, but I did so

many retakes of *Tenderly* I'm so nervous about which one they'll
finally use for the final cut. They said they might even splice it all
together - using just the very best parts of each take. Isn't that dear
for the soundmen to work so hard to make Joan Crawford sound her
very best for the fans? My fans deserve it, though. They aren't all
rich so a movie ticket means a lot. My fans want *my* voice. It has that
distinctive emotional quiver, yet it is *always* stable and in key because
I make sure it is. I'm not a lazy singer who lets her voice warble off
to anywhere. It's mine and it's gorgeous. It better be. Do you realize
how long now I've worked on my voice? Since the silent movies
turned to sound movies and I didn't want to sound like some hick
from Texas. I made myself who I am and I'm very proud of that. I
even studied opera and used to sing it at my dinner guests. We had
so much fun in those days. Everything was an experiment and an
adventure." Joan chuckled, sadly. "I had tried to improve myself
and usually worked too hard. But nobody appreciated that. They
just called me a phony."

"I have to go now." Marjorie pushed through the crowd and
was gone.

Gangster Al entered the room. Most didn't know who he was,
even though it was all MGM people. He walked up to Joan, and
without regret or sadness, plainly said, "Time to take a ride to the
desert."

"Now?"

"Yes."

"Nope." Joan shook her head. "I have a western lined up.
Practically. I have to do one more picture first."

"That isn't an MGM picture. I don't care."

"I do get my one last party, you promised."

Gangster Al looked around. "This isn't it?"

"This is just the wrap party of *Torch Song* idiot. It's an MGM
party, not mine. And you know I still have to be available for any
re-dubbing that might arise."

"Of course."

Joan glared at him fiercely. "Of *course* of course. You mean to tell me you're going to follow me around like the Grim Reaper to remind me that my days as a star are numbered? You don't think the press is doing that enough, as it is, with my career? You son-of-a-bitch!"

"Come to the car, at least, and get your things."

"What things"

"From your last murder at the Joan Crawford show."

"The what? That wasn't real. I decided."

"It was."

"Oh my god."

"Let's go."

"That was real? I was up all last night thinking about it. That wasn't me! I almost got killed, myself, from Joan Crawford, you lousy bastard!"

Gangster Al said, "It was your letter opener, and your clothes and earrings. You were all over the crime. But I took care of it for you Joan, this one last time. I have them in the car for you. Be glad they're not in some detective's office. That wouldn't look good for you. The press would be all over it and you'd be a monster in all the papers."

Joan went with him to his car to take a look at them, and then frowned, "I don't want that anymore, if people were really murdered in it." She shuddered and then began to cry. "It was horrible! It can't be real, it was too horrible!"

"You want me to destroy this - evidence?"

"Evidence, crap." Joan wiped her tears. "I was almost murdered, too."

"You're slipping Joan. You didn't even call me to report this so I could do my job."

"I didn't kill anybody. I'd *never* do that! I know that now. Joan Crawford is the kindest person I know. I just slap and shoot people a lot in my movies."

"Yeah, yeah, yeah. You're so out of it half the time on booze and diet pills you're not sure, are you?"

Joan slapped his face. "I'm still Joan Crawford and nobody talks to be that way!"

"We'll see, Joan, we'll see."

Joan snatched the jewels from him. "I can boil these in bleach. Burn the rest. Where's my letter opener?"

"It's too sharp for you. I'll hold on to it for you." He drove off.

Joan bawled after him, "You *bastard!* I'm a *big* star and I'll stay on top! Just you wait and see! MGM isn't through with me yet! Look how wrong they were about me ten years ago! *WRONG!* 1943 was a nothing year for MGM because they didn't think to make a Joan Crawford picture! I could have made a great year for MGM, I always had! But Mayer got stupid! He wanted to shove me into a downer picture! I would have played a sweaty starving nurse in a dirty uniform! In the jungles of Bataan! Goddam *Battan!* And I would have been sharing the picture with ten has-beens! They were second-tier contract players! And they would be hogging all the lines and wearing the exact same dirty costume as me! Joan Crawford doesn't play a dirty starving nurse in a chorus line! That's not a Joan Crawford picture! That's crap! And I still got my looks and I'm gonna push it a few years more! You ain't gonna tell me it's time to go take a nap in the desert." Then Joan noticed people had come out and were staring at her. She bawled back at them, "Whatcha starin' at!"

They applauded.

Chapter Sixteen

At the Brentwood house, Joan was on the phone to the florist. Bill supervised the workmen setting up the tables and chairs on Joan's backyard tennis court. He pointed, "Put them in rows *that* way."

Joan finally walked out to him and said, "Those men are all straight, aren't they?"

"How can you tell?" he asked.

She pressed him, "How can *you* tell?"

"Cranberry! You think I have a special radar dish on the top of my head to smell homosexuals? Pansy scope?"

"Sure. Something like that. I know, because when you think you're in the company of straight men, you talk in a deep tone of voice and you don't wave your arms around so much."

"I do?"

"Yep." Joan chuckled. "And pansy scope sounds like it should be a new process to go with Cinemascope."

Bill laughed with her. "With cardboard lavender glasses! All the men's clothes disappear! Cranberry, that's too funny! Starring James Dean!"

"Who's he?"

"He's new. Brand new."

Joan asked, "What studio is he with?"

"Warner Brothers."

"Oh. Then he'll be a nobody. The new ones aren't groomed. They're just thrown to the sharks."

"I agree, Cranberry."

"And remember," Joan warned him. "Tonight, I'm Joan Crawford to you, not some old pet name."

Bill frowned. "I knew you before you knew yourself. But alas, as the greatest poet said, *What's in a name? That which we call a rose. By any other name would smell as sweet.*"

"That's me."

"Tonight, Cranberry. Only for you. Only for tonight I'll call you *that* name – Joan Crawford."

"The way you say it, I sound like an imposter." Joan went inside and called the flower shop back. "They have to be here NOW!" The flower shop truck pulled into her driveway. "That's better!"

Men hauled many crates of fresh fragrant gardenias into the backyard. She yelled orders to the small army of Chinese workmen already there, pointing wildly, having large branches installed along the paths, that were disinfected, painted white, and then hundreds of flowers were tied to their tips. Some flowers floated on the pool along with a hundred floating candles.

"Are you sure this will be wonderful?" Joan asked Bill. "Will it impress the fangs?"

"Is it expensive?" Bill asked.

"Yep."

"It's wonderful."

Joan moaned. "I hope my next picture can pay for all the money I've been blowing out my bank's ass. Goddamn it!"

Bill asked, "Cranberry, did you hire the Joan Crawford imposter? I didn't tell you to do that. That's tacky."

"What? No! Was this Joan Crawford in a hospital gown?"

"And a scarred face like in that movie you made. What's it called? The Ingrid Bergman remake."

Joan spun about. "Where is this Joan Crawford?"

Bill pointed. "I saw him earlier walking across the top of your wall. What a dead ringer for you in the face. Of course his knees are boy's knees. I called out to him and he tripped and fell off the wall onto the other side. I went to see if he was okay and he was gone. I could see where he'd fallen into some rose bushes. That had to hurt. Did you really wear something so flimsy in any of your psychotic episodes as a hospital gown?"

"I do not have psychotic episodes."

"It almost got you another Academy Award."

"Call the police!"

He sensed Joan's fear. "You want to call off your party?"

"No, we'll just have the police here. Call them! I meant to call them earlier."

Bill warned, "But the F.B.I. will get involved if it involves anything to do with any of the homosexual themes. Do you want them here, too?"

"I don't care."

Bill looked scared. "Everybody but Gary Cooper could get his dick fingerprinted."

"I said *I don't care!* Nothing is going to fuck with my party! Nothing!"

Discreet private detectives and indiscreet F.B.I. agents arrived who agreed to stay for the duration of the party. And then MGM's hit man, appeared.

Joan wasn't pleased. "Gangster Al! What are you doing here already? I didn't invite you. I want to see you about as badly as I want to watch *Faust*."

"No, the police called me. We always work together. I hear that the Joan Crawford who escaped the loony bin has been seen around here at this loony bin. I suppose you're going to try and kill that one, too."

Joan said, "I don't know who this one is. Bill told me that he had *A Woman's Face* scars. I've never seen anybody like that before. Really. That's not the same one I saw kill everybody at the big Joan Crawford party. That one didn't have scars."

Gangster Al shrugged, "Then we can all leave."

"Screw you, I'm so scared."

"Not with Gangster Al around."

Joan smiled sweetly. "You care."

"No. But if you were murdered at your own party by a psycho Joan Crawford, it would make terrible press."

Joan said, "So you admit it. You can't always blame me. Why are you always picking on me?"

"You'd be so humiliated to go that way, no matter which Joan is at the safe end of the gun, either way. No. At MGM we control these things as best we can."

"Control what? When I'll die?" Joan shuddered.

Gangster Al said, "And I won't let it be a murder at home by a nobody, that's for sure. At this stage, I wouldn't even let an ex

husband pluck you off. These things have to be done delicately.
A star of your caliber has to leave the legend unscathed, if not
accentuated with mystery. MGM, and Hollywood, has a great legacy
to protect."

"How delicately?"

Gangster Al said, "I won't let you down, believe me. I'm a pro.
I'm the best hit man the world has ever seen."

"Because you work for MGM?"

"Which controls the entire city, and most the nation, which
means much of the free world. We control everything but Pasadena.
We leave Pasadena alone so we can test run our pictures there with
some honesty."

"Well MGM doesn't rule my backyard!" Joan insisted. "Stay out
of my sight! Don't bring me down at my own last party with the
sight of you staring at me like a vulture."

"You'll see me later when I'm ready for you."

She wanted to spit on him. "I'm sure I will."

Gangster Al reminded her, "And you'll leave with me like a lady.
Joan Crawford has to stay Joan Crawford. The legend must stay
unscathed."

"A lamb. A sacrificial lamb to grease the wheels of that damn
studio – this town – the free world!" She downed a glass of vodka,
shuddered, went inside to wash her hands, and then hurried back
out to where the tables and chairs were being set up. She directed
Bill, "And when everyone is eating, I want the slide projectors to
start projecting my faces all over the pool house wall, the theater,
and the white fence. I want giant Joans all around! Giant Joan's
everywhere from all my hundreds of films. I want to look eternal
for my party."

Bill made a face. "I didn't plan that."

"I did. It's a fabulous idea because it's my party and I want me
all over it. Joan Joan Joan everywhere everybody turns."

Bill rubbed his jaw. "Isn't that a bit egomaniac?"

"Don't be redundant. I'm the biggest star, at least according to
the fans and accountants! What else is there? All my old glamour
poses from all my years as the biggest star will be shining all around

everybody until they're just so overwhelmed at what a great star I was and what a magnificent career I had. The classic studio shots and the great stills from my movies – damn I was hot in *Letty Lynton* so there's lots of those. And *Mannequin*. And *Paid*. And *Dance, Fools Dance*! And *Spring Fever!* And *This Modern Age!*"

"Waoh! You're going backward in time, now."

Her eyes clouded over. "Time."

Bill frowned. "Cranberry! Baby! You talk about it as if it's over."

"Over."

"Don't be silly."

Joan nodded sadly. "We all live on borrowed time, baby. And I've spent all the money I have, so they say. I'm not talking about bank loans. Screw them. The MGM devil himself has come to take me home. I had my run with this sick town and I stayed on top. I gained the entire world, or at least that's what I fooled my fans to think. I gained the world and now I lose my soul."

Bill marveled, "Where did that crazy talk come from? Did you read a religious book or something?"

Joan dabbed at a tear. "But I'm not talking about that. I'm just facing the facts as those who have the power present me with them. I'm just trying to swallow some bitter reality with dignity so I don't ruin my glorious flawless image. Regardless of what happens to my body - Joan Crawford has to stay alive forever – and please don't let it be on TV. Keep the classics on the big screen."

"Sorry, Cranberry, but you're confusing me. The only thing I understand right now is throwing a party that will be talked about for days. A party to show that you're on top. And then you go do a horse opera. You did sign on the dotted line for the western, didn't you?"

"Yeah. But MGM may not let me do it."

Bill said, "It's not an MGM picture."

"I know. That's probably why they set the time for now to do me in."

"What time set?" Bill became angry. "Do you in! You're just going crazy. I thought you had all the rest and relaxation you needed. You should have waited another week before we did this party. You're just cracking up!"

"Am I?"

"Just don't worry about a thing. It's too late to call the party off, now. Just let me take care of everything and if you need to go in and lie down, do so and don't worry about the party. If you crack up, we'll just tell everybody you're doing a *Possessed* impersonation, ambulance and all. I'll make sure they clap as you ride off. I'll make sure they use the siren for you so the scene ends real good."

"Bless you." Joan grabbed his elbow. "But I won't miss a moment of this night. I want to smell the air and taste everything and put as much of planet Earth in me as I can, while I can, all I can, while I'm here."

"And you can also just *go to the can*."

"You're rude. You just don't get it. You got out of MGM just in time."

Bill reminded her, "That was over twenty years ago."

"Barely in time."

Judy Garland showed up. "Hi."

Joan rushed over and greeted her. "Honey! You're early. Your hair is so cute. You're always so adorable! What a gorgeous necklace. I'm so jealous of you!"

"Bullshit. Just show me to the kitchen and the potato salad. I need a little nibble right now before I faint."

Joan smiled. She saw that Judy looked heavy and knew it was the baby - she wasn't just letting herself go. "Bless you."

Judy patted her tummy. "I'm so goddam hungry every time I'm pregnant. I'm so happy. I hope it's a boy."

"Is that the only time you've been hungry?" Joan's eyebrow arched whimsically.

Judy laughed. "I thought the MGM publicity department had you think I was so thin all by myself."

"Oh. I thought you were already pregnant when you were skipping down the yellow brick road."

Judy grinned lewdly. "All the way to an MGM abortionist." The two laughed wickedly.

"The old movies were so wholesome," Joan added. "We didn't even get to say piss damn my tired balls!"

"Potato salad!"

"I don't have any. It isn't that kind of party. Lobster?"

"I'll eat your kids' food."

"Go!" Joan pointed to the kitchen. "Anything in the refrigerator is yours." Joan followed, deciding she needed to wash her hands again. In the kitchen, as Judy was nibbling on a piece of bread, Joan put a peanut butter and bacon sandwich under the broiler for her.

"If you wash your hands again," Judy shamed her, "you'll lose your skin."

"Nonsense. With Vinolia, you get cold cream. And it was in all the first-class cabins on the Titanic - the only soap they'd use. It says it's a soap fit for a queen! That's me!"

"Don't bring up the Titanic before such an expensive party!"

Joan asked, "You ever have trouble with Judy Garland drag queens?"

Judy rolled her adorable teddy bear eyes. "Ooooh! The worst."

"What?"

"They're all so pretty." She laughed. "And they're so smart!"

Joan said, "Oh - you're smart."

"No, when I was young, I wasn't. Boy what a dummy. I wish my Mom had bothered to tell me anything but all I heard out of her was, Dance Judy! Dance faster! And I was so clueless. When I had my first pregnancy Helen Rose told me that she and the girls were going to give me a shower. I was just terrified. I was so scared. I thought – you know – but then they caught me finally, even though I'd been hiding out in sound stage two where they were shooting The Courage of Lassie. And they weren't running at me with a hose and sponges - but had presents! And some pretty nice ones, too! I bawled for an hour. I didn't know people could be nice."

"Helen Rose is very nice. Bless her."

Judy asked, "How are the Joan Crawford drag queens coming along?"

Joan frowned. "Some of them are just nasty. But I can't talk about it. I want a happy party." Joan gave her biggest flirty smile and asked, "Perhaps you'll be in the mood to sing, later? Hmmmm?"

"Oh, no. Sorry. I'm all tuckered out. Do you have any white wine? Just a tiny bit. I'm pregnant and I don't want the child to grow up a grim pilgrim."

"Of course," Joan offered, nervously looking out the window at a few of the other guests who were arriving. Bill and Jimmy were greeting them. "Oh good. Bela is here. He needs to show everybody he can still get out. Then maybe some fang will put him in a picture. He needs one so bad."

Judy said, "They don't make Dracula pictures anymore."

"Then put him in something - as a butler. Anything. The poor man needs work."

"Don't cry, Joan."

Joan made herself laugh. "I just worry about people like Bela, who've been around since the early days, and now they're so forgotten and hungry." Joan looked out her kitchen window again. "Oh good. William Holden is talking to him. What a relief. He's not being ignored!"

"Relax Joan."

"I can't!"

Judy said, "Maybe later Mr. Holden will lay face down in your pool like he's dead, for a good laugh."

Joan forced a chuckle, and then gasped. "Oh my god who's that? Oh my god! That old lady? Is that -"

Judy peeked out the window, also. "Yep, that's Miss Burke, my most piquant good witch."

"I thought so! I'm afraid to go out. Why does she look so old?"

"Oh, Joan, maybe because she's about seventy by now."

"She wasn't that old when I worked with her."

"When was that?" Judy asked.

Joan thought. "I guess *They All Kissed the Bride* was a while ago. 1942. That was a good year. They don't make years like 1942 anymore. *Mrs. Miniver. Yankee Doodle Dandy.* I should have played those parts. And that was the year Carol Lombard died and left Clark Gable so sad. What's this goddamn year gonna be remembered for? *Torch Song*. That's it. Not because it's a good script but because it's a full color Joan Crawford picture and I kick my gams up higher than Jesus."

Judy nodded, looking alarmed. "That's high!"

Joan asked, "Do you like the wine? You haven't told me how delicious it is."

"Why? Did you stomp the grapes?"

"Oh you're funny."

Judy asked, "What did I do in 1942? I try to put MGM behind me and now all the studio years have blanded together. All I remember is vaudeville. I was always on that vaudeville stage since I was a toddler. My mother warned me that if I wasn't good enough she'd leave me behind in whatever town we were in. I believed her and it scared the goody gumdrops out of me!"

"I'm the lucky one, here, then," Joan decided. "I *was* abandoned. I think it helps to just get it over with. Screw the threats. Mom dumped me off at a convent, said *spank some Virgin into her*, and I said *Alleluia, I've been abandoned and I know it!* Then the suspense was over with. If you really want to screw with your kids, give 'em suspense."

Judy laughed. "Yeah, screw it. So what did I do in 1942? Tell me. No, don't tell me."

"I'll give you a hint," Joan offered. "Vaudeville."

"But I was at MGM."

"No!" Joan reminded her, "a musical about vaudeville and war and being brave and fighting the war no matter what, even if your fingers get smashed in the wardrobe trunk."

Judy sang, "*For Me And My Gal!*"

Joan winked. "Bingo!"

"That smiling candy coated junk! MGM wanted people to think vaudeville and the war really was a bunch of smiling candy coated junk. And people thought it was real. In one scene I go to an army hospital to sing and all the wounded look up at me and *smile*! Their legs were all chopped off and suddenly they didn't care because Judy Garland was singing!"

"We had to fight Hitler. Now be careful or you'll be branded a commie and won't be able to work anymore."

Judy scoffed. "Me? I'm too popular. They just pick on the little guys who aren't very popular. Or articulate."

"Watch it!" Joan warned, looking around for spies. "The F.B.I. is here. So the C.I.A. may not be far."

Judy made a face at Joan. "You're on too much coffee! And at this hour. Shame on you. If anybody calls me a commie I'll just show up and sing *Over the Rainbow*. That's all I ever need to do when I need to win an argument. Speaking of my old movies, Is Gene Kelly going to be here tonight?"

"Maybe." Joan smiled. "He's so cute."

Judy looked out the window again and asked, "What has Glenda the Good Witch been up to lately?"

Joan said, "They say Miss Burke just did a musical for MGM this year. I doubt she is the lead and sings. Not an old feeble woman with such tiny eyes. Maybe they taped the droopy skin back. It's a great thing to have done to your face! Have you ever had your face taped back?"

Judy shook her head. "Hell no! They just chased me with a chair and a whip."

"It's great! It feels so – so – important!"

Judy frowned. "I just sing. They gave up on my looks years ago."

"I do hope you're in the mood to sing a few songs for the party, later."

"Yeah, yeah, everybody thinks you just put a nickel in my nose and a song comes out my foot. I don't think so."

"Oh bless you, I knew you always love to sing. I have to go now and say something nice to Glenda – I mean - Miss Burke. Maybe I should offer her some moisturizer for her elbows. God knows I have enough in this cabinet." Joan rubbed pink hand lotion in-between every finger then traipsed outside. "Daaarling," she kissed Billie's cheek, "Do you love my party? Tell me you just adore it. I certainly adore your dress. What marvelous colors. You look like a dream!"

"I adore your party, Joan darling."

"Oh, really? Really? How so!"

Billie Burke smiled kindly. "Joan, the party is lovely. Relax. Will you ever learn to relax?"

Joan laughed at herself. "What is the new picture you're in?"

Billie Burke twittered. "Oo*ooo*-o-o-o!"

"What's the new picture?"

"*Small Town Girl.* It's a musical remake of an old movie. It's all very sweet. I just have a small character part, of course. Jane Powell stars."

"Oh," Joan contemplated that. "*Her!* What was the original called?"

"*Small Town Girl.*"

"How very clever. Bless you!"

Susan Hayward and Robert Wagner stepped up beside Billie. "Hi."

Joan didn't know what to say, that might be clever, so she hurried off to find Bill. "This party is a disaster. Nobody is having any fun. Nobody will come. All the real people will go somewhere else tonight and make me feel like a fool! Who's real these days? Who's on top so that I can show them that I'm on top?"

Bill said, "Tonight, Joan's party is the place to be in *all* the land."

"How can you be so sure?"

"Cranberry. Breathe. What's that I smell on you? Something for diaper rash?"

"You're so mean to me! And so crude. Fuck you! That's my new hand lotion and it cost a small fortune!" She waved her hands in front of his face.

"Just trying to lighten you up, Cranberry."

"Yes. I'm so nervous." She forced a laugh.

Bill chuckled, "I'm not nervous at all."

"Because you didn't pay for any of this. Because you have Jimmy and I have nothing." She looked around the grounds in sadness. "Doesn't this all look like a movie set? Soon it'll all come down. Nothing lasts. Nothing."

"Stop it! Don't be glum! Not tonight!"

"I won't if you tell me not to."

"I'm telling you!" Then Bill smirked, "That's probably why *I'm* having such a good time. *You* will have a miserable time, no matter what."

"But I can act!" Joan quickly double-checked her gown. "And I'm gorgeous! How's my hair, still?"

"Your wig could survive atomic tests."

"Balls! And why won't I have a good time no matter what? What do you mean?"

Bill explained, "It's just the rule of throwing a party. No matter how many people show up, you'll get mad about that one lousy person who didn't show up who you thought should have. It's the fate of all hosts. It's never good enough."

Joan agreed, "If Clark Gable doesn't come, I'll feel so sad."

He pretended to slap her, making the sound effect with his mouth. "Tsssk! Snap out of it, woman! He's out of the country. Clark's in Italy."

"Mary Pickford will always shun me, too," Joan grumbled. "She almost warmed up to me when I was married to her kid."

Bill asked, "Do you think ZaSu Pitts will make it tonight?"

"Oh sure," Joan shrugged indifference.

"You two go back to the silent days yet you've never made a picture together."

Joan smiled big. "And she never'stole a picture from me either. I do hope she comes. I don't know. Now I'm a nervous wreck if they come or not. You're right. A fickle pile of Hollywood shows up and eats my lobster and drinks my champagne, and if I hear laughter, I fear they're laughing about me. And I panic." She paused to listen, hearing Katharine Hepburn's loud guffaw. "They're laughing about my tight closeup in *Sudden Fear*. I know it. My freckles showed when the camera did a choker. I knew I should have worn more Max Factor!"

Bill said, "Now have a cocktail and relax."

"What if I forget all those jokes I memorized?

"Leave the jokes to Rosalind Russell. They just spill out of her. You don't have to say anything. Just smile like you mean it."

Joan said, "I paid good money for that joke book! I'm blanking out! I need cue cards for my own goddamn party!"

Bill repeated, "Forget the jokes. Have a cocktail and relax!"

"If I have another cocktail I'll be trying to stand on the wrong side of some table. I better eat something now. God knows I'll be too busy later. Oh look! That's Myrna Loy and she looks lost. I think she does that on purpose."

"Yeah, so she can keep bumping into the same drinks table. We should be greeting our guests."

Joan agreed. "Yes we should, to help them pretend they all haven't seen each other a thousand times before over at Gloria Swanson's."

Chapter Seventeen

Dinner was served outside on the tennis court, and at Joan's cue, the projectors started. Their carrousels had somehow been switched. Giant black and white images of Joan Crawford drag queens flashed up on the fence and walls. The crowd howled with laughter as a Joan Crawford as Harriet Craig wore a cardboard house. A Joan Crawford in a dark wedding dress appeared. A Joan Crawford was dancing the Charleston on a wreck of a piano. There was a shot of a Joan Crawford with a beer belly in a belly dancing outfit with arms straight up doing the *Flamingo Road* carnie pose. There was an especially wild eyed Joan Crawford in a hospital gown holding up a letter opener like a weapon. Then there was a most convincing Joan Crawford in a raincoat and tan turban with fake rubies screaming bloody murder. Then a Joan Crawford in an excellent wig and fur had a letter opener sticking out of his neck.

"This is great, Joan," Bill praised. "The Joan Crawford violence looks so real. Joan? Oh my GAWD!"

She had fainted. Judy Garland stood up and in great gusto, in a voice that cut well above the wild laughter, she began to joyfully sing, "*The bells are ringing - !*"

* * * * *

Joan felt smelling salts blast up her brain, and then she jolted with fear. "Gangster Al, no! Not yet! Everything's gonna be better for me! I'm not washed up! Look around! This town *loves* me! All the stars are here! I'm not washed up! Look! Bob Hope is staring at me! Bless you! And Kirk Douglas came and he looked so good in his pants! And there's Grace Kelly and she looks so well groomed. Bless her!"

"That's enough. Time to go and take an old lady nap in the desert."

"No! I'm still young!"

Gangster Al said, "You're old. The 30s are over." He handed her a drink.

"I was a star in the 40s, too. And I'll prove myself in the 50s, I promise!"

"How many films did you make in the 30s?"

Joan said, "Several a year!"

Gangster Al said, "And in the 40s, you only made several films, total, in comparison."

"I made lots! No thanks to the crap MGM was trying to give me!"

"You were getting old."

"I taped my face up! I lost ten pounds! I got legs!"

"But Joan, you're through - your time that MGM has allowed you has run out - in fact you're a bit *past* due. There has been no more work on *Torch Song* since the wrap party. They cut it together in record time and it's done."

"But I have a new picture already lined up! *Johnny Guitar!* It'll be a great picture! Just give it a chance! It's being shot in Sedona! In Arizona! To look like a *real* western. And I need another drink."

Gangster Al said, "But that silly horse opera won't be for MGM. You can shoot it all in a cow pie, for all I care. I don't care."

Joan explained, "But I have a two picture contract with MGM for $125,000 *each* and I only got one in – *this* one. That ain't fair! You're casting *Brigadoon* right now. Put me in that!"

"You're going over to Republic, now, and we may never see you again - especially with one foot on a banana peel with the other in a grave."

"Give Poverty Row and Republic its respect! It's still a part of this rotten town."

"Republic is already starting to crank out TV more than anything. The B picture is over. The Joan Crawford picture is over. That kind of stuff is all being done for television now."

"*Johnny Guitar* is NOT going to be a B picture!"

Gangster Al grabbed her arm. "Let's go and don't make a scene. You're still a movie star and you want to be remembered well for the history books. The last page will be *Torch Song* and they'll say of your photo, *Oh she still looked okay.*"

"Careful, I bruise! They'll miss me at Republic and come looking for me!"

"Not at this hour. And we'll just let them think you're too big a star for them. You are."

Joan said, "They won't believe it."

"You've been losing a lot of pictures, lately, due to your ego. This will just go down with the rest - like your losing *From Here to Eternity* and *Lisbon*. Over at Poverty Row they'll just figure out that they aren't in your league."

Joan didn't know how to argue that, so she just said, "They won't believe it!"

"Hedda Hopper will publish anything. It'll be announced that your cheap horse opera was to be turned into a TV show and you naturally bowed out. It'll be front page. Republic will deny it but the story will already have hit the street and the public doesn't notice retractions."

"Have you already started this lie?" Joan asked.

"Yep."

"But I wanna make *Johnny Guitar*! I have bills to pay off!"

Gangster Al said, "You don't have anymore bills where you're going."

"I'm gonna go get plucked!" Joan hollered above the loud chatter, but some just applauded, thinking she'd said something else. "Let me get my handbag," she asked. "At least I can freshen up my lipstick before I go lay down for the very last time."

Gangster Al winked at her. "I always like a pretty stiff."

Even though she went upstairs for her handbag, she still beat Gangster Al to his car, her great eyes angry and darting about. "And they'll all wonder why I didn't come back and they'll know you're just a lousy hit man for Mayer." She tried to slap him but he punched her, took her handbag, and threw her into the car. He handcuffed her to her door handle. When he got in, she screamed, "Balls! Nobody will believe your story about me! The world will miss me and wonder where I went! MGM has no right to decide these things for people. MGM has no right to control people like this – like we're just cattle."

"A drag queen that looks enough like you is getting on the train for New York, tonight. His shoulders aren't wide enough, perhaps, but he's a dead ringer. At least he is with bangs and sunglasses. That will be the last anybody will see of you. They will all think you just went away like Garbo." Gangster Al stomped the gas.

"I don't take trains anymore," Joan said. "Everybody knows that - I'm too modern. Didn't you see me in the paper - getting off the plane from New York?"

Gangster Al argued, "Trains have more class. Nobody believed that picture of you at the plane was real. It didn't feel Hollywood. Trains feel Hollywood. They got room for luxury. You can kick up your feet and throw a party. On a plane you ain't even got room to scratch your own balls, let alone somebody else's, huh Joan?"

"Don't be crude. You're with a goddamn lady. What did you do with my fucking handbag?"

"It's on the floor in the back."

"I want it," Joan asked.

"Nope. I felt a gun in it."

"Sure! For shooting up my pool parties. The men just love it when I do a Joan Crawford for them."

Gangster Al chuckled. "That's Hollywood, but I don't take chances. Even a Hollywood bullet can hurt you pretty bad if fired at close enough a range."

"A blank can hurt?" Joan questioned him.

"If too close," he repeated.

"Oh really. How interesting. That's stupid. Nobody will believe anything you're doing, and MGM will put a hit out on *you*! Have you ever worried about MGM's reputation? One day soon they'll find out about you in Washington and the whole lid will be blown off."

Gangster Al said, "Not by you."

"Somebody will figure it out! Nobody takes the train that far, anymore, not if they're a star. I was photographed coming off the plane with a blow-up poodle. It looked gorgeous."

"The dead ringer we're sending out will create just the discrete confusion we need. Few people will be there at that hour, anyway."

"And this dead ringer for me," Joan asked, "was this the same crazy fool who escaped the sanatorium who thinks he really *is* me?"

"Nope. This one doesn't have your eyes so we'll keep him in big sunglasses. Your psycho is someone else. There's lots of you, Joan, out there, aren't there? But don't worry, MGM is gonna find that crazy Joan Crawford and pluck him, too. You don't need that kind of press."

Joan said, "You're going to gun down that Joan Crawford like in some western? If you let me stay around for another picture I get to gun down Mercedes McCambridge in the final shootout! I blow her right off the side of the hill! It'll make western history! Oh let me do it! I'm too young to vanish! I'm far too young to end a wonderful career! I'm Joan Crawford! Everyone will go ape bananas when they notice me gone! And I have another picture with MGM. It's in my contract! I got a two picture deal! Let me just do a screen test with Gene Kelley to show how cute we'll look together! We'll be the new MGM musical team! I can dance just as good as he can. I have so much more experience. I certainly have a stronger singing voice!"

"Always leave them when you're on top. The age of fifty will ruin a glamour puss like you. We caught you just in time, Joan. You were killing streetwalkers, anyway. MGM can't allow that."

Joan insisted, "But it wasn't me! You just know it! It was the crazy psycho Joan doing it all. *All* of it! It has to be! That's what psychos *do*! I must have gotten confused about it from the damn diet pills! Damn what did the studio make them out of?"

Gangster Al said, "Some new experimental chemical that makes the system think it has overeaten by swelling the liver."

Joan cringed. "That doesn't sound safe."

He shrugged. "Glamour Queens are only good young and thin. Who cares if your liver is exploded when you're old? Since you're no Billie Burke who can play a little old lady, be glad we gave you this last chance at forty nine."

"I can *too* play a little old lady!"

He shook his head. "They'd just laugh you off the screen. You spent your whole life creating Joan Crawford. It just wouldn't work. It's over, Joan. Just realize it. Thank me. We caught you just in the nick of time before you went too far. You're far too old to play a gun slinging saloon girl and you know it. You'll thank me from where you are in your *better* place."

"The press will find out what you've done to me! They'll see it was a fake Joan who got on the train!"

Gangster Al didn't seem to care either way. "Maybe. Maybe not. The press can't figure out the difference between subtle things."

"But how are you going to explain where I went?"

"We won't. You'll just do a *Garbo*."

"But she's still seen walking the streets of New York."

"How do you know it's the real her?"

Joan gasped, "It's not?"

"Notice how she always covers her face?"

Joan felt her stomach flip. "NOOOOOOooooooo!"

* * * * *

At the Los Angeles train station parking lot, a Joan Crawford, along with a few undercover elite MGM staff, fought to open the car trunk. "It's stuck!"

The Joan Crawford peeked at it from under his big sunglasses and crabbed, "Well make it open. I need *all* my things."

"Why? Is your knitting back there?" a staff asked.

"I don't knit!"

"The real Joan Crawford did."

"Oh," the Joan Crawford said. "Oh. Open up the trunk!"

"All your drugs are back there, aren't they?" a staff asked.

"I need my shots! Get the trunk open *now*!"

"It won't open!" The MGM staff tugged and tugged.

"Leave it," another staff ordered. "We need to hurry and get out where at least a few witnesses can catch a glimpse of you before you're off. Put those sunglasses back down so you look like her."

"I need my drugs!"

"Can't you go a few hours without a fix?"

"I need my drugs!"

A scarred-faced Joan Crawford, like from *A Woman's Face*, but in a hospital gown like from *Possessed*, appeared out of the dark shadows of a row of palm trees. He ran at them. "Bloody knife! Bloody knife!"

"Run!" a horrified MGM employee ordered.

"I can't run! I'm Joan Crawford!"

"Take off those damn shoes and run!" The impersonator was pushed toward the train station.

"Bloody knife!" the escaped hospital psycho repeated. "*That* is not Joan Crawford! *That* is an imposter! That liar must be stopped!"

The Joan Crawford impersonator soon became breathless. "I can't go any farther! I can't run! I have to go back for my drugs!"

"The real Joan Crawford could outrun a bull," an MGM staff said, tugging his fur.

The psycho was upon them and swung the surgical blade so wildly that their blood started to splatter across the parked car windows before anybody could fall. "Stop!" the Joan Crawford cried, holding a mauve gloved hand up as a shield. The fingers were pared off.

"You *monster!*" the psycho killer yelled, until nobody moved a muscle. The psycho killer stripped the Joan Crawford of the bloody shredded dress, sopping fur and now-fingerless gloves and put them on. "*I* am Joan Crawford!" He grabbed the keys, walked back and opened the trunk with ease. "Joan Crawford was not a junkie!"

He found the drugs and syringes and tossed them onto the ground, then gave it a second thought and put a few of the syringes into the pocket of his fur. The Joan Crawford was so excited that he absently closed the trunk on a few of his fingers. After swearing for awhile, he drove away. He headed towards MGM. "And this time I won't try and crash through the gate, like an idiot! This time I'll be sneaky! HAAAA ha ha ha ha! I'll be sneaky with my bloody knife! My bloody knife! Bloody knife! Bloody knife!"

Chapter Eighteen

"I'm gonna take one of my kids to Utah when I make the western," Joan talked nervously as she watched the flat desert go by outside the car window. "I owe it to my son to have a little man-to-mom time with him. He's grown six foot. He was that tall when he was thirteen. I gave my kids lots of meat – something I never had growing up. He'll love hanging out with all the real cowboys. Nicholas Ray will direct it and his kid goes to Chadwick, too. You have to let me do the picture for Nicholas. I'm gonna sing the theme song. They agreed that Peggy Lee sounds lazy, like she's still in bed when she records. I sing from the heart - she sings from the pillow. I did do such a fantastic job singing for *Torch Song*."

"Your *Torch Song* songs are all being re-dubbed by India Adams."

Joan felt like a mule had kicked her in the gut. "WHAT?"

"Yep."

"Why!! You FANG! There's no goddamn reason to do that!"

Gangster Al stated, "Because you sound old."

"What? My singing? Replaced? Gone? Her? India? India sounds like a - a - a nine year old goat-yodeling boy! You can't have *that* coming out of my mouth! It'll be ridiculous!"

"That entire picture is ridiculous. You're getting too old for this sort of wild nonsense, Joan. Don't be afraid of letting go."

"I've never been afraid of anything," Joan corrected him. "Being dead finally is the easy part."

"There you go. Just give it up and see a stupid rodeo for what it is. An animal show. Give in and give it up and let me help you become an MGM legend before it's too late and you make a fool of yourself and ruin everything MGM did for you."

Joan began to cry. "MGM *can't* re-dub my songs! They just *can't*! That's so horrible! I worked goddamn hard on my voice for thirty long grueling years - and now I'll be dubbed by some lazy shmuck who showed up at the studio yesterday!"

"Just let it go, Joan. Just let it all go. It's already been done."

"Never! Not after all my hard work!"

Gangster Al added, "And just to let you know how funny life is in the movies, India Adams also dubbed Cyd Charisse in *The Band Wagon*."

"But Cyd can't sing. She's only legs. I'm both."

"Well, the funny thing is, the one big number in *Torch Song* – the only *real* number - was a song rejected from *The Band Wagon*."

Joan jolted. "What? *Two Faced Woman*? A reject? That's not possible! I recorded it!"

"She did it first, of course - the real version with full orchestra and chorus."

Joan clenched her fists. "Mine was just with a rehearsal piano. Balls! They said they'd do it up good in postproduction. The liars!"

"Since India sang for both movies, MGM could do the trickle down and save a buck. *More* than a buck!. Boy it saved them so much money on your film - and it let them not seem to waste so much on *The Band Wagon,* a much bigger picture. People always forget how expensive sound is, especially a song for a big number. Hiding the wasted money in your low budget stinker will keep the stockholders happy. And your fans will accept anything. There you have it. The story of your life. More rejects and crumbs from the table for Joan, and happy shareholders that don't know it's you they should be thanking."

"Balls! Why are you always so mean to me?"

"I'm mean to everybody. I'm a gangster."

* * * * *

The psycho Joan Crawford went to the soundstage where Esther Williams' set continued to lay sunken near the bottom of her grand pool. Not knowing where he was or what it was, he was just thrilled to be in a motion picture studio soundstage. He got in the makeup man's rowboat at the pool's edge, laid down on its floor in a languid pose of angst, and recreated the scene from *Strange Cargo* where Joan rested in a rowboat and talked to Ian Hunter, "Then why buzz around me if I'm not gonna die. Do you think I want forgiven by you, you lousy bastard. Do you think my rotten heart turned white just for you? Maybe you wanna tell me about the times I got lost, kicking myself. Will you tell my rotten heart that you're gonna make me a clean sheet of paper again and start me over again, you lousy bastard. What do you take me for? Can you ever picture the day a man tips his hat at me 'cause - he looks like he should? Cause I look like a real lady?"

"Hello?" A security man yelled out over the dark pool. "Who's there?"

"It's Joan Crawford, you lousy bastard! I'll kill you!"

"What are you doing here at a time like this? In Esther Williams' makeup boat?"

"No, you lousy bastard, this is the set of *Strange Cargo*!"

"That was a swell MGM picture, Miss Crawford, but I think that was some decades, past. Now get out of that boat before you drown, and I'll help you call your driver."

"I'm a great swimmer. I won't drown."

"You can't be here right now. It's not safe."

"I'll say. It's not safe for YOU! Bloody knife! Bloody knife! Bloody knife!"

He was dead.

* * * * *

At a pre-dug hole in the desert, the car stopped and Gangster Al opened the trunk. He grabbed a shovel. "Out."

"I'm scared," Joan admitted.

"Don't worry. I'm not. Go." With his gun he steered Joan near the hole.

"I'm a *star*!"

"You were a mean ole' rotten egg monster with a bit of an old waver to her singing voice, but you were truly a star. Yes, you were truly a star."

"The greatest star!"

"The greatest star!"

"The ultimate star!"

"The ultimate star, I'll give you that too." Gangster Al looked into Joan's fervent face. "You're not taking this well. Few do, but I'd took you for a tougher cookie."

Joan stomped the sand. "I just can't believe India Adams is redoing all my hard work! My entire career has been dubbed over! I took voice lessons since 1929 to make myself sound like Joan Crawford. I sounded gorgeous in *Dancing Lady*. To think I'll go away forever out of the public eye and the last thing my fans get is India Adams coming out of my great mouth! Unbelievable! You fangs at MGM are just *unbelievable!*"

"Fair enough." He stepped back and shot her two times. "Huh?" His face went white. "How did this happen? Blanks! How did I get blanks in *my* gun."

Screaming, Joan picked up the shovel and swung at him. "India Adams will *not* come out of my mouth!" He held up his arm and it took the blow. He grabbed the blade but she thrust it into his neck, pushing him hard. He choked as he tried to grab the blade but she was too strong. Joan wildly struck again and again in a frenzy. She went at him until she'd finally cracked him good. Gangster Al fell to his knees, his hands and head all in blood. Joan kicked him until he fell backwards into the hole that had been dug for her. Still screaming, she stomped to the car and threw open the back door and snatched her handbag.

She pulled out her gun and when she turned around, Gangster Al was back up out of the hole. He grabbed the shovel. "I have the weapon now, Joan. You put up a good fight and I respect you for that. You always were a good fighter."

"Bless you. Now have you wondered where the real bullets went?"

Gangster Al finally considered that he was in danger. "What? Not in your gun. You didn't have a chance to switch them."

"Not today. Not yesterday. I did it when I first started the picture and came to your house to use you for a little fun. I saw your gun on your table and I thought *how nice to have real bullets instead of those shitty MGM plugs.* I planned on shooting up the flowers floating in the pool to scare the shit out of my guests at my last party. By now they've seen that act so many times they'd have expected me to have blanks, and they'd have pretended to be scared. The only good actor I've had at my pool lately is Rock Hudson and he'd rather play with my garden hose."

"Joan! So why didn't you use the real bullets up at your party?"

"I might of killed somebody! Bela Lugosi warned me. He's really very sweet."

"Joan!" Gangster Al gasped, as he realized he might really be facing his own mortality.

"And I think it'd be just delicious to shoot you with your own goddamn bullets that were meant for me!"

"You wouldn't have the nerve!"

"You haven't seen *This Woman is Dangerous* enough times. This is the dame who made *The Damned Don't Cry*. I've always believed every word of every one of my movies! This is the bitch who's gonna blow Mercedes McCambridge off the side of a hill! You're slipping. It's time for the King to die and be replaced so Hollywood can be renewed. It's you, not me, baby, who's dragging this town down with your old rusted caboose. I'm tired of always getting the rough end of the pineapple! Today is my day, and you just ran out of goddamn gas! It's your turn to star in a bad movie! It's your turn to be *old old old* and to have to be replaced! I have a western to make, fellah! And then another! And then another!"

He growled, and then ran at her with his shovel raised. She pulled the trigger again and again, even continuing after all the bullets had fired into him, ripping him full of holes and felling him at her toes. She dragged him to the hole and buried him, grumbling, sobbing, repeating, "The fangs at MGM are *not* going to kick me around and re-dub me with India Adams! Joan Crawford is *not* going to die for the sins of MGM, and this damn town, and the free world! Why do I have to always clean everything up? It's always me! It's always me and only the fans know it!"

* * * * *

Back at MGM, Joan emerged through the painted sky backdrop, undecided as to whether she should tell everyone that she'd just saved the studio from Gangster Al - that his being exposed would have pulled all of Hollywood down into overwhelming scandal for all time. Or would the telling of it be just as much a scandal. She couldn't figure it out. "Balls! I need a shower!" She went to her old dressing room and pushed the door open. "I'm better than Superman! I saved MGM!" A few stomps in and a wall was at her face. The place was already being rebuilt back into three smaller rooms, as it had been before.

"Goddamn it! I saved the studio's reputation by hitting the hit man before he was found out! Everybody is found out sooner or later! And this is what they do to thank me! They kick me out!" She tried to push the new partition over, mad that she could so quickly be disregarded, replaced, rebuilt and forgotten. The new dressing room wall wouldn't budge.

"I need a shower! I need a movie! I need fan mail! I need a drink!" She deciding to swim it all off in Esther Williams' pool. "One last time, before MGM can go to hell, anyway, and I become the first Republic cowboy star with balls! Screw MGM, my fans will follow me anywhere everywhere. Even to Poverty Row. They ain't proud! They don't care - it all comes to their hometown theater just the same! All they see is my name hogging up the whole marquee, just the same!"

Inside the swimming pool soundstage, she heard a man say, "What's going on here?" The scarred psycho Joan stepped from the shadows, a sharp knife out.

Joan gasped, "It's the psycho Joan!"

"Goddamn!" he yelled, "What are *you* doing here!"

"What are *you* doing here?"

"It's a soundstage! I'm Joan!"

"No! *You're* the psycho Joan! And ugly!"

"Am not, and I'll kill you! I'm real and you're fake! And I've been meaning to do something about it for quite some time! I've been after you since I saw you in New York! I was minding my own business eating one of my own Joan Crawford cookies and then I saw *you*! The most arrogant imposter *ever*!"

"Yoooou! You were the one who dropped the Joan Crawford cookie?" Joan gasped. "That was a horrible thing to do! All over the sidewalk! My face broken! All those pretty colors of sugar scattered! It was a shock to my system to see such an untidy thing!"

"It was MY face!"

"The cookies were made in *my* honor, for *my* charity!"

"What charity?" the scarred psycho Joan asked. "But, I'm a STAR!"

"I'm the real Joan Crawford, naturally, and I'm always involved in one charity or another, if not three or four. That's what real stars do, you selfish monster!"

"I'm Joan Crawford and you can't prove I'm not!"

"I can too! Look at you! What a cheap and tacky fur! And what tacky makeup on your face to try to look like I'm still in that old movie *A Woman's Face*."

"These scars are real! Real! All Real! I'm the real Joan Crawford!"

"The real Joan Crawford doesn't have scars on half her face! That was just a movie! It was fake! It took two hours to arrange and paint the rubber layer down over the cotton pieces that were fixed on with spirit gum. Of course."

"It's real!"

Joan felt the need to explain. "It came off at the end of the day! Not like you. You look ugly forever!"

"You phony! You'll pay for that!"

Joan asked, "Why did you do such a horrible thing to me? Why did you do something so rotten to me as to switch my slide carrousels and ruin my great party? That party cost me seven thousand dollars and at that price I couldn't afford any mistakes. They're still laughing about it. They're still laughing at me, I just know it! The whole goddamn town!"

The psycho Joan touched his scars, sadly. "I did it to show you that you're no better than the rest of the phony drag queens. You're only *one* of them. I am the only true Joan Crawford."

"I am the real Joan Crawford!"

"Prove it."

"I don't have to prove it. I just am!"

"I am!"

Joan said, "You look like me enough, but your eyes are brown. Mine are blue. That proves it."

"Joan's eyes are dark! They were so beautiful and dark, like a Spanish princess, in *When Ladies Meet.*"

"Bless you. I was gorgeous in that one. The critics called it, and I quote, *loquacious trifle.* And who are they calling me pretentious to use a word like that. If it's wordy then just call it wordy and leave it at that. Balls. And that was all only in black and white. I'm doing Technicolor now, baby, and I got blue eyes! I was born with them and I finally get to show them off good!"

The psycho became confused. He looked like he might scratch his own eyes out. Joan waited impatiently for him to do so. He didn't. When he finally took his fingers away from his eyes, Joan said, "I know what we'll do, sugar cakes. You can prove it beyond eye color, if you have the nerve." She smiled smugly. "If you're the real Joan Crawford then you can easily swim the length of this pool, underwater all the way, under those sunken rings. If you are the real Joan Crawford then you can even do it better than Esther Williams. That's what a *real* Joan Crawford would be able to do. In fact she already did. And I won. I swim better than a fish. And all with an MGM smile!"

"Of course I can do anything better than you can."

"Toss that nasty blade away, first, "Joan ordered. "Throw it in the water! I won't have you cutting me. That's not fair play if we're to have a contest."

The psycho killer tossed the blade into the pool where it spun down to the very bottom. Joan stripped and stood at the edge of the water, smiling, feeling like she now had the clear advantage, ready to go. The psycho killer took off his bloody slashed garments and, dragging the fur along with him up to the edge of the pool, also facing the water as if ready to dive.

Joan said, "You're not going to swim with that fur, I hope. You won't go far underwater with all those baby seals."

"I'm Joan Crawford."

"That fur is damaged. I'd never be seen with something so tatty.

And it looks like it was shot only a few minutes ago." She turned away, irritated by it, and focused on when she would dive, arms out, knees bent, her toosh out. "At the count of three. One. Two."

"My fur is fabulous!"

"Are you ready? Get ready!" Refusing to look his way. Joan focused on deep breathing, staring into the shadows in the pool. "Your fur is tacky, and now dirty. Joan doesn't ever do tacky. Joan doesn't ever do dirty. One. Two."

The angry psycho killer reached into the coat pocket, took out the syringe and quickly stabbed Joan in her butt.

"Christ already! What was that!" She pulled the needle out and threw it into the water. "Balls!"

The man laughed, "Opium or heroin or laughing gas or something like that to keep you from thinking you can swim like Joan Crawford. Because you're not!"

"Shit!"

"Joan Crawford doesn't do drugs." The psycho killer smirked. "So, you'll fail. You're a failure. You're not Joan Crawford. You're on drugs!"

"HELL I'm *not*!" she roared. "Let's go, you nobody! You can't mess me up! I don't care what you do or say! I can swim in a beaded iron lung!"

Now it was the psycho Joan who said, "On the count of three! Only the real Joan Crawford will make it out alive."

They took deep breaths. "One, two, three!"

They both dove expertly into the pool and swam deep to go underneath the first sunken ring. Joan began to feel funny and then silly and then sick and then silly again, and then even sillier. A parade of colorfully bright cartoon Joan Crawfords began to walk across the bottom of the pool, flashing their long cartoon legs. Their lips grew bigger and changed size in an instant, depending on the amount of lipstick she was choosing.

"It's the drugs," she dismissed it. "What the hell did he shoot up my gorgeous duff? A toot-doodle-dee buff - a doo-wop doo-wop dooooooo*ho*ho!"

A cartoon Bette Davis wobbled out but a cartoon Joan quickly bit off her head, sending up a shower of pink bubbles through the water.

"Pink bubbles. Oh that's right," Joan thought. "Bubbles. I'm deep underwater. I shouldn't forget that. Where am I? Oh that's right. I'm underwater in MGM. MGM is always underwater. Why haven't I drowned a long time ago in this sick dream factory? What am I doing here? Oh, that's right, I'm making a picture. No. I finished it. They say it'll be out in October with some twelve-year-old goat-yodeling boy coming out of my mouth. I've been dubbed! Goddamn it. Say - so why am I swimming under a gaudy sunken set. Is this Atlantis? No. I remember. Oh how silly. It's Esther Williams' sunken set. Sunken like her career if she doesn't keep on an MGM starvation and rat poison diet. No. I'm out to make a stupid psycho killer drown himself because he's not Joan Crawford. And he broke my cookie. Broke it all over the sidewalk! It was horrible! My face was shattered! But first I have to not drown, myself. Oh, look at all the lovely cartoons. And they weren't done by Walt, so they have personality. I've always loved MGM's cartoons best!"

She turned back and saw the psycho killer swimming behind her. He looked grim and menacing. Lightning and thunder flashed.

"What an unprofessional swimmer," Joan thought. "The man can't swim and smile real big at the same time. At MGM you have to be able to smile big at all times no matter what, even when drowning, or having your legs cut off while Judy Garland sings at you with that big voice in some army hospital set." At that suggestion, an earnest cartoon Judy Garland marched out, selling cartoon war bonds and stamps. In a barrage of newsreels, crowds of soldiers cheered. Bombs went off. Arms and legs and heads flew through the air. But it wasn't real. It was scratched and it moved funny - and it was grainy black and white.

Joan ignored it and kicked her way under the second ring and suddenly a cartoon parade of brightly colored ribbons turned into eels and they turned into shimmering dresses. Joan chased one until she remembered she was underwater and needed to get to the other side to get back up. She looked behind her again and saw that the psycho killer was just at her heels. She kicked faster and made it under the third ring. She saw the cable that kept the sunken set from sinking all the way, from sitting on the bottom of the pool and covering the drain.

When she saw the psycho killer join her under the third ring, she tugged at the cable until she'd pulled it all the way out from under a rod, and the entire ring began to sink. Joan swam with all her might to come out from under the other side of the giant ring. It just missed pinning her to the bottom.

The psycho killer wasn't fast enough and only his hand made it clear. The rest of him was pushed against the floor and he didn't have the strength to lift the big ring off himself. More lightning and thunder flashed. He blew his last bubbles. Munchkins ran in terror as they were pelted with pennies from heaven. Joan looked back again and saw the hand curl up and shrink away beneath a house sitting on a yellow brick road. A cartoon Billie Burke floated away in a pink bubble. Cartoon Joan Crawfords ran down the road, dressed like they were starring in *Gone with the Wind*, with magnolias floating up from under her skirts. Joan Crawford pulled out a gun and shot all the flowers. The bullets bounced into a cartoon Bela Lugosi who was trying to warn her not to do that. He turned into a rubber bat on a string and was gone. A stagecoach roared down the yellow brick road, driven by cartoon cowboy Joan Crawford with a sock in her pants. She had John Wayne in the back – she was saving him from the Nazis in France, again. She pulled out her pistols, twirled them and shot all the Joan Crawford southern belles full of holes. The yellow brick road was now all red.

Then she saw the studio security guard, and he was real, dead, murdered, and floating in some cables. She tried to scream but just choked. "Oh that's right. Balls! I'm underwater. I better get the goddamn hell outta here. Who knows how long my blood's been out of air. I'm stoned and feel no pain and forgot all about everything." She saw a cartoon Marilyn Monroe. She wondered how full round cartoon breasts feel. She wanted to swim over to her and see.

Joan started to see black dots dance before her eyes. Marilyn vomited beautiful sequins. Joan pushed up off the bottom of the pool and swam with all her might until she was finally at the surface. She crawled out, wobbled over to a director's chair and plopped down. She laughed and laughed in utter delight for a while at some more hallucinations of Bette Davis being too fat to get into a Joan Crawford costume. Then Joan fell out of the chair, passed out, and she slept for many hours.

* * * * *

Lying in bed at home with a gorgeously carved wood tray over her lap, Joan phoned Bill Haines. "Oh baby. Goddamn it! Goddamn *goddamn* it!"

"What."

"Balls!"

Bill asked, "What idiot rattled your cage this hour?"

"My publicists say that I can't peep a word about what happened to me. Goddamn it!"

Bill asked, "Why?"

Joan sipped her breakfast, a bloody mary. "So the insurance companies don't get wind of it. Or some irrelevant crap to do with insurance risk. Can you believe it? What crap! Don't I always get the rough end of the pineapple?"

"What? Cranberry! How *rude!*"

"Yeah! I said so too. But he insisted that if I was to be insurable for another picture, and I start the new one in a few months, I better zip my lips. *Johnny Guitar* will be so uneventful compared to what goes on in real life. In the movie I only gun down one stupid bitch, at the end. We film on location. Is anything fun there? They say the desert is full of radiation from atomic tests so I'm gonna bring the boy and maybe if we're lucky we'll get to shoot a goddamn giant bug. I'll let him shoot it with real bullets so he sees how the world really works. Blow its head off! Just kidding but we're going to take a Geiger counter along and play with that for fun!"

"Wait a minute," Bill interrupted her. "Your publicist wants you quiet so that the western script sounds more exciting?"

"Haven't you been listening to what I've been saying?"

Bill admitted, "I think that's the problem? The western has to sound exciting so you have to be quiet about your adventures. Nothing tops behind the scenes of a musical? What?"

"No, not that. I can't blab on about being *such a psycho magnet* - his exact words. There are so many psychos out there stalking the stars. If I'm killed by a psycho in the middle of a shoot, it'll ruin it. Insurance companies don't like that kind of odds. So we have to pretend I'm always the only Joan Crawford in all the land. And the land is full of peace. And all that official baloney Hollywood would have you think about the world."

Bill added, "I'm sure the insurance company also can't hear a peep about studio issue diet pills, either."

"I'm not a dummy. Of course I already knew to be quiet about that. So what if they were dangerous. The doctor - *my* doctor, not MGM's doctor - said that those pills could turn a living elephant into a dead giraffe. Whatever that means. I think he takes pills, too, to say something like that. I just know I'm toxic right now from too many of them, and I'm in bed until I recover. I have to be good to my liver, now. I don't want to turn yellow. *Johnny Guitar* is being done in Trucolor and it picks up yellow like you wouldn't believe. They say my liver has started to swell and that might pinch off a certain hose in there that lets stuff leak out, that's all yellow. If it gets pinched off it all squirts right up into my eyeballs! I'll have bright yellow eyes! And my eyes are so big there'll be no hiding it - not like Deborah Kerr who has such tiny eyes they could just turn yellow and nobody would notice."

"You poor baby. Cranberry!"

Joan griped on, "It makes no sense why we have to keep everything from the insurance company spies. I'll do the whole damn western in sunglasses if I have to!"

"There's some sense to that - Blondell couldn't talk about falling out of the car while she was driving it for fear it'd make her uninsurable - they'd think she drinks too much. And she does."

"You heard that?" Joan gasped and poured more vodka into

her vegetable drink. "Bless her! I knew it! *Cry Havoc* ruined her career and now she's on the skids. That could be me! I gotta be more careful! I'm glad I got out of MGM just in time! Again!"

Bill warned her, "Everybody in Hollywood has big secrets they keep from insurers. The greedy bastards wouldn't guarantee a single picture if they knew what death defying feats of stupidity you stars were always really up to."

"I beg your pardon. I'm a decent woman."

Bill said, "You'll be so decent that you *will* keep quiet so everybody keeps thinking about you that way. In Ohio and Kansas and Illinois they think you really are Mildred Pierce!"

Joan declared, "I don't care what it is that happens to me - I've gotta tell it. If you don't advertise yourself, I always say, then your enemies will do it for you!"

"But you have to play by the rules, Cranberry, or you won't get anymore pictures. The insurance companies control the purse strings."

She agreed, "Yeah they do. What a goddamn shame. I gotta be good because after the western there'll be another movie. And then another one!"

Bill said in a most dramatic voice. "The world will never know what really went on behind the scenes in the life of a true star - most lurid and dramatic - beyond belief so it must be true - the *Cranberry Murders!*"

"If it stars Clark Gable, I'll goddamn buy it."

"He's in Italy."

"I'll do it next year after the western. I'm sure I'll have new bills. I'll need a good picture so everybody can get good and goddamn jealous of me again, and pick on me until they try to pick me to the bones. But I'm Joan Crawford and I'm made of steel and they can just be jealous of me until they choke on it! Yeah, they should make a movie about me! But nobody would believe it! They'll never make a movie about me, not in a hundred years – who could play me?"

"Cranberry. Calm down. There's no cameras on you right now."

"Cranberry who? I'm ALWAYS Joan Crawford! Day in and

day out with no weekends or holidays off, and certainly even in bed - I'm wearing a Helen Rose gown!" She saw something move in the yard. She sat up and looked out the window. Two Joan Crawford impersonators were running around the pool, chasing each other. "Oh balls!"

VISIT STONEGARDEN.NET PUBLISHING ONLINE!

You can find us at: www.stonegarden.net.

News and Upcoming Titles
New titles and reader favorites are featured each month, along with information on our upcoming titles.

Author Info
Author bios, blogs and links to their personal websites.

Contests and Other Fun Stuff
Web forum to keep in touch with your favorite authors, autographed copies and more!

From the mind of Peter Joseph Swanson
Hollywood Sinners
Book 1 of the Tinseltown Trilogy
(1-60076-041-4 -$8.95 US)

Karin Panotchitch, raised on a sheep farm and married off to a drunken loser, finds her way to 1939 Hollywood at the tender age of sixteen. Along the way to stardom, she meets up with Ramon Classic, who with his many brothers is ready for a hostile takeover of MGM, Mama Gravy, the colorful and opinionated proprietor of the run-down Gold Rush brothel, and Sister Agatha, the mysterious nun who seems to turn up every time Karin rides the trolley.

Hollywood history, flying bullets, and big dreams make for a lively story about what happens when a sheep farmer's daughter tries to make her dreams come true.

StoneGarden.Net Publishing
3851 Cottonwood Dr., Danville, CA   94506

Please send me the StoneGarden.net Publishing book I have checked above. I am enclosing $_____ (check, money order for US residents only, VISA and Mastercard accepted—no currency or COD's). Please include the list price plus $3 per order to cover handling costs ($5 outside of the US). Prices and numbers are subject to change without notice. (Prices slightly higher in Canada.)

Name:_____

Address:_____

City:_____State:_____Zip:_____Country:_____

VISA/Mastercard:_____

Exp. Date and CVS Code:_____ /_____

Please allow 4-6 weeks for delivery.

LaVergne, TN USA
21 October 2009
161586LV00001B/45/P